using u~

After Omdurman

After Omdurman

John Ferry

ROBERT HALE · LONDON

ISBN 978-0-7090-8516-4

Robert Hale Limited
Clerkenwell House
Clerkenwell Green
London EC1R 0HT

www.halebooks.com

2 4 6 8 10 9 7 5 3 1

Typeset in 10/14pt Janson
Printed and bound in Great Britain by
Biddles Limited, King's Lynn

PART I

Fighting the Dervishes was primarily a matter of transport. The Khalifa was conquered on the railway.

The River War, Winston S Churchill

CHAPTER 1

THE COLD OF the desert night was so thoroughly entrenched in my body as to make real sleep impossible. Instead strange half-dreams and thoughts came to me, of Cairo, its smoky tea houses and humid bazaars. Images of England, too, with its grey streets and blissfully wet winters. As the first stirrings of light and consciousness crept over me there was the vague awareness of a soft white ceiling above, while my dust-ridden ears picked up the gentle rippling sound of a breeze on canvas. Could it really be that those seemingly endless days spent on boats and on trains had ended? Had I at long last reached Wad Hamed, from where I could begin my intelligence work?

I grimaced as a sharp stone dug into my back and watched as a disjointed column of grey breath rose up towards the tent roof. My leaden mind was slow to recall the details of the previous evening, but I started to go through the events. There was the weary disembarkation and my wishing for nothing but a billet and a few hours of blessed horizontal slumber. But also, I now recalled, there was a stern-looking colonel awaiting me onshore, who took me to the side as the other soldiers quietly filed past. He had an order for me. 'See Major-General Kitchener at his field headquarters as soon as dawn breaks,' he said. The words, 'As-soon-as-dawn-breaks' were iterated twice.

Immediately I kicked off my field blanket and sat bolt upright. The partial darkness suggested the sun was near rising. There was no time to spare. I jumped up and rushed out in search of the general's headquarters and, after a dash through the murky camp and the rapid questioning of several soldiers on night duty, I found myself at Kitchener's tent, a red Egyptian flag sagging forlornly from a staff above it.

'Major Winters to see the Major-General,' I said breathlessly, to the sentry by the door. The soldier returned shortly and instructed me to enter. A second later and before I had even had time to catch my breath I was standing before the most famous British soldier alive. He was perched up behind a fold-up desk, his eyes lowered to some correspondence. A single oil lamp illuminated his calm face, the corners of the tent still near pitch black.

'Major Winters?' he said, without looking up. His tone was rather sharp and serious.

'Yes, sir.'

Kitchener lifted a pen, wrote something on the document and handed it to a member of his staff, who duly departed so that we were left alone.

'You speak Arabic, Winters, correct?'

'Indeed I do, sir, yes.'

'Learned?'

'Sir?'

'Yes, where did you learn the language, man? Come forward, come forward!'

'Oh, er, in the Palestine, sir, during the time of the surveys.'

'Good. Still up to scratch, is it?'

I had spent almost ten years as an intelligence officer in Cairo and had travelled through many parts of North Africa and Arabia collecting sensitive information. My Arabic was as good as any man not born to that part of the world, so I said, 'My Arabic remains of a very high standard, sir, yes.'

'Good!' he went on, standing brusquely from his chair and turning to stride out from behind the desk. He circled in the gloom to come closer. 'Right, that's settled it,' he announced. 'You're going back to the Atbara. I want you to leave right away.'

I was shocked. For several weeks before leaving Cairo I had thought of nothing but the task that lay ahead in the Sudan, namely co-ordinating efforts for the gathering of intelligence from Omdurman. But I had not prepared myself for this, and I could not for the life of me fathom why Major-General Kitchener wished to send me back down the Nile. 'Yes, I see, General,' I said, a little hesitantly.

He was standing a mere three feet away and looking at me directly, arms folded, heels apart. With his handsome features, smooth forehead and unblemished skin he looked to be in the prime of life. There was nothing in his calm exterior to suggest the great responsibilities that the man currently bore. The long moustaches, just visible in the dimness, were immaculately sculpted. The eyes had an outwardly languid quality, and yet there was an inner intensity also, an energy, that reminded me of a light I once saw from shore when I was moored off some distant coastline on a troopship; far off yet constant, always shining, and always looking to draw one in.

'You should catch a boat easily enough this morning,' he continued.

'But sir, I—'

'Now don't argue with me, Winters. I need you to go and that's that. I'll put someone else in charge of intelligence here.'

'Of course, sir.'

He looked to the scrub floor for a few seconds. 'Fact is, Major,' – suddenly the sharpness in his voice had gone, to be replaced with something more conciliatory, if still very stern – 'one of our supply trains got blown up yesterday – blown to bloody pieces. And I need you to make sure it doesn't happen again.'

This, too, stopped me in my tracks, for I had previously been assured while in Cairo that the railway was secure from enemy attack. Kitchener continued, 'You do realize the importance of the railway, don't you?'

'Oh yes, certainly, General. I know that without it the entire expedition to reclaim the Sudan could quite easily turn into a disaster.'

'Disaster! We wouldn't last more than two weeks, man! Do you think we would be in any fit state to fight by the time we got to the Khalifa, or he got to us? The desert would have our bones.'

'Indeed,' I said grimly. 'Is the line still functioning?'

'It is now. But if there's more sabotage … if we lose more trains or, God forbid, the entire line is put out of action, well … well, it simply can't happen. And you'll have to make sure of it, Winters. Got it?'

I nodded slowly, not quite realizing the significance of the job that I was being ordered to undertake. 'And there's something else,' added Kitchener. 'I can hardly believe this myself, but we're not talking about Dervish sabotage here but some kind of blasted traitorous sabotage. That's right. Seems it was a British soldier who did it.'

This seemed incredible, unbelievable. 'But …'

'Bloody traitor. One of our men spotted him, or at least he thinks he did

– said he couldn't be certain in all the confusion. It was a white man dressed as an Arab riding off into the desert just after the explosion.'

THE RED-GOLD of a Nubian sunrise welcomed me out of Kitchener's tent. There would be no time to contemplate it, but, as I set off down the hill from where the field headquarters had been placed, I did take a few moments to observe Wad Hamed for the first time in the light. The rows of British white tents numbered into the hundreds. Grouped along the river, they were bathed in fine morning sunshine. Beyond them, the grass huts and blanket shelters of the Egyptian and Sudanese brigades were arranged in a crescent shape, and still further in the distance the flatness of the desert then stretched to the horizon.

Tardy puffs of smoke rose up from the large white tents of the field kitchens where breakfast was being prepared. The kitchens had been placed by the grassy banks of the Nile, which ran along the eastern edge of the camp to form a natural barrier to attack. The river itself meanwhile was filled with the barges and steamers and other small boats that kept the many thousands of men supplied with food and munitions. Casting my eyes west then, I noted that the other side of the camp was protected by unwelcoming-looking thorn bushes, while in the north an artificial channel allowed the Nile waters to complete the circle of defence.

The air was still fresh from the night, but behind this lurked the usual stagnant smells of the Sudan which, as the day progressed and got hotter, would no doubt come to the fore.

I was about to rush back to my tent to gather my kit when, taking a moment to assess the situation properly, I stopped for a second. There would be little chance of finding a boat that was ready to leave for Atbara at this time of the morning, I thought, so there was no point rushing to the Nile in search of one. Surely it would be better to take the time to suitably prepare myself for the journey.

I put my hand up to my face. The skin was grimy and thick with desert dust. Even my moustache felt weighed down by the stuff. My uniform meanwhile was so torn and filthy that it must have looked as if I had been dragged along the 1,400 miles of desert that lay between Cairo and Wad Hamed. And I was ravenously hungry, for I had not eaten properly in days. Finally I decided that before setting off for Atbara I would first have to find some breakfast and have a wash and a shave, and so, after acquiring some food from a field kitchen, I returned to my tent.

It is often said that the best way to maintain the morale of a soldier in the field is to provide him with a daily ration of fresh bread. Sitting outside my tent door, observing the activities of the now more bustling camp while eating bread that had been brought out of an oven not an hour before, I really could not have agreed more. The sun, which was by this time sitting quite high in the sky, produced a tolerable heat, and I used this comfortable moment to truly contemplate the challenge ahead.

The information that Kitchener had received from Atbara was scant, but it seemed that explosives had been planted in a part of the train's engine where the blast would ensure derailment. The soldier who reported seeing a white man dressed as an Arab racing off after the incident, could not, he had said, provide a description as the events had transpired so quickly. However, it was Kitchener's belief that only someone with sufficient knowledge of engineering, an Englishman, would have the expertise to do it, and this confirmed to him that a traitor was responsible.

Atbara was the British base at the end of the new railway line, about 100 miles north-west of Wad Hamed. My plan was to gain passage back down the Nile on one of the many supply boats that would be returning there. I estimated the journey would take the best part of a day in one of the faster vessels and perhaps a day and a half if a smaller craft were all that could be found. I would travel light and would try to procure the use of a horse or a camel once at my destination. I would then have to travel further north to where the incident occurred, somewhere between the settlements of Bashtinab and Abadia.

My orders were to get to the bottom of the atrocity and to find and stop the English – if indeed he was English – saboteur. 'When you get the traitor, show him no mercy,' Kitchener had said as I was leaving his tent.

But I must say I was doubtful of the theory that only an Englishman could be responsible. The report from the soldier who had claimed to have seen a white man was not in my opinion entirely reliable. In the carnage of those few minutes, the soldier could easily have imagined seeing a white face beneath a headscarf. No, it was my view that one of the more clever of the many native workers who the army employed to construct the railway could have gained whatever knowledge was needed to plant the bomb. It might even have been the case that some sort of organized Arab resistance group was responsible. This was my biggest fear – far more worrying than the theory of the rogue Englishman – for if this were true then it would almost certainly mean that more attacks were inevitable. But I was in no position to be coming to conclusions until I got to the scene of the incident, so accordingly I made haste to prepare for the journey.

Some short time later I had my kit prepared and was walking towards the river, the hot sun beating against my face. The land was a mixture of grey, dusty rocks and patches of dry grass sloping gently down towards the river-bank. The Nile presented me with a veritable forest of sailing masts and steam funnels; the barges, steamers and small native boats – *gyassas* as they are called – moored many deep starting a few feet from the shore. The boats were clumped together so tightly that they acted as one, the whole mass undulating slowly with the movement of the brown but still glistening waters underneath. At first, all the vessels seemed to be empty. I saw no activity, and all was quiet but for the occasional squawk of a river bird. The crews must all be ashore, I thought, their cargoes unloaded. But then, as I walked along the bank, searching the many decks for signs of life, I heard the sound of British voices emanating from somewhere. I looked in the direction of the sounds. The bright sunshine reflected off the water and made it difficult to see the details of the boats' decks, but using my hand for shade I spotted a crew member standing at the bow of one of the larger vessels. He appeared to be enjoying a cigarette while looking out towards the desert on the other side of the river. 'Ahoy there,' I shouted. 'I would like a word with your commanding officer. Is he aboard?'

The man looked at me and, saying nothing, threw his cigarette into the river, turned and disappeared into the bridge. A few moments later, another man appeared, whom I took to be the officer in charge of the vessel. 'Can I help?' he called politely.

I informed him of my rank and explained that I required passage to Atbara as soon as possible, and would he be willing to accommodate me. He replied, 'Can't do it, I'm afraid. We won't be in a position to return to Atbara for at least a day or two. But you could try the smaller steamer there. I believe it will be setting off shortly.'

The boat that he pointed to was located a short distance down river. I made my way towards that part of the shore, noting as I went that the boat's deck appeared to be empty. Regardless, I clambered over the many small vessels that created a bridge out into the Nile in the hope of finding some fellows below deck. Then, as I was struggling to hoist myself and my kit up the side of the steamer, a member of the crew suddenly appeared from below. This came as a relief, for I was beginning to fear that I did not have the strength to pull the weight of my own body and the weight of my kit aboard, and that subsequently I might lose my belongings to the flowing waters of the Nile. 'Well, don't just stand there, help me up, man!' I ordered. The chap looked most surprised to see a major in such a precarious position, but he made no protest and rushed to my aid.

'I hear you will shortly be leaving for Atbara,' I said breathlessly, once his strong hands had pulled me on deck.

'Yes, sir, very shortly in fact.' The young man, a naval seaman, looked startled and confused by the sight of me.

'I am Major Winters of the Intelligence Branch,' I said. 'Who is commanding this vessel?'

'That would be myself, Major,' came a voice from behind the seaman who, upon hearing his commander's words, stood a little to the side. In the doorway of the bridge, just a few feet away, I found a lieutenant of the Royal Navy. 'How may I assist you?' he asked. 'I am Lieutenant Greenhill.'

I said I was an Intelligence Branch officer and that I was undertaking an important mission for Major-General Kitchener, obviously giving away no details of the mission, and that I required passage to the Atbara as soon as possible. Thankfully the officer asked no further questions. He simply nodded and said that I would be most welcome to join the crew for their journey. 'We will be departing within the hour,' he explained. 'You can store your kit below. Then, if you want, you can either join me on the bridge or rest on the deck. It seems it will be a fine day for sailing the Nile.'

'Indeed it shall, Lieutenant. I am most grateful to you.'

Pleased with my good fortune at finding such a gracious host, I decided to take up his latter suggestion. I had no doubt that the lieutenant would ask me to dine with him later that day, for it was obvious that he was both an officer and a gentleman, and knowing that I would have the chance to properly talk with him then, I did not mind at all using the next few hours for rest and recuperation. When I told the lieutenant that a quiet place to relax on deck for the next few hours would be sincerely appreciated, he ordered one of his sailors to take my bag below.

I found an appropriate spot towards the front of the boat. For comfort I spread out my ragged field blanket, which I had kept hold of when handing over my kit, on the wooden deck. Lying down then, I turned my head to the side and closed my eyes against the blinding sun. I did not intend to sleep, but in no short time began to doze, thinking intermittently of the importance of the great desert railway that Kitchener, the appointed *Sirdar* of the Egyptian Army, had had built from North Africa to the Sudan, that lifeline of our forces – a lifeline of the British Empire itself. If it were to be permanently put out of action at this stage in the campaign then disaster would surely ensue. The forces at the front could not be supplied. A retreat would have to be called and the Khalifa, like the Mahdi before him, would have overcome the might of our great nation, which once again would be made to look foolish in the eyes of the rest of the world. I do not exaggerate when I say that the responsibility upon my shoulders now was immense. Indeed, this was easily the most important mission that I had ever undertaken. I hoped I should not fail.

CHAPTER 2

Diary of the Rt. Hon. Colonel Evelyn Winters, MP
5 February, 1935

TODAY HAS BEEN a momentous day – a momentous calamity of a day! If Lord Linlithgow's proposed bill on India goes through it will be a disaster for Britain, for Empire, for India itself – for mankind no less!

'Count the Empire as one, and we need call no other nation master.' Has this Parliament forgotten the unquestionable truth of this statement? I cannot for the life of me see why Mr Baldwin is not taking a tougher line with his partners in the National Government when so many of his party members are plainly against this bill. One has to ask oneself what this Conservative leadership has come to.

The only good thing about it all is that it has aroused the passions of our elected few. Indeed, I have never seen the libraries and the smoking rooms of Westminster so alive with debate and with argument as they were today. Voices were raised, fingers pointed, brows creased with anger as the members of the House parleyed intensely. The less sophisticated Tory MPs who are against the bill argued that giving India any form of home rule – even the limited amount that the bill proposes – will only lead to other parts of the Empire getting lofty ideas that they, too, can play a part in administering themselves, and that eventually this will lead to complete fragmentation.

Those of us capable of more cultivated debate argued that the bill is not reconcilable with democracy. How can one reconcile the caste system with democracy? The Indian peasantry are so racked with religious prejudices, for instance, that only an impartial British court could be trusted to give a fair judgement when the law is called on to end a dispute. When it comes down to it, as another MP pointed out to me this afternoon, this is a choice of self-government versus good government, and I fully intend to fight this bill all the way, lest posterity judge me to be one of the ones who added a nail to the coffin of the British Empire.

It was around seven o'clock when I finally left Parliament. For duty's sake I would have stayed on longer, but I did not want to keep my young historian waiting. I must say I was glad to get away from the place. I do enjoy the debate, the competitiveness, the trying to get one up on one's opponent. But today it all seemed like extraordinarily hard work, especially for a man of my years. When I got outside, the streets of Westminster seemed dead compared with the commotion of the Commons, but they came as a welcome relief, for my ears were ringing from the continuous arguments, my voice weary from shouting.

It was a pleasant and still evening, although it was very cold, and I decided that despite the slight aching from my arthritic knees I would walk halfway down Whitehall before getting a taxi to Bloomsbury. My young historian had informed me that he would be working late and that I could see him at the library any time before nine. I was in no rush, and with these few minutes I took the opportunity to think about the outcome of the lunch that I had earlier today with my publisher and, as a result, what I should expect from my historian and what he should expect from me.

Mr Larwood was kind enough to take me to Claridges for lunch. He was already seated when I got there. My first thought as I approached our table was how much Mr Larwood looked at home in those splendid surroundings, dressed as he always was, in the finest blue pinstripe and silk tie. I myself felt a little out of place. Fine Mayfair dining-rooms are the haunt of senior Tories, not retired colonels with no ambition beyond the backbenches. Indeed, upon seeing my publisher's exquisite attire and observing the others in the room – among whom I did in fact spot one or two Cabinet members – I have to say that I was a little ashamed of myself. I had neither the expensive clothing nor the power for such an establishment. But alas, what can one do when one is now so old? One can't turn back the clock to change the course of one's life. And anyway, why should I wish to? I may not have achieved high office, my suits may now be worn at the elbows, but I have been lucky enough to have led a most adventurous life, so really, I cannot complain.

Anyway, Mr Larwood welcomed me warmly – he is such a friendly chap. We spent some minutes exchanging pleasantries as we considered the excellent menu, but by the time we ordered we were on to talking about this dreadful India business, and then before long the subject of our conversation changed again, and we naturally came to discuss my book.

'Tell me, Evelyn, truthfully, how is it all coming along?' asked Larwood. 'Sometimes I fear that my giving you that contract might be the death of you. Any sensible man of your age would be taking things easy at this stage. But you, you my dear fellow seem determined to work yourself into the grave.'

I assured Mr Larwood that I had never been in better health and that, contrary to his sentiments, the writing of my memoirs of the Sudan campaign has given me a certain new vitality. In explaining this I was reminded of part of a poem that for some reason lodged itself in my memory many years ago. I do not now recall the poet, but believe it may have been Herbert:

> *And now in age I bud*
> *again*
> *After so many deaths I*
> *live and write;*
> *I once more smell the*
> *dew and rain,*
> *And relish versing: O, my*
> *only light …*

I recited these lines to Mr Larwood, who upon hearing them gave out a hearty laugh.

'*Touché*, Evelyn, *touché*,' he said. As the food came we got on to talking about the young historian, Parker, that Mr Larwood has found to help me with my memoirs. He assured me several times of Parker's credentials: top of his class at Balliol, published in several reputable journals, now a respected historian at the British Museum Library, and so on. I said I had no doubt that he would prove an ideal assistant and researcher.

'He's a rather quiet young man, but extremely capable. And you mustn't be weary of heaping responsibility on him,' added Larwood. 'I do not mind, even, if Parker does some of the writing for you, with you doing the final editing.'

'Oh no,' I insisted, 'I wouldn't dream of letting a single word be put on a page that had not originated in my own head.' I must say I was a little annoyed that Mr Larwood would make such a suggestion. I thought that he of all people would see how important these memoirs are to me. After all, I have told him on several occasions that this is not a mere book that I am engaged in writing but a legacy for the future generations that will serve to maintain the British Empire. This book should inspire the warriors and administrators of tomorrow, the boys that are currently spread across England's boarding-schools, thinking, no doubt, of nothing but their Latin and their field games, completely unaware of the responsibilities that lay before them.

I must have had a slightly peeved look on my face, for Mr Larwood immediately apologized for making such a suggestion. 'Of course, Evelyn, of course it should all be your own words. And the better the end product will be for it, eh?' To which I agreed. He then offered a toast to the success of my memoirs. 'Let's hope it sells in the thousands, and that it is still being read one hundred years from now.'

People reading my book one hundred years from now! Selling in the thousands! Mere dreams at this stage, but one never knows one's luck. I wonder now, as I sit here writing, what Britain will be like one hundred years hence? Will the Empire have grown to bring in other parts of the world, other groups of peoples grateful to be shown the way towards civilization – and I mean here true civilization, not just railways and courts and banking institutions, but tolerance of your fellow man, a belief in personal liberty? Or will it remain static, or worse, shrink in size? Even with the current débâcle surrounding India, I am inclined to believe that the former case will develop in time. After all, it is thanks to England's benevolence that much of the world is currently at peace.

The rest of my lunch with Mr Larwood was most enjoyable. We discussed the structure of the book and how Parker should be able to help me write precisely, in the footnotes, on the movements of various regiments before and during the battle of Omdurman. The food was truly wonderful, but unfortunately I did not have time for dessert as I had to get to the Commons for the reading of the India Bill. I do not wish to go into any more details of this afternoon in Parliament. I have thought enough about it today. But I should note the outcome of my meeting with Parker.

I met him in the reading room of the British Library. When I got there I found it practically empty, apart from a few lonely souls spread out here and there, huddled over their books as if their very lives depended on it. Parker must have been watching for me to come in, for no sooner had I entered that beautiful, scholarly room, with its dim lights barely illuminating the thousands of leather-bound volumes that gird its circular wall, than I spotted a young man towards the back, glancing up timidly towards the door.

I waved a little as I started out towards him, but he had turned to peruse, or continue to peruse, the bookshelf he was next to. I got the impression he knew straight away that I was the one he was waiting for, but that perhaps he was a little self-conscious about showing it – Mr Larwood did after all intimate that Parker is a coy fellow.

'Hello, Parker is it?' I said as I approached.

'Oh … yes that's me,' he said rather nervously, turning to half face me.

'I'm Colonel Winters. Mr Larwood has told me so much about you.' I put my hand out. 'Nice to meet you.'

'Yes … thank you.'

I must say he seemed a rather anxious young man. He barely looked me in the eye as we shook hands, while the handshake itself was really quite flimsy. I would have expected a youthful, firm grip, but actually it felt as if my spotted, wrinkled old hand were the stronger.

'Looking forward to helping me with my researches, are you?' I said, my voice lowered so as not to disturb the readers.

'Oh, definitely,' he said.

But then he went silent again, and I had the distinct feeling that the poor boy really did not know what to say. 'Well,' I continued, determined to get him talking, 'what do you know of the 1898 campaign?'

He looked a little startled for a second. I think I had wrong-footed him, which I had no intention of doing. 'Oh, erm, well,' he mumbled, 'I … I know about all the troop movements, and I've made a catalogue of information sources. And I … well … I am so very keen to learn more about the reconquest of the Sudan.'

I placed Parker's age somewhere in the mid-thirties. He was dressed for the country rather than the city, with a tatty looking tweed jacket, check shirt and bow tie. My general impression was that he is donnish looking in his own way, and there is certainly an air of eccentricity about him. Tall and wiry, he is a strong-featured fellow, which seems incongruous when one is reminded of his reserved interior. He wears horn-rimmed spectacles and sports the most incredible mass of unkempt black wavy hair – which every now and again, seemingly without knowing it, he would nervously try to flatten.

But I was keen to get an idea of exactly how much of an interest he has in the war. 'Studied it formally, have you, my boy?' I asked.

He shook his head rather sheepishly. 'No … not formally. Sorry.'

I laughed a little. 'Well that's quite all right. But I'm sure you've read up on it, haven't you?'

At last the corners of his mouth turned up and he seemed, for the first time, to relax a little. 'Yes … I've read rather a lot of the literature on it.'

'Recently?'

'Yes … well, indeed, erm … always, really. Suppose I've always had a bit of a special interest in that particular fight. As a historian I mean.'

'Really, and why is that? Most young historians these days just seem to be interested in the Great War, or the Boer War even? Why the interest in the Sudan campaign?'

He was silent for a few seconds before he answered. 'Well, it was my father, you see. He was … was killed at the Battle of Omdurman, and—'

'Oh I am so frightfully sorry. My dear boy, I had no idea. I've been so insensitive.' I simply could not believe that Mr Larwood had not thought to inform me of this fact over lunch, and I said so.

'Don't think I told him, actually. But it's nothing, really – that's why I didn't bother to mention it. Don't even remember him at all. My father that is. It's just … well, I always thought I should perhaps learn a bit more about the reconquest. I've read the various books, but I … I don't know everything exactly. I don't know what it would have felt like. Fighting in the desert like that, in the heat and the dust. And it was such a very different war to those that came soon afterwards, so it interests me enormously.'

I WAS PLEASED and encouraged by Parker's enthusiasm for the Sudan campaign, despite the awful circumstances that have brought on his interest, although he was a mere baby at the time of his father's death … I am sure he will make a very able assistant. It is sometimes easy to forget how truly awful war is, especially when one is writing about it as if it is all some sort of romantic adventure. But, as Parker told me, in his own embarrassed and rather guarded way, how his mother was heartbroken right up until the day that she died, I was reminded of the very real horror of war. Still, it must be some comfort to him to know that his father died for the glory of the British Empire. I have been lucky enough to live into old age while others have made the ultimate sacrifice, but I was always ready to have my blood spilled on some foreign field in the name of Britain.

I should add that it was touching to hear such a shy young man open up to me like this – even if it was just a little – when we had only just met. Parker said he did not know exactly how his father, who held the rank of captain, was killed, but I should think he most probably faced death at the end of a Dervish spear. I have seen this done myself and it is a quite gruesome end. I told Parker that his father must have been a truly brave man, a fine example of the brave British officer. He merely smiled a little before going quiet again. I asked him what regiment his father was in, but he said he could not recall.

I spent a further half-hour or so with Parker before coming home. We agreed to meet at least once a week while I am writing my book – although I told him he is welcome to contact me at any time. But really, I don't expect to have to give him much in the way of instructions. He seems to know exactly what I need of him. I also gave him a complete outline of how I wish to tackle the memoir, chapter-by-chapter, for him to read over.

He skimmed through the notes as I was standing there, and I think he was somewhat surprised by them, for he stopped at one point and said, 'A traitor?'

I smiled. 'Surprise you?'

'Eh … yes … yes certainly.'

'It is indeed an amazing story. Who would have thought that an Englishman could be seduced by Mahdism? But I think I should be encouraged by your surprise, no? I do hope that when it is published other readers will also be surprised too and, as a result, take a keen interest in the story.'

'Yes … indeed,' he said, in his sort of awkward way.

I have spent some time writing my diary tonight, but I find it is the best way to wind down after a day of important events. I shall go to bed now and try not to think about the India Bill, or of how I should go about writing the next chapter of my memoirs. But I am full of nervous energy, and I fear that sleep will not come for some time yet.

CHAPTER 3

THE BRANDY CAME as a welcome surprise. 'I'm afraid it is far from vintage, Major,' said Lieutenant Greenhill as he poured liberally from an improvised metal decanter.

I looked at him approvingly. 'This will be the first brandy to have passed my lips in weeks. Are you sure you can spare some for a soldier?'

'I'll hear nothing of it.'

Lieutenant Greenhill was indeed proving to be a most hospitable host, and he was doing his best to make sure that my journey back down the Nile was a pleasant one. Over a private dinner in his small and rather gloomy mess, he recounted some wonderful stories of his adventures on the river. His face came in and out of shadow, the little lantern that hung from the low roof swaying from side to side with the motion of the boat, as he explained some of the difficulties of navigating the Nile, with its annual great flood and associated water movements. It seemed that life for the sailors on that great channel was far more pleasant than for us soldiers in the desert. The constant travel along a major trade route meant that there were always opportunities to barter with the natives, security permitting of course, and the result was that the men on board had access to all kinds of luxuries that the soldier in the field could only dream of. And I too benefited from this trade that day by being presented with fresh meat for dinner, my first in two weeks. A sailor acting as a servant turned up with the brandy not long after we had eaten.

I sniffed the dark liquid before drinking. Its strong oaky scent reminded me of England, of nights sat by the fire of the officers' mess after a strenuous day of polo. That first sip felt as if it were burning my dry lips, but vintage or not it tasted wonderful. I drank but little however. I needed a clear head for Atbara, and also I did not wish to be seen to be taking advantage of my generous host.

Greenhill struck me as a lively sort, who, if we were not at war, would have been frequenting the best dance halls and theatres of London. The conversation turned to the current war situation, and it was then that he brought up the subject of French intentions in Africa.

'You're an intelligence man, do you know what this bloody General Marchand is up to?' he asked, sitting back and swirling his brandy in his cup.

'Not something that I happen to be an expert on,' I told him. 'But they are certainly as intent on empire building as ever. I should say that much.'

Greenhill agreed. 'Do you know what I think? I think they want a stretch of Africa that will run all the way from the west coast to the east coast for themselves. That's what I think they're aiming for.'

I nodded and took another sip of my brandy. 'That's certainly possible, yes. And I have no doubt that Kitchener will get on to thinking about it once he has dealt with the Khalifa.'

'And that's where you come in, eh?' He leaned forward and winked. 'What sort of mission is it Kitchener's sent you on anyway, Winters? Dangerous, is it? You can't be going behind enemy lines, or you wouldn't be heading north.'

I smiled before answering. 'You're quite correct in that I'm not going behind enemy lines. But I couldn't possibly tell you the details of my mission. Top secret I'm afraid.'

Greenhill looked bemused for a second. 'Well, here's to defeating those blasted Dervishes,' and he raised his glass.

We were still at the dinner table, engaged in some deep conversation about the tactics of the war, when a sailor came in to announce our approach to the Atbara camp. I decided to go on deck to observe the proceedings and asked leave of my host, who anyway was also getting up to start handing out orders for the docking.

I was much taken by the exuberant scene that unfolded as I approached the bow, for the sun was now setting and the fading light meant that it was possible to observe the river's progress far into the distance. Even today I remember the scene most vividly – a million twinkling lights snaking out towards a gold and purple and pink horizon. And to the sides of the magnificent Nile, that bringer of life, complete desolation. The infinite, dried-up plains were broken only by the occasional mass of jagged rock. At the parts of the river where the water soaked into the land I could see brief but dense vegetation, mostly palms and thorn-bushes. But the lifeless dust of the Nubian Desert was never far off.

The camp was situated at the confluence of the Nile and the Atbara rivers. It was more of a permanent fixture than the Wad Hamed base that I had left that morning. Here there were more than just tents. Here there were proper fortifications and more permanent buildings made of wood. There was also the customary flotilla of steamers and other boats anchored along the banks of the river. The camp seemed to be winding down for the night, with only a small amount of activity to be seen – groups of three or four soldiers gathered here and there attending to their horses and camels.

Once we had docked I wasted no time in getting ashore, having first thanked Lieutenant Greenhill for his kind hospitality. I could not travel further north that day, but if I could guarantee the use of transport for the next morning then it would save valuable time in the early hours. A visit to the quartermaster secured the use of a camel and an escort of two Egyptian soldiers, which I was assured would be available at dawn – Kitchener's administrative genius ensured that the entire supply route from Egypt to Wad Hamed ran with clockwork efficiency, so I was not surprised to find a request like this from a major being quickly fulfilled. I was also lucky to be given the use of a tent for the night.

I AWOKE EARLY, and in the grey light of the pre-dawn quickly prepared myself for the day's journey. My stomach growled with hunger – but there would be no time for breakfast – as I made my way past the many identical tents and little square wooden huts, then through what seemed like a small street of sacks and boxes full of supplies, to the relatively large quartermaster's block, a single-storey edifice standing alone by the river. I seemed the only soul alive, until I rounded a corner of the block and found my transport waiting for me – two young Egyptian soldiers mounted on camels, with a third beast awaiting me as its passenger. They were standing patiently, the elliptical tip of a new sun just showing itself above the river between and behind them. 'Good morning, men. My name is Major Winters,' I said in Arabic as I approached.

They both looked a little surprised at this. They had obviously not expected an English officer with a thorough command of their language.

'Good morning, sir,' they both eventually said, again in Arabic.

They looked like decent enough soldiers. Their dress was in good order and their camels seemed healthy and well taken care of. One of them was a lithe-looking, tall fellow, the other shorter but just as skinny. I did not bother to ask them for their names, for I would only require their assistance for a short time. Instead I explained that we would be riding north for several hours following the path of the railway.

'Are your rifles cleaned and ready? Good. Three soldiers travelling alone in the desert make an easy target. Ah, and I see that the quartermaster has also strapped a rifle to the side of my camel. That's excellent.'

Although three rifles would offer but little protection in an ambush, I hoped we would at least have enough firepower to lay down a sufficient barrage to cover an escape, were we to suddenly come upon a group of Dervish.

I could feel the first stirrings of the sun's heat on the back of my neck as we trekked out of camp in the fresh light, and it was not long before the Atbara was but a speck in the background and we were making steady progress through the desert. We advanced in parallel with the railway and maintained a constant distance of a few hundred yards to the east of it.

'Keep your eyes peeled, men,' I said, staring at the barren desert. 'Sometimes you can hardly see them until they are on top of you. Even out here.' And when I said this they dutifully sat up in their saddles and looked around.

I instructed the soldiers on what should be done in the event of an ambush or some other such emergency. They appeared to listen intently, which was encouraging.

But then, as the morning wore on and the sun rose high to reveal the crackling, parched desert in all its ferocity, the talk died away and monotony set in. We saw no activity on the railway in those first few hours, although we did pass the small and isolated settlements of Berber and Abadia, which consisted of little more than a few mud houses. I could sense that the two soldiers longed to stop and rest at these places, but I was eager to press on as far as possible, and so with Abadia behind us we faced only a large stretch of desert before the area where Kitchener had informed me that the derailment had occurred. All was quiet but for the gentle tones of the soft Nubian wind as it transported sand from one part of the desert to another. The fiery sun rose towards its zenith, its piercing rays seeming to burn straight through our uniforms, which became increasingly uncomfortable and sticky. After a while I could tell that the young Egyptian soldiers were very much beginning to tire, and eventually they seemed so fatigued that I felt I had no choice but to order that we stop to rest and have some breakfast.

'I think you both need some rest. We'll stop by that group of rocks there,' I said.

But I did not let the soldiers settle for long, as it was imperative that I get to the scene of the incident as soon as possible. Also, each minute of rest brought with it waves of guilt – I could not help but think how disappointed Major-General Kitchener would be if he saw me at this point, sitting in the sand eating hard biscuit and drinking water when my mission was so critical to the success of the entire campaign. The soldiers looked disappointed when I told them we had to move. 'So soon?' asked the tall one dejectedly. I ignored him and mounted my camel, and seeing that I was not prepared to be lenient, the men reluctantly did the same.

We trekked the rest of that morning and into the afternoon, time stretching out so that every minute felt like an hour and every hour like a day. It seemed to take forever. The only distraction during this time was the occasional passing of a train as it ferried supplies to the front. First we would hear a low whooshing sound from afar. Then a little black, wavy spot would appear against the light blue in the distance where the railway met the horizon. The spot would grow and the noise gradually increase until eventually the train would be thundering past like a wild animal on the run, smoke billowing from its top and its wheels screeching on the metal rails. And then suddenly it would be gone and the iridescent landscape would become strangely still again, and we would fix our eyes ahead and continue on.

I had not ridden a camel in some time and I found that it became increasingly uncomfortable. This was not helped by the fact that the incessant sun was sucking the energy out of us like water from a plant, so much so that after a while I noticed the Egyptian soldiers starting to slouch forward in their saddles. But I remained alert, for one could never be too careful.

It was almost three o'clock when I sighted a black shimmering object in the distance that appeared to be lying to the side of the track. The relief at seeing what I took to be my objective made me kick my camel into a gallop, and I was soon speeding through the desert, a warm but refreshing wind hitting my face and neck. It was not long before I heard the sound of high frequency pounding behind, and I knew that I had forced my weary Egyptian comrades to smarten up, spring their camels into action and fall in behind. As the distance closed I found that this was indeed the site of the wreck, for I could see clearly the dark, circular nose of the lolling derailed engine. I could also see now a small wooden hut was situated next to the train, which I took to be some kind of refuelling station.

The engine was sitting a few feet to the right of the railway. It was tilted to one side and, as we got close, I saw that this was due to one of its wheels having been completely blown off. The wheel itself had been left unceremoniously propped up against the side of the hut. I was surprised to find no sign of any soldiers here. Dismounting my camel, I instructed my men to make ready their weapons, for I had no idea what I would find in the hut. I drew my revolver before going to knock on the door. Immediately I heard some movement from within and, as the door opened, was confronted by a black soldier of the Egyptian Army. He looked startled at first, as one would in such a situation, but upon the realization that I was a British major the wide eyes narrowed so that he appeared more bewildered than shocked.

All I can say about this man is that he was a slobbery-looking fellow. I was annoyed to find that he deemed it appropriate to present himself to the outside world bare-chested, his tunic unbuttoned and hanging off his scraggy body as if he were out working in the fields. This was no way for a soldier of the Egyptian Army to be operating. 'We salute officers in this army, have you forgotten?' I said brusquely in English, while putting away my revolver. 'Who is in command here?'

The poor man did not know whether to salute or to leave to get his officer. In the end he tried to do both and ungainly turned away from me while saluting, and stuttering, 'I … I get him, sir.'

I walked into the hut and was immediately confronted by that ghastly smell of male sweat that one associates with soldiers living in close proximity. I could not make out much of the contents of the gloomy place, for the hours of trekking had made my eyes accustomed to the bright sunshine of the desert. But from what I could see I concluded that discipline in this little army outpost had long disappeared. The place was a shambles, with empty ration tins and clothing strewn all across the floor. There seemed to be some other bodies deeper inside the hut, but I dared go no further lest the smell should overpower me.

Presently a young Egyptian-looking man approached and introduced himself as Lieutenant el Masri. I told him who I was and asked him to come outside.

'You are in charge here, aren't you?'

'Yes,' he said softly.

'Well, Lieutenant, I have to say that I have never seen such an ill-disciplined bunch of soldiers as the men at this post. Can you explain to me why this place and these men are in such a poor state?'

He gave me no proper answer, but only murmured some excuse or other. I should have expected as much. The Fellahin Egyptian can make a fine soldier, for he is a naturally physically strong and courageous fighter, and he is patient when it comes to bearing hardship. But a capable officer he does not make.

I had no time to berate the man, despite my anger, for I had far more important things to be getting on with. I told him I was from the Intelligence Branch – to which he at first looked a little worried – and that I was here to investigate the sabotage of the train engine. The lieutenant informed me that he and his men had been placed at the post only after the explosion had occurred in order to guard the train for future salvage and repair.

'I see, so there are no other witnesses here to the explosion?'

'Not here, sir, but witnesses, yes,' and he pointed west. It seemed that a group of friendly Kabbabish Arabs had established a small camp about a mile or so from the refuelling station. They made a living from trading with the soldiers when the trains stopped. I would have to pay them a visit, but first I wanted to inspect the damage to the train engine, and so having ordered my two men to dismount and rest I proceeded to investigate the smashed parts.

I have to admit that I did not know a great deal about the engineering of those great beasts of steam, but I did know a thing or two about explosives and their use in this sort of demolition work. First I looked at the wheel that had been blown off. It showed little sign of damage, which suggested that the explosion was not a particularly violent one. The ruined parts of the engine itself were more interesting. The explosive device had obviously been placed next to one of the steam cylinders, and it was my guess that it was the release of pressure from the cylinder following the explosion, rather than the explosion itself, that had caused the wheel to free itself from the train. The telltale signs of exploded dynamite could be seen around the cylinder, which had completely split. Whoever planted the bomb, whether he be British or Arab, must indeed, as Kitchener had suggested, have had some expert knowledge, either in engineering or explosives or both. But I was still not convinced that only a British soldier could be responsible.

It did not take us long to find the Kabbabish settlement. It was situated about a mile to the west – on the Nile side – of the refuelling station. Here the astute reader may wonder if it were not possible that these people were responsible for the act of sabotage, but I have to say that this seemed, to say the least, doubtful. To begin with, these people relied on the railway to make their living. Why then would they wish to put in jeopardy that source of income? But more importantly, these simple people cared nothing for the politics or ideology of the wider world. Their loyalty lay only with their families and with their tribe, not with the Khalifa at Omdurman. I therefore felt confident enough to approach their camp in a completely friendly manner.

It was a meagre and desperate little place, nothing more than a few tents and some camels stuck on a windswept plain. As we rode up it appeared that most of the settlers were outside. Several children were running around and women looked to be busy attending to their various chores. An old man came to greet us. We exchanged pleasantries in Arabic and then he invited me to share some tea with him – the hospitality of these people is second-to-none, despite their lack of civilization.

In a short time I found myself sitting in one of the tents with the old fellow, whom I took to be the people's leader, enjoying some fine mint tea. Compared with the tents that I had spent the previous two nights in the place was positively palatial. Rugs covered every inch of the floor. There were cushions, and our glasses were placed on a little carved wooden table.

I thought there was a certain wisdom in the Arab's weathered old face, each wrinkle seeming to conceal a different story. I got straight to the point and asked in Arabic, 'I have been reliably informed that you witnessed the explosion the other day on the railway, is this correct?'

The old man answered in the affirmative, so I asked him to recount exactly what had taken place. He must have assumed that I regarded the group as being guilty of the sabotage, for he suddenly looked very scared, but before he could speak I assured him that this was not the case and that I was not here to interrogate him. At this he was clearly relieved. He smiled a toothy grin and then started to speak.

'Yes sir, yes sir, we were there that day. I saw it all. Very bad, very bad.'

'Tell me exactly what you saw.'

'We were not there alone, sir. There were other groups of traders like us, waiting for a trainful of soldiers that we heard was on its way, so it was very busy. There was lots of trading to be done, sir. This war will make me a very rich man,' and he smiled again, only this time the grin was wider than ever. I also smiled and nodded my head. I did not mind in the least humouring him if it meant getting the information that I needed. He continued, 'When the train came along and stopped we were hard at work, selling many things. But I noticed that there was a man, dressed as we were, who walked slowly among us but was not trading. I don't think anyone else noticed him, but to me he seemed strange. I saw him walk towards the front of the train, and then I turned away to continue selling.'

'So you did not get a proper look at this man?'

'Not at first, no, but later, yes, I did. After the explosion he walked straight past me and I looked directly at his face. I was very surprised, for although he wore the *jibba*, he looked as you do, with pale skin, and he had the clearest blue eyes, like the sea. Also, his hair, a few strands of which I saw below his headscarf, was the colour of the sand, only lighter still.'

A blond, blue-eyed man dressed in the Arab *jibba*: it looked as if Kitchener had been right after all. Perhaps it was a British soldier who was responsible. It was not entirely unheard of for an Englishman to be wearing Arab dress in the Sudan. I myself had used Arab disguise many times in the past while collecting intelligence in North Africa, but I could see no plausible reason for an Englishman to be doing such a thing at this location. I needed more details.

'Was this the only time that you saw the man?'

'Yes, sir, yes sir, it was. But when I saw him that second time, after the explosion, I continued to look at him.' After he said this, the old man suddenly sat up very straight and proud. 'I have lived a long time in the desert, sir. I have fought many of our tribal enemies and won, sir. And why have I lived so long?' He leaned forward, his eyes opening wide and, putting a finger to his temple, said, 'Because I notice the things that other people do not, sir. That is why. And so I noticed this man and what he did. He walked quickly through the crowd. Everyone was looking towards the explosion, except him, and except me, who was watching him. He went to collect a horse at the hut, and while all the attention was on the train, he quickly rode off to the north.'

I now thought it most likely that it was indeed an Englishman responsible for the atrocity. But there was one last thing I wanted to ask my host. 'And the explosion, what did you see of it?'

He cast his eyes down to the carpet. 'Terrible. Very bad, sir. I was only one carriage away when it happened. I looked up and saw only smoke and steam, but then later I saw the three soldiers who had been hit by a part of the train that had been blown off. Their mothers will be very sad.'

'Indeed,' I said, 'indeed.'

I thanked the proud old Kabbabish Arab before mounting my camel for the next stage of the hunt. The saboteur had most likely sped north towards Bashtinab, which would also be my next destination. He would most probably then have gone further north again, to the larger and more hospitable settlement of Abu Hamed. I felt pleased with my progress as we sped off into the blistering desert. How many blue-eyed, blond-haired men would there be at Bashtinab or Abu Hamed? I would wager not many. And so it was north in search of the saboteur with hair the colour of the desert sands and eyes like the sea.

CHAPTER 4

Diary of the Rt. Hon. Colonel Evelyn Winters, MP
11 February, 1935

I MUST ENDEAVOUR to note down, in as much detail as possible, the happenings of today. I rose early in order to edit some parts of my memoirs before getting to the Commons to hear Mr Churchill's speech in the afternoon. I must say I found it exceedingly difficult to concentrate on my writing. These cramped quarters are not conducive to literary work at the best of times, but this morning I found it almost impossible – I really must try to get out to Wiltshire soon, where I know I am far more productive. I would find myself trying to visualize some aspect of the 1898 campaign only to have my thoughts being drawn away from Africa towards India, from desert warfare to matters of trade and enterprise, as I imagined what Mr Churchill might say. The content of his speech has been the only talk amongst us rebels for the past week, all of us hopeful in our anticipation of him giving our opponents a good bashing. We all know that Mr Churchill can be a fine speaker – one of the best in fact – when he *is* indeed at his best. But many of us I am sure, in knowing that he has not really been at his best for some years now, and in feeling that the man's once bright star has now waned never to shine brightly again, felt more than a little uneasy about his speech – but in writing this I must acknowledge the fact that he is still by far the most effective orator that our group has, and I am glad to have him on our side.

I was sitting at my desk pondering these matters when I heard the bell ring and, opening the door, was pleasantly surprised to find Parker standing in the hallway, his coat dripping from the rain outside and an umbrella by his side.

His first words were apologetic. 'Sorry … sorry,' he mumbled.

'No, no, not at all. Come in, Parker, come in.'

I had forgotten that I had asked him to check some facts in relation to whether or not the members of a particular Welsh regiment had taken part in the campaign. This sprang back to mind, however, when I spotted the battered brown leather briefcase that he uses for his research notes under his arm.

'I was close by and I, well …'

'That's absolutely fine, my boy,' I said, taking his coat and umbrella off him. 'As I said, I want you to feel free to telephone or stop by whenever you like. We can work most effectively that way. I will be off to Parliament later, but I have some time now. Cup of tea?'

Watching him walk slowly into the study I was suddenly reminded of my age. He seemed so tall, his head only a foot or so from the top of the doorframe. I've always been of average height, but still, noting his lofty, slender frame today made me think that I must have shrunk with age.

I made us some tea and took it to the study on a tray along with some biscuits. As I entered the room Parker very kindly got up to relieve me of my burden – my slightly shaky hands were making the teaspoons rattle about and I think the poor chap felt duty bound to intervene.

It did not take us long to get through his recent researches, and it was after we had finished this, with Parker sitting on the sofa putting away his notes while I was on the armchair next to it, that he gingerly asked about today's business in Parliament – it was the first sign that he is beginning to come out of his shell. 'It seems strange just going off to Parliament like that … I mean … as your working day, I mean. It must be incredibly exciting. Is the debate about India?'

He obviously follows the goings on of Parliament quite closely. 'Yes,' I said, 'it should be electrifying today. Mr Winston Churchill is making a speech.'

'Oh, I see.' He was putting away some notes in his briefcase. 'I think I've read about you in the newspapers. Sorry. Not you exactly. I've read about the rebels, all opposing the government and all that.'

'Indeed, indeed. We're taking the fight right to the heart of government.'

He seemed to muse things over for a bit before continuing, 'Churchill, he must be very old now.'

'Oh, yes, should be into his sixties. Been in the House a long time.'

I mention this idle chat only because of what Parker said next. I find him, with his reserved yet intellectual way, a most intriguing fellow, and I am keen to understand what makes him tick. I have to say, though, that given how much he seems to be lacking in confidence, I was most surprised with what he now came out with. With his eyes firmly lowered, he said, in barely audible tones, 'Not very good these days really … eh … Mr Churchill I mean.'

Well, this was most unexpected. But I must say that although I disagreed with Parker, I was rather relieved to see that he has the strength of character to air his views. 'He's had his bad moments, certainly,' I said, 'but he's a very experienced parliamentarian. And he can be a very forceful speaker when required. I myself have witnessed one of his eloquent speeches making even the most diehard opponent of his views rethink his position. Well, anyway, we're hoping for one of his more memorable performances today.'

I thought that would be the end of the discussion, but I was shocked to discover Parker actually keen to get a bit of a debate going. Lifting his briefcase from the sofa, he said, mumbling the first few syllables, 'I just … well, I just can't see the point of trying to stop it.'

Again he would not look at me as he said this. 'Oh, why is that?' I said, with a sufficiently sceptical tone.

He came back with, 'It's just that, his brand of imperialism … it, well, I just think it's rather dated. Eh, these days at least.'

I did not wish to put any distance between us, especially as we are still getting to know each other, so I said cheerfully, 'Ah, the idealism of youth. But when you are older, my dear Parker, and have witnessed more of life and of this vicious world, I would not be surprised if your views become more hardened and pragmatic. After all, are we seeing the Dutch or the French or the Italians relinquishing control of their dependencies?'

'Well … no, but—'

'And what about the Japanese, on the march and creating their own empire as they ruthlessly conquer?'

Here, as petty as it was, I had scored a clear point in my favour. I think Parker realized this, for he was quiet for a few seconds. 'Yes, but shouldn't we … that is to say, not just England, but well … don't you think that the more advanced nations should be setting the example? That is, I mean, especially after the Great War. Shouldn't peace be our goal rather than war and ... well, expansion?'

'Exactly,' I agreed. 'But it is the maintenance of a beneficent British Empire that will keep the peace, my dear boy.'

I believe this felled the poor chap, as all he could say next was something along the lines of, 'No, what I mean is ... is ... oh nothing.'

I thought it best that we should end it here, lest the young man's emerging confidence with me be dented. I said, 'It is perfectly honourable to agree to disagree,' and we ended the argument.

It became apparent to me today that Parker is very much a serious, thinking man, perhaps even an idealist. But I find this quality really quite endearing. It is right that he should be earnest in his beliefs and be ready to defend them intellectually. The young, after all, need a certain amount of idealism, for how else would mankind progress? If anything, thinking about it now and with the added experience of the rest of today's events, I wish he had been more robust with his argument. But we are still getting acquainted with each other's personalities, and I think this morning he might even have been wary of offending an old man. Perhaps, as we spend more time together, I can bring out a little more friendly antagonism in him. I would like to see what else I can get out of his sharp young mind.

After our talk, and as he was making his way to the door, we made plans for the work that Parker will carry out over the next few days. I think I should ask him down to Wiltshire some time, perhaps in a week or two. The India problem has kept me in London far too much of late, and this has been to the detriment of my writing. I know I will get a lot more done in the quiet and space of the country, and it would be an added efficiency if I had Parker to hand. And anyway, I should enjoy some company for a change – I can't even remember the last time that I had anyone to the house.

MY EXCHANGE WITH Parker served as a good warm-up for the rigours of the Commons, and I left here in good spirits. Even this horrible, wet weather did nothing to dampen my mood, and I felt almost giddy as I taxied to Parliament, my state of mind being one of seeing beauty in almost everything. The sodden streets of Belgravia were a pleasure to the eye. The blackened bricks of the fine town houses dripped with moisture. The drenched squares housed bare and sullen-looking trees. Yet all of it seemed to me to radiate greatness. And as with so much of England's great assets, the greatness came in a restrained and a charming way, which made these scenes all the more pleasing.

I knew, even before I had entered the House, that today was going to be a memorable one, for I could hear the excited shouts and laughs of MPs from far down the corridor. I shall never forget the energy of the place as I turned the corner to walk into the Chamber. The noise suddenly jumped up to deafening levels, and I was confronted with what I can only describe as being one of the wildest scenes that I have ever witnessed in Parliament. Squeezing past the MPs who were gathered around the door, I walked on to the floor and to what seemed like a great sporting arena of ancient Rome. On each side MPs were on their feet, shouting and waving their notes about their heads passionately. I found out later that a member who is against us had just tried to strike an early blow to Mr Churchill's position – before the man had even spoken. Naturally the rebels felt outraged and showed their feelings accordingly.

The place was packed. The sitting MPs were shoulder-to-shoulder, while those standing to wave and shout looked as if the pressure on the benches had become so great that they had simply popped out involuntarily, and thought that they might as well bluster and gesticulate now that they were up. I was lucky to squeeze myself into a seat on one of the rear benches.

As soon as I sat down I glanced around for Mr Churchill. It did not take me long to spot his portly figure. Sitting a few benches back from the front and a little to the right of the Dispatch Box, he was glancing through his notes and occasionally looking up to observe the proceedings. But he was clearly not getting involved at this point. He looked steady, the small movements of his head measured, and there was not a hint of nerves in his relaxed posture – but what else would one expect from a man of his experience, who has served the House for so long?

The excitement present in the House today was the sort that will often bring out the worst in men, especially those of a weaker character who have a tendency to run with the mob. And to look at the faces of those whom I know to have a particular dislike of our cause, their eyes looking keener than ever, their heads turning quickly to observe any new change in pitch or tone from some other member's shouts, I feared that this heightened alertness of the senses signalled that Mr Churchill was in for a particularly rough time.

When at last he was called on to speak there were a few shouts of encouragement from some rebels, but then all went deadly quiet. I watched as, in the unsteady silence, Mr Churchill slowly got to his feet, his head lowered a little until he was fully upright. I hoped dearly that this would prove to be one of his better performances, for I wanted to see those near-sighted men intent on breaking up the Empire sink down into their seats, never again to have the confidence to speak up against us.

I must say that the House at this point seemed to be dripping with tension and expectation, the air inside the Chamber warm and claustro-phobic. I believe I can still recall most of Mr Churchill's main points and shall try to get them down for future reference – they may prove to be useful for forthcoming discussions. Casting his head up, he began by reminding the House of the importance of debate, and that we should try as far as possible to answer each other's arguments. And then, as so often with Mr Churchill, he used humour to win favour with the members.

'I used a lot of arguments when we last discussed this,' he drawled, 'but no attempt has ever been made by the government to answer any of them.'

Immediately there were loud laughs from us rebels, and they far outweighed the despairing groans from those who are against us. But Mr Churchill, with typical character, did not linger to make the most of the moment but quickly moved on by making a very good and valid point against the India Bill. He said that the welfare of the Indian masses is being completely ignored as the bill does not take account, in any way, of social services, of education, of agriculture and so on. 'The imperial power divests itself of interest in, and control over, all these matters,' he said forcefully, adding that Britain, 'with a shrug of its shoulders', would be leaving all the peoples of India to take their chances with inexperienced administrators.

He then came on to speak about democracy. He reminded the House of the utter failure of parliaments that have been set up in the East. And as to his own feelings on democracy, he said something like: 'I accept it. But I am a good deal more doubtful whether democracy believes in parliamen-tary institutions.' He then elaborated by stating that we only have to look towards Europe to see how democracy – and I believe he may have added here, 'in its present manifestation' – can be injurious to the parliamentary system and to personal liberty.

This, I fear, could be the one weak point in his speech. It is all very well to argue that some nations are simply not civilized enough for democracy, for this is undoubtedly the case, but here I believe he merely gave the liberals some ammunition with which to counterattack, with little gain to his own argument. I personally think the speech would have been better had he left this part out – although in the end I have to admit that it is a trifling point. Overall I thought he was doing rather well.

Next he came on to criticize those British officials who see fit to, as I believe Mr Churchill put it, 'take a needlessly poor view of our rights and our position in India'. He then slammed the Joint Select Committee for stigmatizing British rule in India as irresponsible – which the JSC definitely and outrageously is doing.

'We are no more aliens in India than the Mohammedans and Hindus themselves,' he said. 'We have as good a right to be in India as anyone there except, perhaps, the depressed classes, who are the original stock.' He then added that our government is the best that India has ever seen or ever will see, to which there were many 'hear, hears' from us rebels, and equally as many shouts of 'blah' from those against us. And he reminded the House that when Mr Gandhi had his appendix removed, he was very careful to insist that a British surgeon should carry out the operation. Again, another good point.

If I remember correctly, Mr Churchill next turned his attention to the security of the Indian nation. He said, wouldn't it be wonderful if the United States were to place her fleets and her armies at the disposal of the League of Nations so as to protect European countries against an aggressor, and yet it is this very function that Britain performs in India. 'This protection and security cannot be removed from India,' he enthused. 'They have grown with our growth and strengthened with our strength.' He said that if Britain were to withhold this aid then India would descend into the anarchy that it experienced in the sixteenth and seventeenth centuries.

I think he put this point across particularly well, and I did like his analogy with the current, precarious situation in Europe. Mr Churchill's next point was, I believe, a crucial one. He said that the current 'infatuation of the liberal mind', as I recall he phrased it, when it comes to the ideal of self-government is misguided. I shall try to print, as best as my memory will serve me, word for word what he actually said. It was something like: 'Their error is an undue exaltation of the principle of self-government.

They set this principle above all other principles – they press it to the destruction of all other principles. Let satisfaction be given to the idea of self-government and in the end, they assure us, all will come right, and the consequences, however evil, will fade into the background.' To give this point some added authority he gave the example of certain millionaire mill-owners in Bombay who would have a corrupt influence over the Congress Party, and could set up a prohibitive tariff against our own industry in Lancashire.

The rest of Mr Churchill's speech was not quite so memorable and, as he went on, much of the tension that had been present in the House when he had first stood up began to dissipate. He talked of the fiscal situation in India and how the proposed bill would damage it, and he made some analogy with the British experience in Ireland. His finish, however, was something of a grander and more impressive affair. He said that the intention of us – us so called rebels – is to instil in the minds of the British people, and of Indians, a new idea of relations between us. 'We hope once and for all to kill the idea that the British in India are aliens moving with many apologies out of the country as soon as they have been able to set up any kind of governing organism to take their place.' He also said that we are there as honoured partners with our Indian fellows, for their lasting benefit and for our own.

I think that overall it was quite a fine speech. Mr Churchill did not win our cause today but he has certainly helped it along. His points were, for the most part, very logically thought through and relevant. Of course there are those who will take apart every one of his arguments and find some reason or other to state that Mr Churchill was quite wrong, but I think that really, in the end, all will agree that our cause has been given something of a boost. Indeed, it would not surprise me if some of those MPs who were on the margin have now been won over.

I dined alone at Parliament tonight before coming home to try and get some writing done. But I am afraid that yet again I have not been very productive, for my mind has been fixated on India and on today's political business. I really must get out to Wiltshire. I shall ask Parker if he can spare a few days the next time I see him.

CHAPTER 5

A LIGHT MIST SAT mournfully over the steel-grey of the river, and I
remember thinking at the time that this seemed to perfectly reflect my
mood, for I was immensely tired and wished for nothing but rest, which
was clearly impossible.

The train's engine began to hiss and spit as its brakes were applied, and
I had to clutch the side of my seat to stop myself moving forward. Then,
as the train pulled up to a little wooden platform, I got up, stretched and
looked out over Abu Hamed.

The village seemed to cling to the side of the Nile as a leech clings to
its host. The makeshift railway station had been constructed on the outer
edge of the place, so that I looked now from the left side of the train out
over a few hundred mud houses set in a maze of narrow alleys and winding
lanes. The buildings seemed to run right up to the banks of the river a few
hundred yards away. In the early morning light they looked like ancient
ruins. Looking out the other side of the train I noted that a low plateau
surrounded the village on three sides. Atop of this rocky area stood three
stone watchtowers, which had no doubt been erected by General Gordon
in the 1880s, before Abu Hamed had been taken by the Dervishes – it was
retaken again several years later in an inspired assault led by Major-
General Sir Archibald Hunter.

I had travelled with my Egyptian men to Bashtinab and, having questioned several officers there, none of whom had seen anyone fitting the
description of the alleged saboteur, had decided to proceed directly to Abu
Hamed by rail. I had therefore dismissed the Egyptian soldiers with the
camels to return to Atbara. From Bashtinab, I had decided, I would make
far better progress alone.

The train on which I had travelled was returning from the Atbara having delivered more troops and supplies south for the final push towards Khartoum and Omdurman. I contemplated the fact that the saboteur would know that this was now imminent, and so I feared that another atrocity could come at any time. My other chief fear was that the trail was now in danger of running cold. No one knew of any blond-haired, blue-eyed man at Bashtinab. My saboteur, it seemed, had disappeared. Perhaps even the old Arab man that I had questioned had endeavoured to feed me false intelligence with regard to the man's description. If this were the case then there was a very real danger of my investigations coming to a complete standstill. These were indeed gloomy thoughts, but rather than let them lower my spirits further I made a concerted effort to renew my enthusiasm for the chase and as such I wasted no time in seeking out the most senior officer at Abu Hamed, a Colonel Maxwell, at his headquarters on the outskirts of the village.

'Well, I'm not about to refuse to assist you, old boy,' said Maxwell, standing up from behind his desk, 'but I can't for the life of me understand why you are so unwilling to let me in on the whole game. You say that General Kitchener has sent you here personally. And now you are asking for my co-operation to delve into the goings on of this village, and yet you won't tell me any more than that you are investigating sabotage on the railway.' Maxwell's tone, like his stature, seemed somewhat forbidding to begin with. He was a bear of a man, rusty looking and with a nose as red as a vulture's. Clearly he was weary of me. But could I blame him? I looked like a vagabond, and I must have sounded like a man on the verge of losing his senses.

'With all due respect, Colonel, it is not in the interests of this particular operation in which I am engaged to tell any person any more than they need know. I must simply ask that you trust me. If you wish, you may telegraph General Kitchener for reassurance of my word.'

I felt that Maxwell, despite his apparent impatience with me, was actually a practical and understanding man, and I knew that he would come round. He simply seemed a little of the old school. I had to be firm, however, in not giving away any information at this point for, as we spoke, other junior officers were coming in and out of the headquarters. It was not the sort of situation where one would wish to divulge sensitive information. After a short delay and a few mumblings,

Maxwell cast his eyes in the air and answered, 'No, we can't have that. Tell me what you need.'

I wished for three things. One was to have the assistance of a guide for at least that morning, someone that knew the area. Second, I wanted to send a telegraph to my Intelligence Branch colleagues in Cairo. And third, I wished to breakfast. Maxwell, as I suspected, said that he would act as my guide. 'If whatever this thing is that you're involved with is as important as you make out then I better look after you myself,' he said. And so after a hot breakfast, which proved to be a magnificent boost to my spirits, and a trip to the wiring post, Colonel Maxwell accompanied me in a walk around the village.

In my telegraph message I asked that my colleagues compile a list of British men whom they knew to be fluent in Arabic and to be in the Sudan. Whoever the saboteur was, he would most likely be on our files some-where. I also sent a short message to Kitchener's headquarters, updating him on my progress.

Abu Hamed's narrow little streets were just starting to come to life as Maxwell and I ambled our way through them. Weary-looking soldiers who had stopped off on their way to the front passed us, heads lowered with exhaustion, as did tatty-robed townspeople going about their daily business. Maxwell was in his element in these surroundings. He seemed to have complete command of the streets, the people naturally moving aside for him as he strode through, his massive chest pushed out and leading the way.

I decided that it was in the best interests of my investigation to inform Maxwell of my hunt for a blond-haired, blue-eyed saboteur – he was, after all, turning out to an extremely helpful fellow. The colonel, as I had been, was astonished to learn that we could have a treacherous Englishman in our midst. 'Sorry, old boy, but I can't for the life of me recall seeing a man of such looks here,' he said.

'Have you noticed anything unusual in the area, anything at all?'

'No, nothing.' We had stopped by a small clearing at the edge of the village that commanded a view of the entire area, the railway running behind us. Both of us stood looking out across Abu Hamed, over the now sparkling Nile and to the desert beyond. It was very quiet here. Maxwell looked to be in deep thought for a few seconds. 'No. Sorry, can't think of anything.'

'Any Egyptian soldiers acting suspiciously? Anything at all?'

He rubbed his large chin. 'There are so many soldiers who pass through here that … I'm dreadfully sorry I'm not helping much.'

'That's quite all right.' I sighed. 'Seems I'm stuck, unless Cairo can come up with anything. You will let me know if you see or hear of anything suspicious though, won't you?'

'Oh yes indeed. I'll have my officers—'

'No!' Instantly I checked myself. 'Forgive me, Colonel, but please, you mustn't inform anyone of what I have told you. This is a very sensitive issue, and the less people who know about it the better.'

He nodded. 'Understood perfectly, old boy.'

THE FOLLOWING HOURS were frustratingly wearisome, as there was literally nothing that I could do to move my investigation forward. I returned to the telegraph office, and having sufficiently irritated the communications officer there with my impatience at not hearing from Cairo, decided to go for a stroll through the town in the vague hope that I would notice something out of the ordinary. But it was getting towards midday at this point and the streets were burning, driving most of its inhabitants, including its soldiers, to seek cooler air indoors. I decided to join them and returned to Maxwell's office.

'Ah, there you are, Major,' said Maxwell, as I entered. He was engaged in talking with some of his junior officers. 'Gentlemen, if you would be so good as to leave us for a few minutes.' The young lieutenants and captains dutifully departed with a few quizzical looks. 'Any progress, old boy?'

'I'm afraid not.'

'Nothing from Cairo?'

I shook my head. 'Where has my saboteur disappeared to?' I said mostly to myself, placing a hand on Maxwell's desk. 'Where the devil has he got to?'

My discontent was obvious. 'Now look here,' said Maxwell, 'there is nothing that you can do until you hear from Cairo, correct?'

'Correct.'

'Then in that case, there's no point in your worrying about all this until you have some new information. Why don't you stick with me for a bit? I'm expecting the Heavy Camel Corps to reach us today, and I'll have to go about getting them sorted out. I have to say that seeing them riding in formation is one of the most impressive spectacles I have ever seen. Why don't we have some lunch and then you can come out with me and we'll watch them make their approach?'

'Splendid,' I muttered, at once thankful for the colonel's concern while also regretting that there was nothing better for me to do.

The first contingent of the Camel Corps had been raised in Dongola a few years before, being made up of a mixture of the Royal Sussex Regiment and part of the Mounted Infantry. Since then, however, the unit had expanded to bring in many parts of other regiments. I had seen elements of the corps once before in Egypt. I remembered it vividly. A group of perhaps two hundred sturdy-looking men preparing to voyage out into the vast deserts to the south. I remembered thinking then how vulnerable the men seemed as they set off, the dry horizon seeming to draw them in as if to digest and then discard them. But I had never, until now, seen them in operation, and I was actually rather grateful for the opportunity.

After lunch, the colonel and I took a horse each and rode out beyond the outskirts of the town and over its little surrounding plateau. We stopped about a mile to the north of Abu Hamed, by the palm-fringed banks of the Nile.

'We can shade here by the trees until they come in,' said the colonel.

We got our horses out of the sun and settled ourselves down to drink water and eat some dates that we had brought out of the mess after lunch. With my back against a palm tree, the colonel busy scanning the horizon for any sign of the Camel Corps, and with all being quiet but for the gently rustling palm leaves above and the low steady swish from the nearby river, I closed my eyes and relaxed, feeling eternally grateful for this moment of peace following the morning's anxieties.

'I think ... yes, there they are,' I heard from Maxwell after some short time.

Feeling a little dazed, I picked myself up, donned my hat and mounted my horse. And what a sight it was that awaited us as we emerged from the comfortable shade of that palm grove! The colonel's romantic vision of the splendid Heavy Camel Corps was entirely accurate. As we trotted along by the side of the Nile we had a clear view of them in all their glory. Two lines of riders, each led by an officer, meandering their way down a slope about a mile ahead. There must have been at least a hundred camels, all with identical field kit. Each beast was protected from the sun by a large, dark red tarpaulin that had been placed below the saddle to rest along the back and hang by the sides. The saddles themselves meanwhile were overly large, with leather handholds rising up to the front and the rear almost to the height of the men's chests, creating something of a sheik-on-the-move look. Each beast was like a large vessel, a ship sailing blissfully through the desert.

The riders too were identical, with their brilliant white helmets, light desert breeches and tunics and riding boots, each man with a bandoleer of fifty rifle rounds, sword bayonet and scabbard, water bottle and haversack as their standard kit. What a splendid sight to behold, I thought. The noble beasts were placid, their movements measured and calm, perfectly at ease in the stifling heat while carrying a heavy load, the riders sitting high and proud. Sporadic twinkles emerged from the column as the sun reflected off various bits of metal; a soldier's button; a glittering epaulette.

'A fine sight, is it not?' said Maxwell.

'Wonderful,' I replied, gazing in awe at the beautiful picture that had to lift the spirits, surely one of the finest sights in the deserts.

'You made it without any adverse adventures, I trust?' shouted Maxwell, as we approached the column.

The officer at the front, sitting far higher in his saddle than Maxwell and I, saluted promptly. 'Good afternoon, Colonel. No trouble from the enemy. Splinters of rock in the camels' hoofs, that's been the only trouble.' He was the same rank as Maxwell, a rather short fellow with a bushy black moustache. He glanced at me and I responded with a polite salute.

'Splendid,' said Maxwell. 'Let us ride with you to town. How long will you be staying?'

'Just one night, I'm afraid. I would have liked at least two to give the camels a chance to recover. But we are under orders to get to the front as soon as possible.'

'Yes, quite, quite. Well, we shall look after you. Ah, and here comes one of my captains now to find out what you might need.'

I turned my horse to face Abu Hamed and observed a fiery column of dust with a soldier on a horse galloping at its front. Maxwell must have told one of his officers to be on the lookout for the Camel Corps' approach then ride out to meet us.

More salutes and welcomes from the young captain. 'I was wondering,' said the head of the Camel Corps, 'if it would be all right for me to house some of my men in those old watchtowers there.' He pointed his gloved hand towards the plateau surrounding Abu Hamed and the old stone watchtowers that Gordon had had erected years before. 'It's better for the camels if they stay out of the town. The men can billet in the towers with the camels on the scrub surrounding. That's what we did the last time we passed through Abu Hamed and it proved most satisfactory.'

'Why certainly. They are lying empty and I shall—'

'But sir—' It was the captain. Maxwell's face suddenly turned very stern and he swivelled to face the young man.

'Yes?' he said seriously.

'Why, sir, it's simply that the towers are not all empty. Some Egyptian soldiers are using one of them to bivouac in.'

'No, you're mistaken, Captain. At no point have I given permission for any of the towers to be used by soldiers.'

'But I've seen the men going in and out, sir. They must be billeted there.'

'When did you see this?' I butted in ungraciously, my interest instantly aroused.

'Well …' stumbled the officer while patting his restless horse to calm it, 'I … I've seen them going in and out several times over these last few days.'

'With what? Were they carrying anything?' I continued, looking at Maxwell to find that it was obvious he knew what I was thinking.

Well … some bags of things, I think. I really didn't take that much notice, sir.'

'Do not touch anything, Colonel!' I said, as soon as we entered the watchtower. Realizing instantly that we might have stumbled upon a significant find when I spotted two boxes of dynamite stacked in a corner, I did not wish for the colonel to disturb what could turn out to be an important area for my investigation. The good chap that the colonel was he dutifully obeyed my command, despite my junior rank. 'Can you think of any reason why dynamite should be stored here?' I said.

'Clearly, it should not be,' replied Maxwell, looking around. 'Only the quartermaster should be storing such material.'

'Exactly.' The place was tidy, very organized – well-disciplined men, I thought. The billet was in complete contrast to the one that I had witnessed the previous day at the refuelling station. The square tower was reasonably well lit with windows in each wall. Inside, the tower was more spacious than one imagined it would be from the ascent up the hill towards it and, despite having a dirt floor, it seemed to be a comfortable enough dwelling-place for a soldier. I asked the colonel to keep watch at the door while I had a snoop around, lest the tower's occupants, whom I assumed were probably off breakfasting somewhere, should return and surprise us.

Field blankets with accompanying kit were neatly stored against the walls, and it would appear that the lodgings housed three men. The wooden lid of the top dynamite box was loose, and upon lifting it I found around twenty sticks of explosives packed efficiently next to one another. A plan for my next course of action was already beginning to form and, as it required that the place be left exactly as I had found it, I proceeded with the utmost care, diligently replacing the lid of the box.

Looking around the room once more my attention fell upon something else of interest – a small green notebook, which was sitting next to a metal cup and a rolled-up field blanket. Opening the pages, my eyes widened when I saw what it contained. There were writings and notes in Arabic. Train times, destinations. I quickly flicked through the rest of the contents. There were more detailed descriptions of what particular trains contained. But, and most sinister of all, there were sketches. My heart jumped as I saw what they were of – Kitchener's Nile gunboats that had already proved such effective fighting machines against the Dervishes, and which the general was relying on for the final battles that would decide the outcome of the entire campaign. A million questions raced through my mind. Were the gunboats their next target, or at least one of their intended targets? It certainly seemed so. Were there only three men, or more? If there were more, were those men already on their way south with a deadly cargo of explosives? I knew the answer to none of these questions but would have to find it as quickly as possible.

My next course of action was now quite clear: I would have to leave the place as if it were untouched and keep watch from some concealed area in the hope that its current occupants returned. Then, hopefully with the assistance of the colonel or of some of his men, I could capture the fiends.

IT WAS ALL arranged in a short time. The colonel was indeed most helpful, and rather than calling on some of his men to help, he insisted that he personally be at my side as I watched over the tower. This was as I had hoped, for I did not wish for anyone else in Abu Hamed to know of our plan. And anyway, I felt that we were both sufficiently armed – I with my field rifle and hand weapon, and Maxwell with his revolver – to take on three men.

The colonel returned briefly to his headquarters to check that the Camel Corps were being attended to and his officers had sufficient duties to be getting on with – and to instruct the young captain that had come to meet us with the Camel Corps to keep his mouth shut. By the time he returned I had found a small dugout, located two hundred or so yards from the tower, which would serve as our observation point.

'I say, Winters, this is all rather exciting,' said Maxwell, as he stepped into the dugout upon his return. 'I haven't been on the front line for a long time. Been stuck in places like this little village, far from the action, sorting out administration and what not. Not the sort of thing that a man wishes to be doing, you know.'

'Quite,' I replied. The dugout was rather shallow, which meant that we would have to take particular care to remain low if we were not to be seen. Importantly, however, it offered an uninterrupted view of Abu Hamed, the surrounding country and the tower. It was simply a matter of waiting and of being observant.

The time passed slowly. Maxwell and I chatted a little, but I was vigilant that our conversation should not become too robust lest the noise should give away our position. At short intervals I would observe the goings on in every direction using a spyglass. Over the next few hours there were movements of troops and people around the village, there were trains entering and leaving and there was lots of activity on the river, but I saw no men come up towards the plateau.

Thankfully, the colonel had had the foresight to bring water back with him from Abu Hamed. And by God I was glad of it, for not having the benefit of shade as we had earlier in the day, the heat in that little dugout of ours was becoming quite intolerable. Indeed, if Colonel Maxwell had not supplied us with water, I fear we would have had to retire to the village.

But, as it happened, we had enough to maintain body and soul, if only just. And after a few hours in our uncomfortable position our luck finally changed when I spotted three men emerge from one of Abu Hamed's alleyways and start to ascend the hill towards the tower.

Not wishing to excite the colonel – the last thing that I needed was to have Colonel Maxwell go charging down the hill with his revolver drawn – I at first remained silent and watched. As I had hoped, the men casually made their way towards the tower. They were dressed in Egyptian military uniforms and looked to be Arabs of some sort or other. Once they had entered the hut I informed Maxwell of their presence. He had been lying at the bottom of the dugout, exhausted from the heat.

'Well let's get after the wretches,' he said, getting to his knees and reaching for his revolver, having suddenly found some energy.

I had to calm his enthusiasm. Touching his shoulder, I said, 'Yes, yes, of course, but please, Colonel, slowly. We must proceed with care. We don't want them running off into the desert and getting away now, do we?'

This seemed to do the trick, for Maxwell instantly calmed himself, muttering, 'No, no, of course, we don't, Major.'

I had the utmost confidence in the colonel despite his susceptibility to excitement, for he was an experienced soldier and he had a certain air of gallantry about him that I liked. We had one last drink of water before we left the dugout and proceeded to slowly make our way towards the tower, along the top of the plateau. I had my rifle slung over my shoulder and my revolver at the ready, which I had decided was actually a more appropriate weapon for this situation.

'What's our strategy, Winters?' asked the colonel in a hushed tone.

'We simply open the door and walk in,' I said. 'I hope they will be so shocked that they offer no resistance.'

'And if they do resist?'

'Then we must use whatever force is necessary to defend ourselves. But these men are no good to me dead, Colonel. I need at least one of them alive.'

In my time gathering intelligence in the Arab world I had been in numerous situations far more dangerous than this. I would be lying, however, if I were to suggest that fear was not stalking me at this moment, for it certainly was. Indeed, it took some effort to put a brave face on things.

I led the way. As we approached the tower I slowed our pace to the point that our steps produced no noticeable noise whatsoever and, upon reaching the door, I looked to the colonel to seek assurance that he was ready for what we were about to commit ourselves to. He declared his approval with a stern look and a slow nod of the head.

I threw the door open and was inside less than a second later, revolver at the ready. The next few seconds were chaotic. Three Arab men as expected. One to my right side, the other two ahead and in my line of fire. 'Hands up!' I shouted. The men ahead of me instantly complied but the man to my right made a break for the door, only to be confronted by the colonel as he was entering. With magnificent control, Maxwell refrained from shooting the man but rather used his bulk to pin him against the wall.

'How would you like a bullet between the eyes?' he asked the frightened looking young Arab. The man did not resist.

I WAS TRULY elated at the capture of these three men. It was my first real progress in my quest to get to the bottom of the train derailment. And, as one of them had actually tried to evade capture, and also given the facts of the other evidence that I had seen in the tower, I felt sure that the three must be part of the conspiracy. What was needed now was to interrogate them, and so with the men firmly bound, Colonel Maxwell returned to Abu Hamed to get some officers to accompany our captives to his head-quarters. I asked that they be placed in separate rooms, that they be blindfolded and that no one should speak to them.

The colonel, too, was overjoyed at the outcome of our adventure. 'Stunning piece of work, Major, stunning,' he continued to say. He asked if he could be present during the interrogations. I said that he could – after all, he was strictly a senior officer – but asked that I alone should question the men.

The first man that I interrogated was called Mahamet Achmet Ibrahim. 'You are in a lot of trouble, young man, do you know that?' I said to him, speaking only in Arabic.

He was tied to a chair in the middle of the room. He uttered not a sound in response, so I slapped him, hard across the face. 'Answer!' I shouted. I did not mind at all using violence on the vermin. Still, he said nothing. I removed his blindfold. 'Why are there boxes of dynamite in your quarters?'

Still nothing. 'Very well,' I said, 'remain silent. It only implicates you more. But I'll get it out of you yet.'

The room that had been provided for this particular chap's interrogation was not ideal for this sort of work. If I had had more time I would have insisted on a smaller room containing nothing but a chair in which to place the captive. As it happened, this room had a desk, a map hanging on the wall and other miscellaneous items that could help the man take his mind off of his interrogator.

Regardless, there was a look of extreme fear and disillusionment in my captive's boyish-looking face. He must have known that his fate now was to eventually be paraded in front of a firing squad.

'I know who is leading you,' I said, my back to him. 'A British man with hair the colour of the desert sands and eyes like the sea. My men are working to find out his name as we speak. Now why don't you help me – why don't you help yourself – by telling me his name?'

As soon as I said this I turned and cast my eyes upon him. Lifting his head slightly, he looked at me directly. I moved closer and knelt in front of him, as eventually he opened his mouth to speak. 'God is on my side,' he whispered softly.

'And what side is that?'

His distress brought a wretchedness to his face, a face which I was sure would have been a handsome one in easier times. Sweat dripped down his forehead and from the end of his nose, making a small pool at his feet. 'We have no name,' he continued. 'We simply fight you because we have to. We could not live otherwise.'

'And it was your group that was responsible for blowing up the train?'

His answer came to me as a smile. 'Bastard!' I said, slapping him again and thinking of those British mothers who would soon be mourning the loss of a son.

The force of my blow almost knocked him off his chair. 'Let me shoot the fiend now,' said Colonel Maxwell, who was observing the proceedings from the corner of the room.

'No,' I said. 'We shall not make a martyr of him yet.' Then I addressed Achmet Ibrahim once again. 'Your next target, is it the gunboats?' As I said this I produced from one of my pockets the notebook that seemed to prove the men's guilt. But my captive had returned to being silent and would not even look at me.

The next captive was similarly reticent. But our last man, who went by the name of el Kadhi, and who looked to be the youngest of the three, was somewhat more forthcoming with information. As soon as I saw him I knew that he did not have the confidence of the first two. Indeed, the anxiety displayed by the first captive was nothing compared to the terror that was writ across this man's face. His fear was pleasingly palpable, and I was certain that I could make some progress with him.

'How does a young man like yourself come to be caught up in a nasty business like this?' I asked in Arabic.

He was crying. He shook his head pathetically. I was about to ask a further question when I was interrupted by a young officer who had come to inform us that a telegram had arrived for me from Cairo. I left our young captive with Colonel Maxwell so that I could read the message in private.

The telegram consisted of a list of six names. Three of them were the names of officers whose units were serving at the front. The other three, however, were names of officers who were attached to units engaged in building the desert railway. The uniforms of the captured men indicated that they were all from the same unit – a unit engaged in constructing the railway. Was the saboteur one of these men: a Captain Dawson, a Major Cathcart or a Captain Henry? It seemed perfectly plausible.

Armed with this new information I returned to my third, more amenable captive. 'Neither of your friends are prepared to help me,' I said as I closed the door. 'Indeed, they say that it was you who blew up the train.'

'No,' he said pitiably. 'No, it was not me.'

'Then who was it?'

He was silent for a few seconds. He seemed to be contemplating an answer, but then he simply shook his head in anguish.

'I don't believe it was you either,' I said calmly. This surprised him. 'I do not believe you to be as bloodthirsty as these other two, who will certainly face a firing squad. Their fate has already been decided. But your fate, well, that is yet to be decided. If you help me now then I could save you from those executioners' bullets.'

He said nothing, but he looked at me in such a way that I knew he had agreed to help me. I folded the telegram so that only the names Dawson, Cathcart and Henry were showing. Then I held the list before his eyes.

'Which one is it?' I said. 'Henry?' He shook his head. 'Dawson?' And he made no move. I had my man – Captain Dawson.

MY INVESTIGATION NOW began to move quite rapidly. My new informant, in wrongly believing that I could save him from the firing squad, began to spill out information. He, it seemed, had not long been recruited to the gang of would-be saboteurs by one of the other two men. He had never met this Captain Dawson, although importantly he did confirm that the man was leading the group. He admitted that he wanted to see the British leave the Sudan. Indeed, he wished them to leave all of Africa. 'They do wrong here,' he said.

He claimed not to know how many men Dawson had managed to recruit in total. Further, he claimed to know nothing of Dawson's future plans for sabotage. But he did provide me with one very interesting piece of intelligence: Dawson had arranged to meet one of the three – which one they had yet to decide – at a location in Wadi Halfa, further to the north, in two days' time. As soon as he said this a plan began to form in my head. I would accompany my informant to the location of the rendezvous where, somehow, I would set a trap to capture Dawson. Exactly how I would do this I did not know. But of one thing I was certain, now that I had Dawson in my sights, it was only a matter of time before I caught him. My worry was that he, or some other of his sympathizers, would commit further acts of sabotage before I could get to him, perhaps against Kitchener's Nile gunboats, perhaps against our desert railway, or even against some new target that I had not considered.

CHAPTER 6

Diary of the Rt. Hon. Colonel Evelyn Winters, MP
2 March, 1935

I AM PARTICULARLY fond of Wiltshire at this time of year, when winter is yet to retire and the joys of spring are on the horizon. There is a stillness to the countryside that is really quite calming. It is as if nature has taken a break in order to ready itself for the vast efforts of March, April and May, when it must thrust life back into everything.

And I am glad to be away from London for a bit. Glad to have escaped its politics. Glad to have the chance to concentrate fully on my writing. This morning, as with the last few mornings, I was extremely productive. I was at my desk and writing by 8 a.m. I worked right through until 10, when Mrs Jenkins brought some tea to my study. But even then I did not stop working, but rather read over the material that I had written in the previous hours while supposedly taking rest. I then continued to work until Parker got here at around 11.30.

I went out to meet him in the drive, and found him standing with his little suitcase admiring the Georgian architecture of the exterior.

His first words: 'Beautiful ... so beautiful.'

It is at times like this that I fully appreciate just how much of a blessing it is to have a house in the country, even if the maintenance of a constituency home can at times be a burden. 'So much space,' he said charmingly, then, taking a large, deep breath, 'And the air, it's so ... so very pure.'

The way he was looking so approvingly over the place one would have thought that my country residence was a grand estate rather than a modest house with just a few acres.

'Somewhat different from London, eh?'

'Oh, indeed, yes … yes I should say it is.'

I went to take his bag from him, but Parker insisted that he could manage – I do tend to forget that I'm getting on a bit.

Once Mrs Jenkins had shown him to his room and we had had a spot of lunch, I invited Parker to join me for a stroll around the garden before we got to work. After all, the weather this afternoon was quite fine and I did not wish to put the poor boy to work when he had only just arrived.

We took a wander down to the stream. It was all very pleasant and made me think how wonderful it is to have a bit of company for a change. We chatted about nothing in particular at first. Parker was interested in how I maintain the gardens in the summer. He commented that he misses the greenery of Sussex.

'Now that Mother's gone, I'm never really out in the country,' he said.

He comes across as being a rather sensitive young man, probably the result of not having had a father to guide him through his youth. It strikes me now that he obviously reflects a lot on things, and I think I may have to keep in check my previous inclination to try and bring out the debater in him – although I still hope to convince him, as it is important to convince all of his generation, of the need to maintain Britain's position in the world.

He is very inquisitive though. It showed itself today when he asked me how I came to be recruited to the Intelligence Branch. I, with my tired old legs, had perched myself on the bench that looks out over the stream, while Parker stood on the bank.

'It was not long after my time in the Palestine,' I explained. 'The newly formed Egyptian Army Intelligence Branch needed fluent Arabic speakers, and, well, I fitted the bill.'

He seemed quite impressed. 'It must have been so exciting, taking part in such wonderful adventures in exotic lands. Hardly been out of England … me, I mean. Just the, er, odd trip to France really.'

I think he rather admires some of the things that I have done in life, and perhaps even wishes he had had more of an adventurous time of it himself. I was reminded then of something that Milton once wrote, and I quoted accordingly: 'Peace hath her victories no less renowned than war.'

'Milton?'

'Indeed. There is much that an intelligent young man like you can achieve, my dear Parker, even in these relatively benign times.'

But I am noting down what we said today only because of the turn of direction that our conversation subsequently took, for what Parker said next truly got me thinking. He was looking out over the stream, his hands in his pockets, when he said, 'Is that why you've never married? Because you were in Intelligence, I mean? Sorry, I should … I should really mind my own business.'

'No, no, not at all,' I said.

He turned then to look up the lawn towards the house. 'It's just that, this house … it's so beautiful and, well, I can just picture children running up and down the garden, playing in the stream here in the summer and … oh, but I'm sure it must have been so very difficult, spending so much time away, and, of course, there was the danger.'

He mumbled these last few words, as he has a tendency to do, as if they were more for his benefit than mine. He had a point though. I have often thought about whether my life would have been more fulfilling had I had a family, had I fathered children. And as woeful as it may be to admit now, I have come to the conclusion, over many years of contemplation, that overall my life would indeed have been much more satisfying. Most men of my age would have children and grandchildren coming to visit on days like today rather than their writing assistant – although I am glad that Parker at least is here. And anyway, a house like this deserves to be full of family life, not a single old man with nothing but a housekeeper for company.

'The truth is,' I said, 'when I was a young man, I never really gave much thought to such things. I was too busy, as you say, having adventures. But then time passes so quickly, Parker. Before you know where you are it is all too late.'

After I said this he came and sat at the other end of the bench. He was looking not at me but out across the stream to the row of trees and to the fields beyond. He was obviously reflecting hard on something. We were both silent for a while, but then he said, 'Do you … do you regret it?' His eyes were still fixed on the distance.

I am not one accustomed to talking about one's inner thoughts. Indeed, my years working in intelligence conditioned me to give away as little as possible about myself. I think, however, that old age may be changing me – or perhaps it is simply that I feel comfortable in Parker's company – for I found being invited to open up like this, which is a real novelty, somewhat refreshing. 'That's a very difficult question to answer,' I said in response. 'I am not sure if I would go so far as to say that if I could somehow go back I would change the course of my life. But in general, yes, I think there is much that I have missed out on as a result of not having had a family. I believe that most men, when they get to my age, come to truly appreciate the benefits of a family. It must be very reassuring to know that there are people out there thinking of you.'

'Yes … yes it must be,' he said thoughtfully.

There was again a period of silence between us, when all that one could hear were the light tones of the winds as they passed through the trees. And it was then that I decided to ask Parker if it were not about time that he himself settled down to have a family. 'After all, my dear boy,' I said, 'time passes quickly, you know. It seems like little more than the blink of an eye when I was your age.'

He laughed a little before answering. 'Yes, yes, I think it is rather. The only trouble is I haven't, erm … haven't met the right woman yet. Yes that's it.'

He said this in such a way that it was obvious that he wished dearly to meet 'the right woman'. I must say that my heart went out to the boy. With his mother now departed and with no other close family to speak of, there is obviously a wide gulf in Parker's life, a space that would most suitably be filled by a good woman and perhaps some children. I sincerely hope that in the not too distant future he meets a kind young woman to complement his own good nature.

I intimated this thought in as much as I leaned over and patted him reassuringly on the shoulder, saying, 'I'm sure she's out there somewhere. Don't you worry, my dear Parker. Men like you, unlike men like me, I'm sure are destined to enjoy the love of a family.'

It is strange to write these words as I have never been one for, how would one put it, exploring one's feelings. But there is something about young Parker that makes me feel that I can be more open with him than I am accustomed to being, and which in turn makes me think deeply about issues that I would normally try to suppress at the back of my mind. There is something quite endearing about him; a sadness perhaps – a certain innocence. I do hope that once this writing project of mine is completed we keep in touch. Perhaps Mr Larwood will wish me to write another book, to which again I should invite the assistance of Parker.

*

AS WE MADE our way back up towards the house I was fearful that our rather serious conversation would put something of a cloud over this afternoon's work, so in an effort to lighten the mood I decided to show Parker the project that I've been working on sporadically for the last few months.

'Well, my boy, what do you think? Not bad for a man of my years, eh?' I said.

Parker looked a little bemused for a second. 'Yes ... not bad at all really,' he said, observing the results of my labour. 'But ... well, I don't wish to be rude, but, what is it, exactly?'

Here I had to laugh – we both did. At the moment it may indeed be nothing but a small hole in the ground, but I would have thought it should have been obvious what the endgame is. 'Are you blind, man?' I said teasingly. 'It's a pond!'

'Ah,' said Parker, finally catching on. Then he added, rather sarcastically, 'Yes, indeed, very impressive ... very impressive.' And we both laughed again.

This little interlude did much to lift our spirits, and the result was a highly productive afternoon of revisions to my writing. Although he made fun of my aspirations to build my own pond, Parker promised to help me with some digging tomorrow. I think the prospect of engaging in some real physical labour in the country has got him rather excited.

We worked right through until dinner, when Mrs Jenkins served up a wonderful roast for us. Afterwards, I left Parker alone to read in the sitting-room while I got on with some work in my study. He has retired to bed now, as I shall do in a few minutes.

I am so glad I managed to convince Parker to spend a few days with me here in the country. I am enjoying spending time with him, and I have to say that he seems very much at home in these surroundings. Indeed, I would go so far as to say that I believe Parker to be a countryman at heart.

3 March, 1935

It is indeed rare to have a day that one can look back on with utter contentment, a day that seems perfect in every way. Today, however, has been one of those exceptional times.

Mrs Jenkins woke me just after seven. She had prepared a full breakfast for Parker and me in order that we be properly nourished for our morning of toil in the garden. My plan was to spend a few hours digging out the pond, have some lunch and then spend the rest of the day working on my memoirs – but things did not quite turn out as I had contrived.

The weather this morning was perfect for outside work. It was clear, the air crisp and with an honest smell to it. But it was not so cold as to make the ground hard. The sun was still sitting low in the sky when we ventured outside, so that it cast great beams of pale yellow across the lawns and across the fields beyond the house. It was such a pretty and welcoming sight that it had to make one feel good about the day's prospects.

I find that I feel the cold far more these days than I did as a younger man – which is a sad thing to admit to – and so I was dressed in a coat and scarf for our work. Parker, blessed as he is with the hardiness of youth, wore his usual tweed jacket, although he did supplement this with a woollen jumper.

We must have looked an odd sight, the two of us. The old and the young, shovels in hand, tenaciously working away in the early morning. I, of course, do not have the strength of young Parker, and I have to say I was very impressed with his ability to labour. Still, I think I did rather well, with my old arthritic knees, for a man of my years.

There was no strict method to our digging. I showed Parker what should be the rough dimensions of the pond, and after that it was simply a case of getting the old head down and getting on with it. 'Good man, Parker,' I said encouragingly, as my youthful helper got stuck in.

We talked as well as laboured. At first we chatted about my memoirs and how the research and writing was coming along. It was then that Parker mentioned he would like to write his own book some day. 'Probably something on the Crimean. Most interesting,' he said, as he worked his shovel enthusiastically, his breath rising in a cloud above him.

Although he is well aware of his talents, I shall nevertheless have to put in a good word for the boy to Mr Larwood the next time that I see him. We then talked a bit about politics and world affairs, and yet again I saw the ideologist in Parker shine through, when he intimated that he is worried about the increasing support that the fascists are getting in this country. And on this view, unlike on India, I was glad to agree with him.

It was then, when we were both rather tired from digging and had stopped for a few minutes' rest, that Parker, leaning on his shovel like a hardened labourer, asked me if I intended to make a speech in the House against the India Bill. He had no idea that it is years since I have spoken in Parliament. 'If I am being perfectly honest with you, Parker, I don't have much of a speaking reputation in the House,' I said, as I rubbed one of my knees to try and get some heat into it.

I hoped he would not push the point, but he did. 'But ... sorry, I don't understand.'

I could only be honest with the boy and so, with a sigh, I told him that it has been three years since I made my last speech. 'There are other, far more effective speakers than me,' I explained. 'And anyway, I am quite happy to limit my debating to outside of the House, when I can talk to members one to one.'

I did not wish to say outright that I no longer feel confident in my ability to speak to the House. I think, however, that Parker surmised this from my rather enigmatic answer to his question.

Thankfully he did not labour the point further, but he did go on to question me, once again, about my thinking on the British position in India. 'I just ... just don't understand it.'

'What?'

'Why you are so against people ... native peoples I mean ... why you're so against them making their own decisions. They're just as capable ... surely just as capable as us, aren't they?'

I almost smiled at how much his confidence to engage in debate with me is rising, but I had to press my point. 'Of course they are. Of course they are, my boy. At a basic human level we are all the same, and I have met many impressive people from all races and countries. But I have also seen how the good nature that I believe we are all born with can be sullied when nourished by a culture that has become perverse and corrupt over many centuries. Trust me when I tell you that, having travelled a great deal, having immersed myself in the customs of other lands, I have concluded that there is no higher civilization than our own. And it is therefore our duty to lead others not fortunate enough to have been born to our advantages.'

He shook his head. 'No, no, it's just not right. How can you be so ... so completely certain of that ... that our civilization is higher? And if there's just the slightest, just the smallest possibility that you're wrong which ... which I think there is, then people should be left alone to live however they wish. Even if you think it's not right.'

I simply reiterated that it is our duty to lead those blighted by barbarism. Parker shook his head again and took up his shovel as if to stop talking and commence digging. But it was at this point that I thought I would be brave and ask him a rather sensitive question. 'What do you think your father's position on the matter would be, if he were still alive? Forgive me, my boy, if I am being insensitive.'

He looked somewhat startled by my question. He had certainly not expected it; it was after all really quite bold of me. He was staring at the ground when he quietly answered, 'No, no quite all right, quite all right.' He stopped and pondered the question for a few seconds, then answered nervously, 'Well, I … I really couldn't say. I never knew him and … well, Mother never talked about his politics. Sorry, but I really don't know whether he would have been against it or not.'

I could only imagine that his father, who fought and died for the Empire, would indeed have been against the India Bill. Also, I am sure he would not have wished that the deaths of his fellow soldiers-in-arms – for he would undoubtedly have seen comrades die on the battlefield before he himself was killed – should ultimately be in vain. These were my thoughts on the matter, but being somewhat careful not to offend Parker's liberal sensibilities, I did not venture to confirm this supposition. Rather, I asked him if he had managed to find out which regiment his father had been in.

'Er, no,' he said quickly, 'but I'm sure it'll come back to me.'

'Do you think about him often?' I then asked, rather unsure whether I should progress with the theme. But I had a suspicion, which proved to be correct, that it must be very difficult for Parker to research the military campaign in which his father was killed – after all, at the moment he is being reminded of his father's death on a daily basis.

He said that in recent weeks he has indeed been thinking about his father an unusual amount. 'And also,' he said, thrusting his shovel into the ground to commence work, 'you remind me of what he might have been like today. Had he still been alive, I mean.'

This was a rather forthright thing for Parker to say, and I have to admit that I was a little surprised by it. But now that I think about it, it makes perfect sense. Parker's father was a military man after all, just as I was, and we would have been around the same age now were he still alive. Yes, in retrospect it seems like a perfectly obvious statement to make.

Although I did not wish to linger on this uncomfortable subject, equally I did not want Parker to think that I was not interested in something that was obviously important to him, so I asked him if he found this disturbing.

His answer was really rather nice. 'No,' he said. 'Find it quite comforting, really, in a way.'

We left the conversation there for a while and concentrated on our digging. We made thoroughly good progress; so much so that by lunchtime I was amazed at how much dirt we had managed to get out of the ground. I estimated that the pond would need only one more day of excavation.

Pleased with ourselves, we put our shovels away and went for lunch, satisfyingly ravenous from our exertions. Parker had obviously enjoyed the morning as he kept commenting on how nice it was to be out working in the country. Also, I think he was proud of how hard he had worked. And to be fair to him, his young muscles had indeed put in far more effort than my tired old things.

At the end of lunch my intention was to suggest that we have a short rest before going to the study. Little did I realize, however, that Parker had other designs. 'We could finish it,' he said, sliding his plate to one side.

'Finish what?'

'The pond.' He looked nervously at his now discarded food. 'Oh no, no of course not. It's a silly idea.'

I sat back in my chair. 'My dear boy, I think it's a wonderful idea.' I had obviously underestimated just how much he had enjoyed the morning's activity, and although I found his sudden enthusiasm quite bemusing, I could only readily agree to his suggestion. 'Let's forget all about the book and go out there and finish our digging.'

And so rather than adjourn to the study we fetched our shovels and went back to the garden.

I began writing my diary tonight by stating that today was a perfect day. It was, and I can explain this as follows: there is something utterly fulfilling for a man, even an old man, to engage in the sort of physical work that Parker and I engaged in this morning and this afternoon. Even now as I write, with stiff shoulders that I know I will barely be able to move tomorrow, I have a feeling of complete contentment.

We worked right through until six when, finally, exhausted and aching, the job was done and we laid down our shovels. It was wonderful. Working and talking together, occasionally sharing a laugh and a joke, and to top it all achieving a common goal. It was indeed a perfect day.

CHAPTER 7

THE SUN WAS just starting to show itself above the Nile as our train pulled out of Abu Hamed. It was a new horizon in so many ways. For me it seemed like a turning point, and I could almost smell success looming. For my prisoner it may also have seemed like a new and brighter beginning. Certainly, he must have imagined that he was in a far better position today than when he was first captured. I had successfully fooled him into believing that by assisting me he would be spared treatment as a traitor. In reality his fate was as cruelly definite as that of his two comrades. And I cared nothing. I hoped also that this morning's horizon would prove to be a dark and ominous one for Captain Dawson.

When I had first arrived at Abu Hamed I was worried that my investigations were set to come to a complete standstill. But now as I left the village in the sombre early morning, prisoner in tow, I felt sure that events were moving towards a speedy and positive conclusion. I had the traitor Dawson in my sights. Surely I would have him captured and would be triumphantly reporting my victory to Kitchener within twenty-four hours. How wrong I was.

Having completed my interrogations of the prisoners and with all three safely locked up, I had dined with Colonel Maxwell in the officers' mess. I was then given officer lodgings, where I spent a very comfortable night before getting up prior to dawn the next morning, my intention to get my prisoner and myself to Wadi Halfa in time for the pre-arranged rendezvous with Dawson.

As I breakfasted, again in the officers' mess, I tried not to dwell on the fact that the day could quite possibly turn out to be the most important of my life, for my performance – whether I successfully captured or killed

Captain Dawson – could certainly have an effect on the outcome of the entire war. Experience had taught me, however, that these sorts of profound thoughts in situations such as this were a waste of time, and so I forced myself to think only of the job at hand.

My main concern lay in working out how to get my prisoner and myself to Wadi Halfa with the least amount of fuss. I had no choice but to treat el Kadhi as a potentially dangerous man, despite his apparent lack of zeal. Accompanying a bound soldier in Egyptian military dress would certainly raise the suspicions of any other troops who may be on our train, and I did not want anyone asking questions, even if it were only British soldiers displaying some natural curiosity. I wanted the journey to be made quietly and without trouble – the less people who knew what I was up to the better.

The solution lay in dressing el Kadhi in traditional Arab dress. This way I would simply look like an officer accompanying an African prisoner who had been a nuisance in some way or other. And so, having had one of the colonel's men acquire for me an Arab *jibba* – I have no idea where he got it – and with el Kadhi dressed in it and firmly bound, I said my goodbyes to the colonel.

'Good luck, old boy,' he said as we were leaving. 'And make sure you get the bugger!'

I would miss the colonel. He had been such a good chap. But now my business lay in Wadi Halfa, some thirty-odd hours north by train from Abu Hamed if there were no hold-ups. The entire journey would be across barren and empty desert. But there was one last thing that I wanted to do before leaving the village. On the way to get the train I called in at the telegraph office to send another message to my Intelligence Branch colleagues in Cairo, asking them to garner as much information as they could on Dawson within the next day, and to send me a telegram at Wadi Halfa should they discover anything of significance. The more information that I could get on my enemy – even if captured – the better.

The train was transporting several companies of troops who had been relieved of front line duty back up north. Most of them were asleep when we boarded, slouched against the sides of the train, against each other, or against baggage. I was mindful to make as little noise as possible as I pushed the prisoner past the various bodies in the gloomy carriage, eventually placing el Kadhi at a window and seating myself next to him.

I often find that the rhythmic pulses of a train's engine as it pushes out its steam can bring on a type of lethargy that can easily lead one to sleep, and in those first few hours I knew I would have to be careful not to nod off in the company of my prisoner. Although I had slept well the night before, I still felt generally exhausted, as I had done since leaving Cairo. Clearly I had to maintain the utmost vigilance, but as an added precaution I decided to secure el Kadhi's bound hands to his seat.

My prisoner obviously also found train travel sleep inducing, for just a few minutes after we had got ourselves settled in and the train was starting to get on its way, I noticed him rest his head against the rattling window and quickly fall into a deep slumber. I was not surprised. The man had been through a lot the day before and must have been exhausted. It also suited me perfectly, for I wished to keep communication with the prisoner to a minimum. It would not do to become too chummy with the man, especially when I was ultimately intent on sending him to his death.

The landscape through which we travelled was utterly featureless – the epitome of desolation. There was little to do in those first few hours other than observe the troops in the carriage as they slowly came to life, the rising heat and brightness causing them to waken, the sounds of men conversing gradually overtaking the noise of the train's engine.

At one point I sensed that a chap, a private, sitting behind me, was looking round and keenly observing my prisoner and me. It seemed that not stirring the interests of other troops had been wishful thinking. Still, I hoped that if I ignored the man he would keep his interest at the level of observation only. But, alas, this was not to be the case.

'Excuse me, sir,' came the inevitable utterance. The man's accent seemed to be broad East London. 'I don't wish to be nosy or nothing, but what's 'e done then?'

'He?'

I turned to find a rat-like little man whose mouth and chin seemed out of balance with the rest of his dirty face, being far smaller than they should have been.

'The man next to you there – your prisoner. What's 'e done?' And he pointed at el Kadhi.

'Oh, him. He's just been a bit of a nuisance, that's all.'

'Oh,' he said, turning away again. I thought for a second that my vague answer would be enough to satisfy the man's curiosity. But he had no sooner put his back to me than he again turned round to say something else. 'I just thought it might have had something to do with last night's bombin', that's all.'

Last night's bombing? The man was obviously getting confused. The train derailment had taken place a few days ago now, not last night. 'You mean the derailment a few days ago,' I corrected him.

'Oh no, sir, not that one. What, ain't you 'eard?'

I was astonished to hear these words. And I must have looked it, for the soldier's eyes widened when he realized that I had no idea what he was talking about. He moved round a little more in his seat and leaned forward towards me. I too, leaned, over towards him, getting a whiff of his rotten breath, which almost made me flinch.

'There was only another one,' he said.

'What, another bombing of a train?'

'Yes. Oh, bleedin' hell, sir, I can't believe you ain't 'eard. This time it was to the north of Wadi Halfa. We 'eard about it when we stopped at Bashtinab. There was some sailors killed this time as well as some soldiers. They was transporting the parts for one of our gunboats to the front. I felt safer on the front line than I do sittin' 'ere.'

Another atrocity! And this time the target *was* the Nile gunboats, which I had wrongly assumed would be attacked, if at all, at the front, once they had been assembled and were on the water. But, of course, they could be attacked while in transit by rail. How stupid of me not to think of this scenario. It was devastating news. My mission had been to stop another incident such as this occurring. I had failed. And to make matters worse there had been further loss of life. My heart sank. Kitchener would be enraged. This latest atrocity, if it led to a delay in the deployment of the gunboats, could hold up the entire war. In a matter of just a few hours it seemed that Dawson had gained the upper hand – and things had looked so promising this morning. But there was still, I hoped, the possibility of capturing him in Wadi Halfa.

'Do you know where the bombing took place?' I asked the soldier.

'I don't exactly, sir, although I believe it weren't that far to the north of Wadi Halfa.'

What to do. I knew that there was little action I could take until we reached our destination. Once there at least I could try to capture Dawson. Unless, I thought, perhaps there would be a communications officer on the train who could arrange for a telegraph to be sent from some stopping point before we got to Wadi Halfa. At least then I could inform Major-General Kitchener that I was well and truly on the trail of the saboteur, and that he could expect results soon.

As he seemed to know so much, I decided to consult my new friend. 'Ask for a Captain Newcombe in the front carriage, sir. He should be able to sort you out,' he said.

'I am most grateful to you. Watch this chap for a bit, will you?'

'Oh yes, sir. I'll keep an eye on him for you.'

My prisoner was still sleeping when I left to find the communications officer. I had no faith at all that my soldier friend would keep a vigilant eye on el Kadhi, but I did have faith in my ability to tie a secure knot, and so all-in-all I felt quite confident that I could safely leave him alone for a few minutes.

When I was a young soldier we carried far less kit than the modern fighting man of 1898, a point which made itself particularly apparent when I tried to make my way through the train, for there seemed to be pieces of equipment and other field materials taking up any and every available space. It meant that the going was slow and frustrating, and I seemed to be apologizing continuously for stepping on feet. It was also uncomfortable, for the train now was becoming extremely hot. Add to this the desert dust that was flying around everywhere, and moving through the train really was something of an unpleasant experience. But eventually I did get to the front and, after consulting a few of the soldiers at the back of the carriage was directed to Captain Newcombe, the communications man.

Newcombe turned out to be probably one of the least obliging communications officers in the Sudan. I found him slouched in a chair with his feet resting on a field bag. When I first asked him if he could help me transmit a message, he attempted to brush me off with some feeble excuse or other to the effect that I would be better waiting until I got to Wadi Halfa. 'Sorry, Major, but I just don't think we could manage it,' he said blithely.

This infuriated me, for I knew that he was taking little professional interest in my plight.

'Look,' I said, 'I happen to be engaged here in an extremely important mission that has been instigated personally by Major-General Kitchener. Now I demand – I order you – Captain, to put whatever resources that you have at my disposal, or by God I'll have you paraded in front of the man.'

This put the wind up the sod, for he immediately straightened himself up and said, 'Forgive me, Major. I had no idea that … I'll get on to it right away.'

'Yes, you do that,' I said.

Newcombe arranged that one of his communications men would leave the train at the next stop in order to transmit a message for me. Leaving sensitive intelligence with a soldier with whom I was not acquainted was far from ideal, but I felt that at this point I was left with little choice. I did not want Kitchener to delay the deployment of the gunboats for instance, when it was still possible that I could bring matters to a close that very day. And I could not leave the train myself, for I had to get to Wadi Halfa to try and catch Dawson, and anyway it would have been completely impractical to do so, beset as I was with a prisoner.

Once I had noted down my message for Kitchener and given it to Newcombe – with a quiet but sternly given warning that what was contained inside was top secret and should not be shown to anyone other than the soldier charged with transmitting it – I made haste to get back to el Kadhi. I estimated that I had already left him alone for at least twenty minutes, and although there was no immediate cause for this to be of concern, it nevertheless did make me feel somewhat nervous.

Moving through the train was excruciatingly cumbersome. It was now getting so hot that men seated next to aisles, in an effort to catch some fresher air, were starting to make their way towards the windows located between carriages. This impeded my progress further, making movement slower than ever.

When I eventually did get to my carriage I found a number of troops crowded into the passageways, which prevented me from immediately seeing el Kadhi. I began forcing my way through, expecting very soon to start catching glimpses of my Arab prisoner's white dress through the gaps between soldiers' bodies.

But there was something not quite right. Depending on my movements and that of the soldiers, I could only catch a glimpse of where we were sitting for a second at a time, but in none of these brief instances did I see my man. He must be there, I thought. What about the soldier from London whom I had talked to? I moved my head to try and search out the gaps between troops. Yes, got him. He had his back to me but it was definitely the same soldier that I had conversed with earlier. But where was el Kadhi? I could not for the life of me see the man. Had he gone? I panicked and rushed through the crowd to where I had left my prisoner.

The seat was empty.

'Where is he?' I said loudly to the cockney soldier.

'Oh, you're back, sir,' and he calmly turned in his seat to half face me.

'Yes, I am indeed back! Where is my prisoner?'

'But your friend came to collect him, sir.'

'Friend?'

'Yes, sir. Said he was with you and that he had been sent to collect the man.'

I was infuriated, so much so that I grabbed the soldier by the lapels. 'I have no friends on this train,' I said angrily. 'Now who took him? Where did they go?'

The soldier, not surprisingly, looked profoundly shocked by my behaviour. 'They went out that way, sir,' and he pointed in the opposite direction to which I had just come, towards the back of the train. 'He said that you was sitting somewhere else and that he was taking the prisoner there. I thought ...'

But I had now completely switched off. Any other information was superfluous. I was about to start making my way towards the back of the train in pursuit but then stopped. 'What did the man look like?' I asked, more calmly this time as I partly regained my senses.

'You mean the man who came for your prisoner?'

'Yes of course I mean him. What did he look like?'

'Well, I suppose he was quite a short fellow. And he had blond hair. I remember that much.'

Blond hair! Was it Dawson?

'Eyes?' I said.

He thought about it for a second. 'Blue, if I'm not mistaken, sir.'

It must be Dawson. It had to be. But why and how was he here? I had no time to think. I rushed off in pursuit, shoving and pushing my way through the crowds with shouts of, 'Move man, move yourself there!'

I knew I had to be at least two or three carriages from the back of the train. It was two or three carriages of potential hiding places and two or three carriages of potential danger. Perhaps Dawson would try to ambush me. Perhaps the men had jumped from the train – although I thought this highly unlikely, for being stranded in this part of the desert could easily prove suicidal given the sheer desolation of what lay outside.

I seemed to be some kind of conveyor of carnage as I fought my way through that oven-hot train. Any man not getting out of my way was liable to end up on the ground or on top of some other seated fellow. I believe I may have made many enemies in those few minutes, but this could not be helped, and nothing could stop me in my pursuit.

I got through two carriages and saw no sign of my enemies. There was only one carriage left. If the men were not there then they must have jumped from the train – unless they had somehow and very cleverly hidden themselves, and I had already missed them.

The last carriage. Again full of soldiers. As this was the most likely place in which I would find my men, I decided that it would be unwise to go charging my way through it blindly. Rather, I stopped by a large equipment bag that was stored near the entrance. Placing one foot on top of it and bracing my hands against the walls for balance, I hoisted myself up so that I had a clear view down the entire length of the carriage.

Immediately I spotted them, around two-thirds of the way down, facing away from me and moving towards the back of the train. It was the first time that I had seen my enemy – my real enemy. But I had little time for contemplation other than to register that the man with el Kadhi did indeed have blond hair. Strangely though, by the way that he moved it seemed that el Kadhi's hands were still tied together. The only way that I could fathom what was happening was to assume that Dawson must have been in Abu Hamed while I was there, that he found out somehow that I had captured his three men and had embarked upon some sort of botched rescue attempt, and further, that in trying to escape now was pretending to be an officer in charge of an Arab prisoner. It seemed callous indeed for a man who had seemed so well organized before, for the chances of success were monumentally slim.

From my vantage point I launched myself into the carriage, simultaneously drawing my revolver. There were shouts of, 'What's going on there?' And I believe there were also general shouts of alarm that an officer was suddenly and quite aggressively brandishing a weapon.

Regardless, I pressed on towards my target. Men were now pushing towards the sides of the train to make way for what must have seemed like a madman. And now I could see my foes once again. They were rushing towards the door at the back of the carriage, el Kadhi at the front being continuously pushed by Dawson. They were surely intent on jumping.

For a brief second Dawson looked round and observed me. My dark and what must have been wild eyes met with his steely light blue. He had a look of sheer determination on his face. And then they were at the door and through it. I had to get there before they jumped.

Just a few seconds later I too was nearing the door. I expected to see nothing but train tracks and desert extend into the distance through the door's window, but I had not realized that there was one last section of train to go. It was not a carriage but a flat wagon for transporting equipment, and it was empty as the train was returning from the front having delivered its cargo.

As I got to the door I saw my men once more. They were around two-thirds of the way down the wagon. Dawson seemed to be trying to force el Kadhi to the side as if to make him jump, but el Kadhi seemed reluctant, perhaps because his hands were still bound.

'Hold it there, Dawson!' I shouted, when I was through. I had my revolver raised. Dawson turned. He too had a revolver. He began to raise the weapon. I had no choice but to fire. The noise of the train's movements here was almost deafening, and it muffled the crack of my shot. But the bullet went wide. It was difficult to aim effectively when the train's motion kept moving me from side to side.

I dropped to one knee in an attempt to make myself a smaller target for Dawson's returning fire. But no bullet came near. Dawson did indeed raise his weapon, unsteadily as he struggled to retain his balance, but rather than point it at me I was stunned to see him place the gun next to el Kadhi's temple and calmly shoot the man dead. The Arab did not even see it coming.

I watched as the body collapsed and fell off the side of the train, tumbling inanimately into the desert and leaving a trail of dust in its wake. Dawson's next shot would surely be for me. But before he had a chance to aim his revolver I got off another shot. This time it was on target, hitting the man in the lower chest area.

Dawson fell to his knees then keeled over on to one side. I raised myself slowly and began to move towards him, careful lest he should suddenly spring back into life. But he seemed clearly to be dead.

I kicked his revolver off the side of the wagon, and looking at him concluded that he had most definitely expired. The eyes were lifeless and staring towards a blue sky that seemed to be a perfect reflection of them.

I decided to search the body to see if I could find any evidence of Dawson's sabotage activities. I was completely bewildered by the events that had just taken place. In little less than ten minutes I had gone from being in a completely controllable situation to having killed a man and caused panic on a packed troop train. And I could not understand why Dawson had killed el Kadhi, whom he had apparently been trying to save.

I began rifling through his pockets. I found a Swiss watch, some cigarettes in a silver holder and some gold sovereigns. I unbuttoned his sweat-stained tunic to search inside and came across a gentleman's wallet. Here I discovered some money and, strangely, several cards for hotels in Casablanca and Algiers. I was about to place the wallet back in the tunic when something made me pause for a second. I thought I had felt the faint outline of another item in there that I had almost managed to miss.

Looking carefully around the area I noticed that an opening had been neatly cut along one seam of the wallet, giving access to the lining within. I squeezed my fingers inside and felt what was apparently a very small and thin notebook.

I pulled it out. It was not so much a notebook as some pieces of paper held together by just a few strands of thread. Peeling back the first tiny page I was astounded at what my eyes fell upon – it was nothing less than a codebook! A line of tiny numbers ran along the top of the page, a line of letters horizontally down one side; the middle filled with letters, numbers and symbols. I could not decipher the code, but I had seen something similar used in North Africa.

As far as I was aware only one group of people used such codes, and those people were agents of the French State. This man was no British Captain Dawson. In those few seconds it became shockingly clear that the man who now lay dead next to me, the man whom I had just killed, was a French agent.

PART II

'France is, and must always remain, Britain's greatest enemy.'

Lord Salisbury, British Prime Minister, 1885-6, 1886-92, 1895-1902

CHAPTER 8

'A FRENCH AGENT? Come on, Evelyn, you can't be serious.'
'I am quite serious, I can assure you. Have a look at this.' I handed Major Jonathan Lloyd, my Intelligence Branch counterpart based at Wadi Halfa, the tiny notebook that I had retrieved from the body of the dead French agent.

Lloyd carefully opened the notebook and looked through some of its pages, then raised his eyebrows. He had obviously come to the same conclusion as I had. 'Am I not correct in saying that those codes are unmistakably the work of the French?' I said.

Lloyd nodded knowingly. He was a phlegmatic man with whom I had worked in Cairo, his most obvious feature a long vertical scar that he sported on his right cheek, the result of some dangerous mission he would never discuss. 'Do you know,' he said, 'you might just be right. Well who would have thought … and you say you took this from the man that you shot on the train?'

'As I said, I thought I was on the trail of an Englishman, but it seems that this conspiracy runs far deeper than I – and indeed Major-General Kitchener – had first thought.'

'And this Englishman whom you say is leading the conspiracy—'
'Dawson.'

'Yes, Dawson. Don't you think your informant could have lied about him in order to put you off the trail?'

Lloyd was sitting behind a desk in a tiny, bare room that had been provided for Intelligence Branch use. We were alone and drinking tea. 'I don't believe so,' I said, in answer to his question. 'My instincts tell me that the man that I captured, the one who was also killed on the train, was telling the truth. I cannot explain why exactly. Let's just say ten years of experience in getting information out of Arabs.'

He placed the little codebook on the desk and leaned back in his chair. He looked thoughtful for a few seconds. 'You know, Evelyn,' he said, 'the more that I think about it, the more this thing actually seems to make sense. The French obviously have designs on the Sudan. I've read the reports on General Marchand's movements.'

He was quite correct. As I had discussed not long before with Lieutenant Greenhill, it was clear that the French wished to extend their influence further east into the Sudan. We would only find out after the war that, under the orders of French Foreign Minister Hanotaux, General Jean-Baptiste Marchand was ultimately intent on having a strip of Africa from the Red Sea to the Atlantic Ocean under French control. Although Kitchener's energies at this time would have been for the most part focused only on taking Omdurman and Khartoum, on crushing the Khalifa and his Dervish army, French imperial designs were no doubt also taking up space in some part of that great analytical mind of his.

'And we cannot beat the Khalifa and finally avenge General Gordon only to find ourselves outmanoeuvred by the French,' I added.

Lloyd agreed. He also agreed that given the importance – and now the added importance – of my mission, to put himself at my disposal. I was grateful for his offer of help, for there was much now that had to be done. I instructed him to contact our colleagues in Cairo and to inform them of this latest development with the French. I added as a suggestion that our Cairo station should get in touch with the Foreign Office in London with a request that its diplomats put pressure on Paris to answer for its agent's activities, for what was now taking place was most serious in terms of Britain's political relationship with its neighbour.

I then asked Lloyd what he knew about the latest bombing to the north of Wadi Halfa. 'Well, it's certainly going to take longer than Kitchener had hoped to get that particular gunboat to the front and assembled,' he said.

'Was the gunboat itself damaged?'

'Not that I know of. But the real problem will come down to how to replace the sailors who were killed. I've heard that these are pretty sophisticated vessels, and very difficult to navigate on the Nile.'

'Indeed, I'm sure they are,' I said, feeling guilty that this latest atrocity had even occurred. The incident it seemed had brought the entire rail line north of Wadi Halfa to a complete standstill for almost the entire day. Five sailors and two soldiers had been killed in what must have been a far larger explosion than the one that had derailed the train further south. 'Do you know if Kitchener has changed his plans in any way for the march on Omdurman and Khartoum?'

'We've heard nothing,' said Lloyd. 'Although if he had changed his plans I'm sure Kitchener would let very few people know about it.'

I agreed, adding, 'He did, after all, work in Intelligence.'

Now fully up to date on this latest bombing and with the telegraphing details taken care of, I was quickly on my way. There remained a small chance that Dawson would turn up for his meeting with one of his recruits, although in reality I felt sure that the news of the commotion that I had caused on the train to Wadi Halfa would have filtered through to him by now, and that consequently he would stay away. Still, as I had made it to the town as planned, I felt I had little choice but to be at the rendezvous point at the pre-determined time.

It was dark when I left Major Lloyd's office and ventured into Wadi Halfa's maze of streets. It has been said that the fight to reclaim the Sudan was won not on the battlefield at Omdurman but in the workshops of Wadi Halfa, where the Sudan Military Railway was forged. It was from here that the engineers and rail workers had thrust the line away from the Nile and into the heart of the Nubian Desert, from here that that great feat of engineering – performed under the harshest conditions, on a meagre budget, with old rolling stock and with the constant threat of Dervish attack or of running out of food and water – had begun, the rifle being laid to the side and replaced by the pick and the spade as the soldier's weapon.

My informant had given me the location of a mud hut lying just beyond the western outskirts of the town, between the Nile and the section of the railway that went south-west towards Kerma – as opposed to the main line that went south-east to Abu Hamed. The place, he had said, would be standing with just a few other buildings and would be located next to a track that led out of the town. He had added that I would further be able to distinguish the meeting place by looking for an empty flagpole protruding from its roof.

I am not afraid to admit that I felt extremely nervous as I made my way through Wadi Halfa's narrow and darkened streets. Most of the town's inhabitants had by now retreated indoors, so that the only people to be seen were Arab men dotted in doorways here and there, alone, smoking silently. It was a place of shadows and mystery, and it made me alert and on edge. I had an ill feeling that Dawson and I had now switched roles and that I was in fact the hunted rather than the hunter. Was it not possible that Dawson, with the knowledge that a British officer was on his trail, was now seeking directly to eliminate him? Perhaps he had managed to get an accurate description of his pursuer from one of the soldiers on the train. After all, I had certainly given many of those men cause to take a particular interest in me.

Any one of these Arabs that I am now so casually walking past could turn out be an assassin, I thought. That man there whom I am approaching now, did he not just give me a deadly glance? And that man whom I can just make out there, why is his right hand concealed under his clothing? Is it actually clutching a knife that in a few seconds will be thrust up towards my throat?

Such unnecessary and quite irrational thoughts began to crowd my mind, and I have to admit that I had to struggle to maintain my nerve in those narrow alleys with their gloomy doorways, each one seeming to be an enclave of danger. In the end I placed my hand on top of my holster for comfort and pressed on through the inhospitable streets, for it was all that I could do. But every step of the way I had to struggle against thoughts that I knew could easily overcome a man.

Eventually, and with much relief, I reached the westernmost point of the town. I then turned left and skirted around the buildings on the edge of Wadi Halfa until I came to a track leading out into the pitch-black desert. I walked along the track for a hundred yards until I came across the outline of three mud huts lying in a line. Although I could not see it, I knew that the railway to Kerma ran parallel to the huts, around two hundreds yards to the front, while directly behind flowed the Nile, again in parallel. As I walked towards the buildings I saw, in the little illumination that there was, a thin area of more dense darkness sticking up from the middle hut, which I took to be the flagpole. No light emanated from any window.

It was my guess that the building had been used as a military post at some point, perhaps as a checking area for those entering and leaving Wadi Halfa. It looked, however, to have been uninhabited for some time. It was double-fronted and had a wooden door, to the sides of which there were situated two square windows. It also had a small wooden veranda with a slated roof that looked to be almost falling apart.

Slowly I drew my revolver, the weapon that I had already used to kill one man that day. I then walked around to inspect the backs of the huts. Here, too, there was no sign of life, the only noise the soft flowing sound of the river. Returning to the front I stepped up on to the middle hut's veranda. The creak of the wooden boards under my feet seemed deafeningly loud, and this heightened my nervousness, for if anyone were nearby they would certainly have heard.

Staying close to the wall of the building I made my way towards the window nearest to me. I saw nothing but blackness within. But this was as expected, for there was half an hour to go until the appointed time – 10 p.m. – that el Kadhi had informed me that the meeting was due to take place.

I made my way to the door and entered cautiously, then moved to the back of the room, where I remained still for a few minutes until I was certain that I was alone. I then proceeded to light a small candle that I always carry with me.

The flickering light showed a bare, decaying and unwelcoming space. There was a hole in the top corner of the building, and I noticed also a gap in the floor close to where I had entered – I had been lucky not to lose a leg to it. It smelt of disuse.

I decided to place the candle down near the door and to place myself in one of the back corners of the hut. In the unlikely event that Dawson did turn up, I fully intended that I should see him before he saw me. Further, if he did appear, I hoped that the sight of a light coming from the hut would lead him to believe that one of his recruits was awaiting him inside.

I have already mentioned how tired I felt at the start of this day – the sunrise that morning, that at the time had seemed so hopeful, now felt as if it had occurred months ago so much had taken place. As an intelligence officer I was perfectly familiar with being in situations where there was little to do but wait, watch and listen. And in such situations the self-discipline of a good intelligence officer should be second-to-none. Here, however, I must confess that as I crouched in the corner of that dim little hut, my nerves exhausted from the previous hours' constant excitement, I found it extremely difficult to keep my eyes open and to remain alert.

Perhaps this lack of control stemmed from the fact that in my heart I did not expect Dawson to appear. Or perhaps, and more likely, it occurred because I was so fatigued that my body felt as if it were close to collapse. Whatever the reason, there was no excusing my unprofessionalism in allowing sleep to gradually take its dangerous hold. If I had known that I were losing consciousness I would have acted to remain awake, but I did not, and so gradually I began to doze.

It was the scrape of shoes on the veranda's floorboards that brought me back to life. As soon as my ears picked up that awful rasping noise my eyes shot open and my heart began to beat faster. Slowly I raised myself as the sound of whoever was outside got closer to the door. I had my pistol, which had been on my lap, in my hand. Would I be required to use it for a second time this day? I was not even sure that my nerves could take any more drama.

The door slowly creaked open to reveal the black figure of a man in its entrance. I could see no details at this point, only that the outline suggested that he was dressed in western military uniform. 'Hello, Captain Dawson,' I said softly and in my best Arabic.

Immediately the head turned to face the corner where I was standing, but still the man did not enter the hut. There was silence for a few seconds before I got an answer. 'Good evening,' he said in perfect Arabic. 'And which one are you?'

This was what I needed. Surely now there was no mistaking that this was Dawson, and that he was indeed the leader of the traitorous group. It took all the self-control that I had not to raise my revolver and shoot the man right there. 'Mahamet Achmet Ibrahim,' I said.

'Have you brought the dynamite?' He took a step into the room. The step forward meant that he was now partially illuminated by the light of the candle. I could clearly see the left side of the body. The uniform was certainly British, and from the three pips that appeared on the shoulder it was obvious that he held the rank of captain. The face, however, remained for the most part in the shadows. From what I could see it seemed that Dawson had dark hair and a strong chin, but I could make out little else.

My aim was to maintain my cover for as long as possible in the hope of extricating some information from the man, so rather than answer his question, I said, 'The Frenchman is dead, have you heard?'

The reply: 'Ah, so it was him who was shot on the train today. Well, then they must be on to us. He did some good work for us in the south; I wish we could have used him more.'

'We have no more French agents to help us?'

'Not yet, but ...' and there was a pause. 'Look, why don't you come out of there? Let me see you.' He sounded a little suspicious.

The game was up. I now had to make my move and try to capture Dawson. But the few seconds of silence must have been enough to convince him that something was amiss, for in little less than the blink of an eye he had jumped back and through the door.

I moved to start off in pursuit, but here I was felled by one of those cruel acts of fate that occur only rarely, for I tripped over a raised wooden plank in the wasted floor and fell flat on my face, my revolver tumbling to the ground in front of me. This gave Dawson a vital few seconds with which to get a head start and, by the time I had recovered myself and reached the door, he was striding off into the desert towards the railway. What is more, in that short timeframe my ears also picked up the unmistakable pounding noise of an approaching train.

I looked to my left as I jumped off the veranda and saw, from the little light that emanated from the town, first a plume of smoke moving horizontally across the rooftops of Wadi Halfa then the engine itself as the train emerged from the outskirts. Dawson would also have seen this, and he would also have realized instantly, as I did, that it was his best chance of escape.

I could just see Dawson's figure in the darkness ahead of me, running at an angle towards the railway. I could have stopped then and tried to get off a shot. He was certainly within range, but I was not at all confident of accurately hitting a moving target that I could hardly see. Instead I ran, as fast and as hard as my body could muster.

I seemed to be gaining on him, but the gain was marginal. Meanwhile, the noise of the steam locomotive was getting louder and louder. I glanced around in mid-stride. The dense front of the locomotive was thumping down the track and growing larger. Desperately I tried to work out the odds of Dawson reaching the train, of both of us reaching the train. But I could not be sure of anything. I doubted if I would get there, but there seemed a small chance that Dawson might make it.

And then the train was hurtling past me, about a hundred yards to my front, the noise of its rolling carriages competing with that of my heavy breathing. Dawson had around fifty yards to cover if he were to get there. My heart felt as if it was about to explode and it seemed impossible to get as much air into my lungs as I needed. But still I ran on through the desert.

Dawson was getting close to the train now. He might just make it. The last carriage of the train, which looked – in the darkness at least – to be a supply train, started to move across my field of vision, Dawson sprinting towards it. I must have been no more than thirty yards from him, but by now it seemed clear that Dawson was going to get to the train and that I would not. He reached up his hand to what might have been a bar protruding from the back of the last carriage, and then he was up and on board. I kept running until I reached the train tracks but there was no possibility that I would also reach the carriage. I stopped, facing the back of the train. I could still see Dawson's outline, crouched down on a small platform. I raised my weapon but then decided not to fire. There was little point. It would have been a wasted bullet, for it would never have hit its target.

As the train with my enemy aboard sped off into the darkness I collapsed to the side of the railway line, completely exhausted.

I SPENT THAT night in the mud hut where I had confronted Dawson. Not having the energy to return to Wadi Halfa, it was all that I could do to drag myself back to that uninviting place, as unpleasant as it was, to sleep on its rotting floor. When I awoke the next morning, stiff and not feeling at all rested, sunshine was flooding in through the windows to illuminate the dust in the air around me.

At once I made my way to Major Lloyd's office. The previous day had turned out to be probably the most eventful of my entire life. I hoped dearly that this day would bring no more surprises.

'Evelyn, you look like a wreck,' were Lloyd's first words upon seeing me. 'What has happened to you, man? And where did you get to last night?'

I tried to explain as clearly as I could my adventures of the previous evening. My colleague had a look of complete astonishment on his face as I told him how I had actually confronted Dawson and described the incredible circumstances of his escape. We now knew for certain that the French were involved and that Captain Dawson was leading the group of saboteurs – although we still knew little of the group itself, its size, its motives and ultimate intentions and so on.

'Did you contact Cairo?' I asked.

'I did, and they in turn have contacted London, where I understand a formal complaint has been made to the French ambassador. I expect further communications this morning.'

I was about to launch into the plans that I now had for catching up with Dawson when Lloyd stopped me. 'Evelyn, have a look at yourself,' he said, in a manner which suggested that my welfare was of some concern to him.

'What?'

'Just stop for a second … stop and have a look at yourself. You're in a mess, man.' He was absolutely correct. I looked down at my uniform. It was filthy and dishevelled looking; far worse than a few days before. My hands too were thick with dirt. Lloyd continued, 'Now why don't you have a wash and a shave in my quarters then join me for breakfast? We can discuss what to do about Dawson then.'

I WAS GLAD that Major Lloyd had forced me to stop and take stock of the situation, and I felt thoroughly refreshed after taking up the offer to use his lodgings, which were really quite comfortable by the standards of the Sudan, to wash and shave. At the start of that morning my intention had been to get a train south to Kerma as soon as possible, but after conversing with Lloyd over our meal I decided that such a rash move could turn out to be counterproductive. What would I do once at Kerma? How would I locate Dawson? After all, I did not even have a proper description of what the man looked like. 'Best to stay with us for a bit, at least until we hear from Cairo,' he suggested.

But there was no telegram from Cairo awaiting us when we returned from the officers' mess to the Intelligence Branch room, and it was several frustrating and useless hours later that we did finally receive a communication. Even then, however, all the telegram said was that negotiations with the French were ongoing and that we would not hear anything conclusive until at least the following day. 'Damn it!' I said. 'Those bloody bureaucrats. How they love to talk. Can't they see that every minute counts out here?'

Yet again I found myself with nothing to do until a new lead came my way – or perhaps even a confirmation from London that they would not be providing my next lead! That afternoon, I believe in an attempt to counter my increasing frustration, Lloyd suggested we go out on the plains to the south of Wadi Halfa to watch some firing practice that was taking place. 'The War Office have, as wisely as ever, issued the artillery on active service only with shrapnel ammunition,' said Lloyd sarcastically, as we walked across the sand towards a line of men with their accompanying artillery pieces arranged in a line about a mile from the town.

'And what difference does that make?'

'Oh, quite a difference, I believe. Shrapnel rounds are no good for breaching defences, you see. But some of our officers have found a way to overcome it. Quite ingenious really. Stop here. You see that stone wall in the distance there?'

I narrowed my eyes against the strong sun and observed a square block, perhaps ten feet high, and from the angle that we observed it I estimated it must have been around the same again in thickness. 'Yes, I see it. And that represents the walls of Omdurman, correct?'

'Precisely. The men have been building these to practise on. They can't practise any further south, as no ammunition could be spared there, so this is their last chance to test their firing skills. The men are loading now. Keep your eye on the wall when they fire.'

With perfectly timed precision the line of soldiers, three to each gun, loaded the heavy artillery pieces. Soon after came the shout, 'Fire!' and the shells were let loose. A massive pounding noise as they fired simultaneously, the guns leaping back to throw up clouds of dust around them, and then a few seconds later the square block in the distance disappeared as the shells exploded around it. When the dust had settled I could see that the target had been completely destroyed, and the rubble that remained seemed to have spread, from our vantage point at least, over quite a distance.

'Very effective indeed,' I confirmed.

Lloyd explained. 'The shrapnel shell you see is a steel case, containing about a hundred and twenty bullets of various sizes. Down its centre there is a narrow tube, which contains the bursting charge and is ignited by a time fuse. So the shell bursts in the air you see, scattering its contents over an area of ... oh, about a hundred yards by fifteen. The common shell, on the other hand, although it also has a hollow centre containing a bursting charge, only ignites when it hits something. Now, you may not know this, but one of the interesting developments to come out of the Turko-Greek war was the almost harmless effect of using heavy artillery on massed troops when shrapnel was not employed. But when it is necessary to breach a wall or other fortification, the shrapnel shell bursting in the air is useless. These ones, however, work extremely well because a percussion fuse has been used. As I say, quite ingenious.'

'And I assume the regular shrapnel shells are for use on the Dervishes?'

'That's right.'

I thought about the effect of all that deadly hot metal flying through the air. 'I pity anyone on the receiving end of that.'

THE BOREDOM AND frustration of that night in Wadi Halfa was almost unbearable, and despite Lloyd's attempts to keep me occupied with a card game I could not put my mind to rest even for a few hours.

Thankfully, however, we received a telegram the following morning. I let Lloyd read the message first and, as he did so, I noticed a smile gradually develop on his face.

'Evelyn, I think we've got them on the run,' he said, handing me the note. It stated that French diplomats had formally apologized for what they described as 'an unofficial operative' getting involved with British affairs in the Sudan. Further, in an effort of appeasement, the French had agreed to gather whatever information they had on the man whom I had killed and his activities, and hand it over to us. The details of this handover were still being worked out and another message would follow.

'My guess is there was nothing unofficial about it,' said Lloyd.

I agreed. 'Clearly this would all have been planned from the very top. But we can let Paris and London play out their diplomatic games, so long as we get that information.' This latest development was extremely important, for the intelligence with which the French now planned to provide us, could – unless the offer were disingenuous – turn out to be the key to getting to the bottom of Dawson's activities. There was one problem, however: it was I, and not our intelligence people in Cairo or London, who needed the information if we were to stop Dawson. If the French handed over a file on the man then I wanted to see it. I did not wish to rely on second-hand transmissions by telegraph. I explained this to Lloyd.

'I'll go back to them,' he said. 'Perhaps we can engineer some sort of handover right here in the Sudan, which you could deal with directly.'

The next few hours were again immensely frustrating, for I could do nothing but wait in Wadi Halfa for further news from Cairo. With each minute that passed I knew that my enemy was getting further away from me. I also knew that in that time he could be plotting – or even carrying out – further acts of sabotage against our forces. I suspected that the Nile gunboats would still be his main target, for Dawson would have known that strategically they would form a key part of Kitchener's offensive, and that without them any march on Khartoum would be an extremely risky venture indeed.

Eventually, and after the sending and receiving of many messages from Cairo, who were in turn communicating with London, it was all arranged. I would leave the next day for Kerma by rail. I would then have to travel on by horse, camel or boat to Dongola, a total journey of some two hundred miles. There I would meet an agent who had travelled from French West Africa who would supply me with the information on Dawson and his activities.

Lloyd and I were somewhat surprised by the speed of the climb down by the French. One would have expected them to have put up a more spirited defence of their interests, but as events were to prove a few months later at Fashoda, when Marchand and Kitchener were on the brink of going to war with each other, the French would always choose diplomacy over a fight with the British. And also, it occurred to me at this point, there was no absolute certainty that the French would actually supply us with accurate intelligence, even though any move to further implicate themselves in the débâcle would be political suicide.

My Intelligence Branch colleagues in Cairo also sent a message that day on what they had managed to find out about Dawson. He had, it seemed, actually been engaged in some sort of intelligence work in the past – which I suspected – and was an expert Arabist. Overall, however, very little was known about him.

I was about to leave Lloyd's office to prepare myself for the next day's journey when a junior officer appeared with yet another message for me. This time it was from Kitchener himself. I could not help but feel somewhat ill at ease as I opened it. It read:

> FINAL ADVANCE WELL UNDER WAY.
> GUNBOATS MUST BE SECURE.
> THERE MUST BE NO MORE ACTS OF SABOTAGE
> I HOLD YOU PERSONALLY RESPONSIBLE.

I showed the note to Major Lloyd. He sighed as he read it. 'The man did not get where he is today by not taking risks,' he said. 'But this last line seems a bit harsh on you, Evelyn.'

'No it doesn't,' I responded. 'He is perfectly correct. I have a task to complete and so far I have not achieved it. And I almost had him last night too.'

Lloyd was really quite sympathetic, probably because he knew first hand what I had been through the day before. He told me not to be so harsh on myself. 'And this latest development with the French, it could turn out to be a real blessing,' he added. 'It might even lead you straight to Dawson.'

'I certainly hope so.'

'If you need anything else from me here then do let me know,' said Lloyd, as I left his office to start out on yet another weary journey.

As I walked through Wadi Halfa in the bright early afternoon sunshine, reflecting on the events of the last twenty-four hours, it struck me just how incredible the previous day's adventures had been. Things had seemed so simple yesterday morning, but now the game had completely changed and had become far more complex. I had killed and had almost been killed, and yet ahead lay possibly even more trying times. I would have to have my wits about me for the meeting with the French agent. And then there was still Dawson, probably the most dangerous man in the Sudan after the Khalifa himself. I had already failed to stop him committing another atrocity. I had already let him out of my grasp once when I should have had him. And I had already let General Kitchener down. I simply could not fail again.

CHAPTER 9

Diary of the Rt. Hon. Colonel Evelyn Winters, MP

15 March, 1935

ANOTHER WEARY AFTERNOON and evening in Parliament. I seem to be spending longer and longer there each day – to the detriment of my writing – as these debates on India continue to heat up. At the moment it seems like something of a gladiatorial match between Mr Churchill and the Secretary of State for India, with the former speaking sometimes three or four times within just a few hours. Both men are highly accomplished speakers and are equally committed to winning their arguments, and I have to say it is a fine thing to see them parading their intellectual abilities before the House.

The debates are now so frequent that my time spent listening to the speakers is becoming almost routine. Today, however, something rather unusual happened to break the cycle.

I was out on the terrace by myself having decided to steal a few minutes away from the debating Chamber. It must have been around five in the afternoon and I was enjoying a cigar in the cool air while taking in the fine views out over the Thames. I had my eye on a little steamer coming down the river. The big red sun behind it reminded me of the sights that I had seen in the Sudan, by the Nile, all those years ago. Indeed, if it had not been for the buildings along each side of the Thames and the trees further along, I could almost have imagined that I was back there, engaged in some marvellous adventure. I was contemplating this strange thought when I heard, from directly behind me, a voice say, 'Evelyn, how are you, my dear fellow?'

Turning, I was surprised to find the Secretary of State himself addressing me. I think I must have looked a little taken aback, but I greeted him amiably all the same.

'Taking a break from it all, are you?' said Hoare, coming and standing next to me so that he too could look out over the river.

'Yes, yes, I am,' I said. It was perfectly obvious why he was talking to me now, and I am actually surprised that he has waited this long to see me.

'Your Mr Churchill's putting up a good fight as usual,' he said. 'He's like a bulldog that man. Once he gets his teeth into something he simply will not let go.'

'I think it is one of his great strengths,' I said.

'And one of his greatest weaknesses,' the Secretary of State returned quickly, the fire of the debater automatically kicking in. But he seemed to check himself, for he immediately fell back into sounding more congenial. 'Oh, I have nothing against the man personally, of course, although his rant last year that myself and Lord Derby had somehow managed to persuade the Manchester Chamber of Commerce to change its evidence to the Joint Select Committee was really quite ludicrous.'

He was referring to Mr Churchill's charge on the floor of the House last April that Hoare, through his relationship with Derby – the shrewd Lancashire political tactician that he is – had persuaded the Manchester delegation to fall in line with the Government's stance on India. It is no secret that Hoare was a bit miffed at being referred to the Committee of Privileges, even though in the end it came to nothing and did him no harm. I remained silent when he said this, watching the smoke that I was blowing out fly over the balustrade to float along the river. I was really not at all interested in talking about the events of last spring when what is truly important are the arguments of these last few weeks. But Hoare clearly wished to draw me into some sort of discussion. He went on, 'Yes, I think Churchill's blustering last year was the act of a desperate man, who knew even then that he was defeated.'

'You think so?' I said. 'But are you not forgetting the way that the voting went at the Conservative conference in October? I seem to recall that we got five hundred and twenty votes to your five hundred and forty-three. Hardly a landslide, Mr Secretary of State.' I think I was guilty of saying this a little sarcastically, but it had the desired effect, for Hoare nodded slightly, accepting my point. 'And anyway, you have heard him speak recently. He has been most effective,' I added.

Hoare then turned to face me directly. 'Of course he has been. But he is also at this time the *enfant terrible* of the House, Evelyn. But you know, I have to say that I am a little surprised by your continued support for the man. You strike me as being far more sensible than many of the others who are currently gathered around Churchill as if he has the divine rights of a king. And you are certainly no nostalgic sycophant. I know that much.'

'No, no, I am not. And I like to believe that I am a realist. But that is precisely why I am supporting him. With the greatest respect, Secretary of State, I have heard Churchill complain that people on your side see history as simply an extension of the past, where in fact he, and I for that matter, see history as being full of unforeseeable twists and turns and retrogressions. He predicts a dangerous future where England shall have to fight for her self-preservation, and he quite rightly regards your actions on India as being misguided at a time when dictatorships are replacing democracies in industrialized countries, and yet again we are witnessing a rush to arm and to extend power and influence.'

Hoare actually seemed to listen to these points quite earnestly. Perhaps he still had hopes of swinging my opinion away from Churchill and towards him and the Government. From what he said next this certainly seemed to be the case. 'But surely a man of your experience and presence of mind can see that we are simply trying to create a better world; one that will be free from great wars and from the subjugation of other peoples?'

I have heard these arguments before, many times, and indeed Hoare's words reminded me of some of the arguments that Parker has made when we have discussed the India situation. They are old hat. I said, 'I admit that there is a certain nobility in some of these ideals, but my worry is that that is all that they are – ideals. Many of us had great hopes for world peace after the armistice, but these, I am afraid, quickly turned out to have been illusions.'

'But don't you think that we owe it to the Indian peoples to at least give them some say in how their country is run?'

He was determined to press his argument, but so was I. 'Secretary of State, the only reason that India operates as one country is thanks to the stewardship of we British. Some men want to see it become a single independent nation, but that is impossible. We made that country. Its natural state is to be an area comprised of fifty nations, not one self-governing one. Only the British can administer it as a single nation.'

The Secretary of State sighed, saying, 'And I thought that you would perhaps see sense and vote with us.'

'I can see perfectly clearly, thank you, Sam, and I shall continue to vote against this bill.'

Hoare turned to again look out over the river, and there followed a few seconds of uncomfortable silence. I contemplated returning back to the House, but I did not want him to think that I was running from a debate, so I remained where I was. Then the Secretary of State turned to address me once more. 'I hear you're currently writing your memoirs, correct?'

I confirmed that I planned to publish my memoirs of my time in the Sudan campaign. 'And when you cast your mind back to 1898 now,' he continued, 'do you not feel a sense of shame?'

Here I was most taken aback. 'Shame? But why on earth would I feel ashamed? On the contrary I am proud of our performance in that war.'

Suddenly he became somewhat more animated. 'This is what I am getting at,' he started, his eyes narrowing. 'The way that you imperialists talk of war, one would think it was just some jolly game of sport, where all that matters is showmanship and winning. Do you never stop to consider the wider picture, the moral implications of that campaign?'

'And what would those be?'

'Well, was it right for instance to kill all those thousands of Dervishes purely to avenge Gordon's death?'

As soon as he uttered these words I recognized that the man had left himself wide open to the charge of naïveté, for there was much more to the war in the Sudan than simply avenging Gordon. I think the Secretary of State recognized that he had blundered for, as he tailed off the sentence, his voice went quieter, his confidence dissipating. I immediately capital-ized.

'Secretary of State, if I had been asked to put a price on the value of your stock of knowledge and appreciation of our history a few hours ago, I fear I would have grossly overvalued it based on what I have just heard. Have you forgotten the imperial ambitions of the French in North Africa at this time? Would the French rather than the Egyptian flag be better flying over Khartoum? And what about the people of the Sudan? Would it be right for them to still be ruled by the Khalifa or one of his descendants, with all their cruelty that has been so well documented?'

It was a pleasure to see the Secretary of State look so uncomfortable as

I said these words. There was no comeback for him. All he could do was utter something about my not understanding before shuffling off again.

Now that I have had time to think about the happenings of today, I am glad I had this chat with Samuel Hoare, for I believe I defended my thoughts and feelings rather well. But as I write now and go over what Hoare said, it occurs to me that he did make one very good point when he said that Churchill was supporting a lost cause, for in the last few weeks it has become apparent that the Government seems determined not to move an inch on India. I do hope we can still have an effect on the bill and can perhaps water down some of its parts before it gets its final reading. Ah, but how small-minded these people are! They simply cannot see the bigger picture. But I shall fight on for what I believe in, as I always do.

I SHOULD ALSO note one other development from today. I invited Parker to have lunch with me at the club before I went to Parliament this afternoon. I noticed immediately that he was not quite his usual self. He almost bounded to the table and seemed to be extremely pleased about something. Also, he was wearing a new jacket rather than the tatty old thing that he is normally attired in.

'Well, you look very pleased with yourself,' I said. 'Has Mr Larwood offered you a contract on your first book and not told me?'

He seated himself and laughed a little at my question. 'No, no, no, no, no ... nothing like that.'

'Then what is it?'

'Oh it's just that I ... well, happen to be in a fine mood today, that's all. Yes, yes, that's all.'

He was still smiling broadly as he said this. It all seemed really quite unusual for Parker, and I could not take much more of the intrigue. 'Come on, Parker, out with it. What's this all about?'

He had been sitting back in his chair, but he suddenly leaned forward very attentively. 'I've, er, I've met someone,' he said, almost as if it were a secret.

So he has met someone at last! This was wonderful news, and I told Parker so. Her name is Margaret Bellingford and they met at the library. I think Parker is really quite taken with her.

'Very, very nice. Very nice indeed,' he said excitedly. 'I was in the history section. She couldn't find her book. On plants. It was a book on plants ...

that she was looking for I mean. Can you imagine? She asked me to find her a book on plants. Anyway, I don't know the first thing about them, but I didn't leave it there. Got one of the librarians to tell me where the section was so I could show her.'

I have never seen the boy so animated, and indeed I was glad to see this side of him, for so often in the time that I have known Parker there has seemed to be something of a dark cloud hanging over him. Perhaps Margaret Bellingford will be the one to release him from this constant sobriety. I sincerely hope so, for I would like to see him happier and more settled.

'And Miss Bellingford, what does she do?' I asked him.

'Oh ... she's a secretary. Down in Whitehall.'

'But with an interest in plants,' I added jovially.

Parker laughed. 'Oh yes, yes quite. With an interest in plants, as you say.'

'Pretty?'

He pushed his shoulders back in mock offence. 'Well, naturally.'

I was going to suggest that we look at the menu, but Parker seemed so keen to talk about the new lady in his life that I thought I should wait until he got everything out that he wished to tell me. 'I saw her and, well, I just liked her ... straight away I mean. Liked her from the start,' he said. 'Soon as I saw her I knew that she would be ... well, very nice, very nice. You must meet her.'

'I would be delighted to.'

'No, I really would very much like for you to meet her. She is really quite wonderful.'

He said this in such a way that it was obvious that he is very keen for me to meet Miss Bellingford. I must say I felt rather honoured by this pronouncement. I would not for a minute have imagined that Parker would have thought it important that the new woman in his life should meet me, but as I say I really do feel quite honoured.

I asked him how long they have been seeing each other. 'Oh, er, so far we've just met on a few occasions,' he said. 'But I think ... well, that is to say I can't be sure, but I hope she likes me as much as I like her.'

The poor boy – he is completely smitten but clearly still feels insecure. 'I am positive she does, my boy,' I said, to which Parker smiled.

Parker was wonderful company over lunch. Our conversation would range from one thing to another, but every now and then he would come back to mentioning Miss Bellingford. I really am happy for the young man, and I am most looking forward to meeting this new woman in his life, for she sounds like a charming girl.

CHAPTER 10

THE ARABS HAVE a saying that when Allah made the Sudan, he laughed, and as I made my way to Kerma by train on the next stage of my mission, I was reminded of how accurate this sentiment is. On my right-hand side there was the Nile, beautiful in its command of the landscape. But its sublimity made the barrenness of the Nubian desert to my left – a place sporadically afflicted by plagues of flies and plagues of locusts, a place that on the rare occasions when it is not bone dry is shattered by torrential rains – all the more palpable.

I had managed to gain passage on a train that was carrying wood to supply the hungry fires of the gunboats as they made their way up the Nile to the front. I therefore did not have the comfort of a seat in a carriage, but rather had to spread my increasingly torn field blanket out on top of some logs in the open air for a journey that would last several hours. There was little to do in this time other than observe the landscape and think about my meeting with the French agent. I also thought about Dawson. Where was he now? What was he plotting? Was he moving north again or further south? There remained so many uncertainties – it was most disconcerting.

The arrangement agreed upon was that I would meet the Frenchman at the British military station in Dongola. Only then could I work out a plan for how I could next tackle my enemy.

I spent the night at Kerma in officer lodgings and set off for Dongola first thing the next morning. In order to avoid a set of rapids known as the Third Cataract, I had to travel a few miles by horse – one of the officers from Kerma was kind enough to escort me – before getting a boat. The only water transport that I was then able to muster was a place in a *gyassas* towed by a steamer. This part of the journey was really quite pleasant, and

I welcomed the opportunity to put my thoughts back into focus following the excitements of Wadi Halfa. I had the *gyassas* entirely to myself, which meant I could simply lie back and enjoy taking in the wildlife of the Nile, which was more ubiquitous than one would perhaps have imagined for a waterway surrounded by empty desert.

I took my tunic off and placed it in the v-shaped bow to rest my back against. Sitting down then I had a clear view of the expanse of the Nile, the steamer leaving a wide wake as our trail. Most of the banks were bare, but occasionally a row of palm trees would appear as if they had been placed there solely to salute me as I passed. I closed my eyes to take in the warmth of the sun, made bearable by a prevailing breeze, but then opened them again when I heard squawking sounds to my right. Turning, I found a beautiful group of white pelicans at the edge of the river. Then I heard tweeting sounds from above and looked up to see some scarlet birds, which reminded me of humming birds, flying overhead. Languidly I watched as other birds floated past on the sparkling water, bouncing over the waves produced by my little boat. How wonderfully simple their existences are, I thought, compared with my own. These simple creatures do not have to bear the weight of Kitchener's expectations – and by extension the expectations of England herself. Not for them the responsibility of ensuring that the most powerful army in the world is triumphant in its attempts to reclaim a great area of land for the Empire.

As the morning wore on the sun grew intensely strong, so that even with the wind it became unbearably hot. The sun's fierce rays beat down from the sky but also reflected off the water. In order to provide some relief I erected a kind of makeshift canopy by hanging my field blanket from the sail mast and pinning one end of it to the side of the boat with my knife. It was here in the shade that I spent the remainder of the journey, arriving at Dongola in the early afternoon.

The eastern bank of the Nile as I approached the settlement was lined with a thin strip of cultivation and palm trees, the little brown town sitting behind. It was not as significant a place as Wadi Halfa, and was made up of the usual assortment of mud huts mixed with the occasional fortification. When I landed I at once made my way to the British military station, a two-storey building situated in the heart of the town.

My visit and that of the Frenchman was, to all intents and purposes, being kept top secret, and as such none of the officers at the station was expecting me. I thought it best, however, to introduce and explain myself to the most senior officer there, who turned out to be a rather stuffy and owl-like old colonel by the name of Warton.

'I don't much like you intelligence sorts, you know,' he said to me, as soon as we were alone in his office, a cluttered room full of maps, old furniture and other junk. 'All this snooping around that you do. Don't see the sense in it myself. Better to confront the enemy head on, that's what I always say.'

I brushed aside these comments, as it was important that I did not give the man any reason to impede what I was doing. 'Yes, yes, I'm sure,' I said somewhat flippantly. 'Nevertheless, I must ask that you co-operate with us, at least for now, for I am engaged in matters that are most serious. A Frenchman is due to arrive here some time this afternoon. He—'

'A Frenchman! Now look here, what on earth do you think you're doing inviting a Frenchman here?'

It was clear that the colonel was going to try my patience. 'He has been sent by his government,' I said, trying not to sound too brusque. 'I cannot divulge the details, Colonel, but what I can tell you is that this goes to the very highest levels of government in both London and Paris, and indeed my mission now has been instigated personally by General Kitchener himself.'

'You refuse to tell me what you are up to, even though we are both on the same side, and yet you expect me to help you?'

'Certainly.'

'Well, I don't see why I should.' He was stroking his moustache as he said this, which I found most irritating. Indeed, I had now had enough of the bothersome man – if only he were as co-operative as Colonel Maxwell had been at Abu Hamed, I thought.

'I shall require the use of your office when the Frenchman turns up,' I said, as if I had not even heard his last phrase. 'He should be here within a few hours. I should not tie you up for very long after that.'

Warton looked a little shocked. 'Need I remind you that I am a colonel and that you are a major, Major?'

'Why of course you needn't … sir. And I am sure that I need not remind you of how severely Major-General Kitchener treats those who see it as their business directly to get in the way of his plans.'

The old colonel was not at all pleased by this, but he knew he would have to co-operate, which indeed he did, albeit with many complaints about the Intelligence Branch.

I did not expect the French messenger to arrive for a few hours yet, so I took time to visit the station's field kitchen for lunch. It was situated a few hundred yards from Warton's headquarters, down a relatively wide dusty street lined with mud houses, which constituted the main thoroughfare of the town. There were few people on the street as most of Dongola's citizens had retreated from the strong afternoon sun, and so it was very quiet.

As I was making my way back towards the military station, which sat squarely at the end of the road and stood out, with its domed roof, as being the most distinguished building in Dongola, I noticed that a man in western clothing was standing at the station's large metal gate, talking to one of the guards. As I got closer, however, I noticed that the man, who was dressed in a white suit and hat, was actually arguing rather vociferously with the soldier. He seemed to wish to gain access to the station, but the guard would not have it. 'I don't know what you think you're doing here, sir, but you can't come in,' he was saying, or words to that effect.

I immediately suspected that he could be my contact, but I thought it best to remain silent as I approached, for my suspicion could have turned out to be entirely wrong.

Was this man English, or did he have a French accent? As I got close enough to properly hear his voice I thought that surely he had to be British, for he seemed to be very well-spoken.

'But I am expected here,' he was saying. 'I insist that you let me in.'

I was now close enough for the two men's attention to be redirected towards me. 'Excuse me,' I said, looking directly at the man in the white suit, 'I am Major Winters.'

I awaited a response. The soldier looked utterly perplexed by the situation. Thankfully, however, a look of realization appeared on the other man's face. He was indeed my contact.

'Olivier Lamoureax,' he announced, extending his hand.

'THE FRENCH GOVERNMENT very much regrets the actions of this unofficial operative,' Lamoureax said, once we were safely ensconced in Warton's office, 'but it wishes to make it absolutely clear that he was not working under the orders of Paris.'

This sort of denial was exactly what I had expected, but I raised a sceptical eyebrow all the same. 'Your government had no idea what this man was up to?'

Lamoureax smiled a little. He was a little overweight, with greasy-looking, jet-black hair, and was distinguished by a silver monocle that sat precariously in his left eye. 'We know a great many things, Major. But as I say, this man was acting independently of my government and of our intelligence efforts. Call him a rogue element, if you will. But you are an intelligence man, you know how these sorts of things work.'

The wry way in which he said this told me that despite the requirement that he give me the official line on what had happened, Lamoureax clearly also wanted me to know that in reality the man I had killed was working on behalf of the French Government. 'Yes, I know how these things work,' I said.

I took the colonel's seat and invited Lamoureax to place himself in the chair opposite the desk from me. Observing him then I was very much taken by what a strange-looking fellow he was, for he seemed to be full of contrasts. His white suit looked expensive and could easily have come from a fine Savile Row tailor, and yet it was dirty and creased from his desert travels and looked tight on his squat little body. And although he did indeed look French, with his pencil thin moustache and dark hair, to hear him speak one would have been forgiven for thinking that he had been born and brought up in the Home Counties. I certainly found him an intriguing fellow, and was eager to know more about him before we got on to seriously discuss Dawson – I was also eager to learn as much as possible about our intelligence competitors, for it was not every day that this sort of opportunity presented itself.

'I was born in Paris but schooled in England,' he said, when I asked how he came to be such a fine English speaker. 'I went to Winchester. My father was something of an industrialist, you see, and for a number of years had to base himself in London.'

'And now you are an intelligence agent working in French West Africa?'

He smiled again. 'You may assume that, Major, but I couldn't possibly confirm it. I am simply an English-speaking representative of the French Government.'

This evasiveness combined with the occasional piece of enlightening information set the precedent for my entire conversation with Lamoureax. He would not, for instance, explain how he had apparently managed to get to Dongola from French West Africa so quickly for our meeting. I could only surmise that he had been lurking somewhere within British – or perhaps even Dervish – territory, and as such was able to reach the town relatively fast. How he communicated with his superiors, I had no idea.

I was hoping that he would turn up for our meeting with some sort of previously prepared file on Dawson, but it seemed that any intelligence that the French were willing to impart would be done by word-of-mouth, for nothing was forthcoming – I was glad I had insisted that I be the British representative for the handover. I began by asking about the man that I had killed.

'His name was Portart,' said Lamoureax, producing some French cigarettes from his jacket and offering me one, which I accepted. I think the lighting of our tobacco did something to ease the slightly strained atmosphere.

'A colleague of yours?' I asked, sitting back in the colonel's chair.

'Not as such. He *had been* a colleague of mine, but as I said, he went his own way. Certainly we knew that he was up to something, but he was no longer under our control.'

I thought this most probably a lie. It did not really matter, however, for it was irrelevant – at least for my purposes as our man on the ground – whether Paris was sponsoring the man or not. What I needed to know about Dawson was what this Portart fellow was doing working for him. 'Tell me what you know about him,' I said.

Lamoureax drew heavily on his cigarette. 'We had a suspicion for some time that Portart was not quite right. His behaviour was becoming very strange. Unlike myself and those whom I represent, who accept – and indeed welcome – the British position in the Sudan, Portart was very much against your expansionism.'

To hear him say this one would have thought that the French had no imperialist ambitions of their own in Africa. I remained silent, however, for Lamoureax was starting to convey the information that I was looking for. 'It seems that he somehow managed to link up with your Captain Dawson and began to help him with his attacks on the British.'

'Then it was Portart who blew up our train in the south?'

'Yes, we believe so.'

'But how can you be certain?'

'We have our informants just as you do, Major.' Again the smile which showed him to be an untrustworthy sort – but then I could not hold this against him, for he was engaged in the same mischievous work as I.

'And what about Dawson and his saboteurs, what do you know about them?'

'You know the name of the group that he established?'

'No. I was under the impression that they had no name. And if I am being perfectly honest with you, I was not even sure that Dawson had established the group, although I assumed as much.'

'Oh he started it all right, but ...' He trailed off mid-sentence and leaned forward in his chair. A comical moment then ensued as his monocle fell from his eye and he scrambled about frantically to replace it. When he had done this he half-pointed his burning cigarette at me and said, very sternly, 'Major Winters, I am prepared to convey some important information, but first I need an assurance from you.'

'Yes, go on.'

'The death of Portart ... the circumstances surrounding his death ... has placed the French Government in a very, how should I say it, tricky situation.'

Now we were making progress. 'Indeed it has,' I said, with the tiniest hint of satisfaction in my voice.

He sat back again in his chair. 'Yes, yes, it is all very tricky. We don't wish to be seen by other nations as a state that engages in this sort of clandestine work against its neighbour – not that we have done, of course. But you know how an incident like this could easily be misinterpreted by others, don't you?'

'Indeed.'

'What I mean to say is that in this day and age there is no need for great powers like France and Britain to be fighting each other. These days the politicians sit down to discuss our disagreements rather than reaching for the generals at the first hint of trouble.'

This was a time when the leading European powers made accords on where their imperial boundaries would sit, as indeed the British and French did on Africa just several weeks later. And in our own smaller way, Lamoureax and I were also reaching a diplomatic agreement.

'You want my assurance that we shall keep secret what happened on that train to Wadi Halfa,' I said, interrupting his monologue.

Lamoureax seemed almost relieved that it was I who had said it and not him. He nodded. 'Yes, Major, that is precisely what I want.'

Giving him such an assurance meant little to me. I still wanted to make sure, however, that I was getting something of value in return. 'And if I give such an assurance, how much information are you willing to impart?'

'Believe me when I say that you will not regret it. I happen to know where Dawson is *en route* to now, and I know what he has planned. If I were in your shoes, Major, I would not hesitate.'

He sat back and smiled. I did not have to think about the offer for long. 'Very well, you have my assurance. But I should warn you, that if the information that you are about to give me subsequently turns out to be untrue, then we would have little choice but to inform other governments of Portart's actions.'

Lamoureax agreed. 'They do have a name,' he began. 'They are called the *Mulazemin*, after the Khalifa's personal bodyguard, for they regard themselves – or at least Dawson regards himself – as being just as committed to the cause as they are. I have to say that we do not know an awful lot about Dawson. Portart ... and you must understand that this has to remain absolutely secret ... Portart was observing the construction of the railway for us when he first reported that an Englishman was attempting to recruit Arabs clandestinely to his own *Mulazemin*. Naturally we found this extraordinary, and we refused to believe it at first. But, as you well know, it has turned out to be true enough.'

'Do you know how many men he managed to recruit?'

'No, we don't, exactly. But I don't think it could have been very many, for not long after he got the group going, most unfortunately he managed to convince the wayward Portart to blow up that first train.'

A likely story. But we were just getting to the important part. 'You say you know what Dawson's plans are now. What are they?'

'Indeed. He is moving south. From what our informants tell us he has gathered together his small group of followers and is on his way to Omdurman to defend the Khalifa.'

So he was on his way to Omdurman for the final showdown with Kitchener! These words actually came as something of a relief, for if Dawson and his band of followers were ahead of the British lines then that at least meant they could not, for now, carry out any more acts of sabotage. And also, as we spoke, Major-General Kitchener was marching to crush the Khalifa at Omdurman, which I was sure Lamoureax, with his informants, was well aware of. 'Then they will be annihilated,' I said.

I expected the Frenchman to agree, but to my surprise a look of scepticism actually appeared on his face. 'I would not be entirely sure of that, Major.'

I was truly surprised by this. 'Oh really, why?'

'Our informants have provided us with one crucial piece of intelligence, which I have been instructed to pass on to you. It is no secret that Kitchener's strategy for taking Omdurman and Khartoum will rely heavily on the use of his gunboats, yes?' I agreed. 'And Captain Dawson has already made an attempt to sabotage one of these vessels while it was being transported to the front.'

'So the main target remains the gunboats?'

'Indeed, Major, as far as we know, it does. We have received intelligence that the Khalifa has already attempted to set a trap for the gunboats, but that it failed. It seems he planned to have a boat filled with explosives sunk in the middle of the Nile, slightly to the north of Omdurman. The intention was that the charge would be set off from shore once the British vessels were over the top of them. But whoever set the charge did a poor job for, as the boat was being taken out to its assigned area, the dynamite went off prematurely, killing a number of the Khalifa's men. Dawson, though, *does* have the expertise to set these charges safely, and we believe that this is his intention.'

It was really quite extraordinary. If what Lamoureax was telling me were true, then it seemed that French military intelligence efforts were far ahead of our own. But I was unconvinced.

'Monsieur Lamoureax, how can you be sure of all of this?' I said. 'The detail of your intelligence seems exemplary, but you will forgive me if I am a little sceptical about it. Perhaps you are trying to throw me off the scent in order to give Dawson a chance to plot further acts of sabotage against us.'

Lamoureax stamped his cigarette out in the ashtray on the desk. 'That is your privilege, Major. But I am not looking to convince you of these things but merely to provide you with intelligence that we know to be correct. And—'

'But why should you help us? After all, there can be no denying that we are in competition.' I was keen to press my point, for already I was beginning to plan my next course of action based on what Lamoureax had just said, but I needed to be as certain as possible that this was indeed the correct course of action to take.

'Yes, we are in competition. But the fact is, Major, it would simply not do for the French Government to be linked in any way to Dawson, if the man's actions led to some kind of humiliation – or even another military catastrophe – for the British in the Sudan.'

And now it all fell into place. 'You mean he is now more trouble to you than he was worth.'

Lamoureax said and did nothing to either confirm or deny this, which told me that what I had suggested was the case. It meant that Dawson was indeed most probably on his way to the Khalifa to help him halt the gunboats – which meant he could yet severely disrupt, if not completely stop, Kitchener's final attack. But there was another crucial question that now presented itself to me.

'I was not aware,' I said, 'of Dawson having been in contact with the Khalifa until now. If what you are saying is true, then the Khalifa must trust Dawson, which suggests they may already have met, or that at least he is aware of his sabotage activities and has some kind of admiration for the man. But I cannot for the life of me understand how Dawson, an Englishman, could have come into contact with the Khalifa.'

'Neither do we, I'm afraid. We do know that Dawson easily commands the respect of the Arabs who have chosen to join his group. We also know that the Khalifa would find Dawson's commitment to the Mahdi's cause a most attractive quality. But as to how they first came to know of each other, perhaps that is something for you to investigate further, Major.'

'Indeed it is.'

I LEFT THE Frenchman at the gates of our military station to wander off into Dongola and then on to who knows where. It certainly was interesting meeting my French equivalent, and it was now perfectly clear how I should proceed. As soon as I had sent a telegraph message to Cairo to report on the outcome of my meeting, I would have to speed south as fast as I possibly could to try and reach Dawson before he had a chance to lay those charges. Immediately, however, a dilemma was posed. I was in Dongola, and if I were to travel south by rail I would first have to go north to Wadi Halfa, then south again towards first Abu Hamed and then the Atbara. I would then have to travel by boat back to Wad Hamed and then further by horse or camel to the front line – at this stage I was not entirely sure of exactly how far south Kitchener's forces had advanced. A journey like that would take days. Ideally I would have been able to travel directly from Dongola along the river to the Atbara, with no need to use the railway, but I was prevented from doing this by the fact that the Nile after Merawi is unnavigable.

This was indeed a great problem, for it seemed that in the time that it would take me to travel towards Omdurman the battles would have already been fought and either won or lost. But wait a minute, I thought. If Dawson was able to hastily travel to the Khalifa from here – for the train that he had scrambled aboard that night when he escaped my grasp would have taken him to Kerma – then surely there must be another way through the desert to Omdurman. And that was when it struck me. There was another way: the caravan trade route that the Bedouin Arabs used to travel from Korti to Metemma, straight through the desert. Dawson must have bribed his way across it. Perhaps he had even disguised himself as an Arab to get through our lines.

My next course of action was now obvious. I would go at once to Korti, from where I would attempt to pay to accompany some travelling Arabs through the desert towards Metemma. And if I disguised myself as an Arab, perhaps I could even secretly gain passage behind Dervish lines, where hopefully I could still save the gunboats and put a final stop to the menace that was Dawson. It would be a most dangerous enterprise, but I had little choice in the matter.

CHAPTER 11

Diary of the Rt. Hon. Colonel Evelyn Winters, MP

2 April, 1935

I HAVE BEEN all over town today, to Fleet St to see Mr Larwood, to Parliament and then to St James's for dinner. The time has passed so quickly that it seems like only an hour ago that I breakfasted. Looking back on it now, it has been one of those days of interesting and yet subtle developments, the sort of day where one may regard the events that have taken place as being inconsequential, when in actual fact they could lead to some rather important changes. I should note down in detail what took place.

I wished to get some work done on my memoirs before going to see Mr Larwood, and so was up and working before eight. I then took a taxi to my publisher's office for our meeting at eleven. It is the first time we have managed to talk face-to-face since that day I met him for lunch at Claridges. He was his usual jovial and energetic self. 'Evelyn, good to see you, good to see you,' he said, getting up from his desk and coming round to shake my hand vigorously. It never fails to surprise me how cluttered his little office looks, with its stacks of books and papers piled up here and there. It seems strange for a man who is so neat in his appearance. 'Everything all right with you? Good.'

He had asked for the meeting to check on the progress of my memoirs, which I informed him were coming along nicely. 'This India business in Parliament not keeping you away from your writing desk too long, is it?'

'It has served as something of a distraction,' I admitted, 'but I am still managing to make fairly good progress. Parker tends to keep me on my toes, you know.'

'Ah, yes, young Parker. Proving to be a good help, is he?'

'Oh, indeed, a marvellous help. He is a very bright young man. Seems to remember everything. We're getting along splendidly.'

'Good, good.'

Mr Larwood asked at what stage I am at exactly with my writing. I told him that I am now working towards covering the day of the Battle of Omdurman itself, and that we should have progressed to this point in the not-too-distant future. 'Parker is getting stuck into all of the research for that part at the moment,' I said.

'Marvellous, and is he keeping you well informed with regard to what he's doing?'

'Certainly. We see each other regularly. I've even had him down to Wiltshire a few times. As I say, we're getting along splendidly. Indeed, I think we've become firm friends since we started work on my book.' This brought me on to what I wished to get out of our meeting. I continued, 'Yes, yes, I really do like the lad, and I have the utmost respect for his intellect. I was just thinking the other day how surprised I am that he hasn't written his own military history book.'

Mr Larwood did not catch on. 'Well, he's still a young man, Evelyn. He has plenty of time for that sort of thing. Perhaps he will decide to write something at some point.'

'Well, that's the thing, you see. He sort of has decided to write something. He is most keen to do some kind of history of the Crimean War and, well, I promised to put in a good word for the lad with you.'

Now there are several ways in which Mr Larwood could have taken this. He could have been somewhat annoyed that I regarded it as my place to recommend young writers to him – although I could not even imagine the man being as such. He could have been grateful for the recommendation, or he could simply have been polite about the suggestion but essentially brushed me off. Fortunately he seemed to take it rather well, even though he was a little surprised.

'Let me have a look at our publishing list for the coming year, then I'll have a chat with him. Can't promise anything of course, but I'll certainly look into it.'

'That would be marvellous. He will be most pleased.'

I am so glad I managed to convince Mr Larwood to consider Parker's proposal for a book of his own. I really would like to see the boy get on and do well in life, for he deserves to, which almost brings me on to the rest of today's events.

I left Mr Larwood and went for a bit of lunch at the club before stopping off at Parliament. I do not believe there was anything of significance to report from today's proceedings. Many of the arguments are now being repeated, and I have no recollection of any of the speakers coming out with anything that was either new or out of the ordinary. Still, I remained there until about seven, when I taxied to St James's for dinner with Parker and his new lady friend, Miss Bellingford.

I thought I should take them to Whittakers, which is all very plush and expensive, but I did not want Parker to feel that I was skimping. I managed to get there before they arrived and spent the time over an aperitif, watching the other groups of well-turned-out, cheery-faced diners and the white-tied staff as they scurried between tables.

I saw Parker's head glide past the window before they came in. A second later and the door opened and there was Miss Bellingford, Parker holding the entrance for her. She was radiant. Petite, slim and very delicate-looking, with fine gold hair and pretty features. She was dressed in an appealing, full-length, wine-red dress.

I don't think I have ever seen a man look so proud as Parker did when he came through that door. He was positively beaming from ear to ear. He looked around, and when he saw me he waved excitedly, then led Miss Bellingford to the table.

'Hello, Colonel,' he said. Then moving nervously to the side, 'This is Margaret. I'd like you to meet Margaret.'

I stood to take her hand.

'Hello,' she said softly. 'Wilfred has told me so much about you, Colonel Winters.'

Over dinner we got to know each other a little. I asked Miss Bellingford about her work as a secretary in Whitehall and she asked me about my work as an MP. And then something very interesting happened when Miss Bellingford asked me what sort of work I was currently involved with in Parliament. I shall try to note down precisely what was said.

'Well, my main preoccupation at the moment is with the proposed India Bill, where I am involved in efforts to fight its progress,' I began.

'Oh, yes, Wilfred has mentioned it.'

'Has he now. And has he mentioned how he is all for the thing and I am all against it?' I said this jovially, as Parker and I have more or less agreed to disagree on India.

'Yes, he has,' she said. 'But what about your speech? When do you intend to present it?'

'Speech?' Naturally this took me by surprise. I could only conclude that the poor girl was horribly mixed up in her thinking.

But then she continued with, 'The speech that Wilfred is going to help you with.' As she said this she looked over to Parker as if to check her facts. In return he gave her a somewhat pained look.

I myself was completely in the dark, and was about to correct the girl without, I hoped, causing her to feel foolish, when Parker actually piped up with, 'Oh, er, no, Margaret, that was just a thought … yes, just a thought I had.' He looked highly embarrassed, as did Miss Bellingford when she realized she had said something that she should not have.

'Oh yes, a thought with regard to what?' I said. I believe Parker expected me to be somewhat annoyed, but I was merely interested, as I hope my tone suggested.

Parker placed his fork on his plate. Suddenly it all seemed very serious. 'It's just that … well, I know you haven't made a speech in Parliament for quite a while, and … well—'

'Three years,' I reminded him.

'Indeed. Three years.' He moved a little uncomfortably in his chair. 'I just thought that perhaps, if I helped you write a speech … in the same way I help you with your memoirs, I mean, then perhaps … perhaps we could come up with something really quite good. But I'm sorry, it's not my place to …' and he trailed off.

I have to admit I did not know what to think, and I can honestly say that I was completely bowled over by the suggestion. Some stubborn part of me wanted to tell him to mind his own business, while another part – a much larger part – felt eternally grateful at the boy's thoughtfulness. Indeed, I was really rather moved, and I believe I may have looked a little silly by not responding at first. 'No, nothing to do with me, nothing to do with me,' he added, before I had managed to collect my thoughts to form a response.

'No, no, not at all,' I said eventually. But now I was perplexed, for Parker is all for the India Bill. Why then would he wish to help me formulate a speech to be made against it? I asked him directly why he felt a need to help me.

He said, 'I simply get the feeling that you miss it. Miss the speaking I mean. Now I know that you can easily write your own speech, but I just thought that … well, if I can be frank, I thought that if you had a bit of assistance with it, with the writing I mean, then perhaps you would be more confident – more confident to stand up there.'

He was indeed being frank, and I am sure there are many men who would have found this deeply offensive. I have to say though that I found it rather charming. 'But what about your feelings on India?' I asked. 'You've always seemed to feel so passionately about it.'

'Yes, yes, I have,' he said, with a small smile. 'And I still do. But, well, despite my own feelings, I would like to help. I really would. And anyway, I can't pretend that you haven't made some good points on it, on the whole India thing.'

This really is something of a turnaround. I was positively amazed. Now I know that young Parker is bright, but I did not for a second think he could read people's minds – how on earth could he have guessed that I have secretly been yearning to make another speech, but have always found one reason or other not to do so? I decided I must accept his invitation, his challenge, whatever one wishes to call it. 'And I must say it's very good of you, Parker my boy, very good of you indeed,' I added.

As I said this and thought about what a fine young fellow my writing assistant is, I suddenly remembered the outcome of my meeting earlier today with Mr Larwood. It was so fitting, for now I had something of a gift for Parker in return. I told him that Mr Larwood has promised to look into publishing something on the Crimean. 'Said he can't promise anything, but he wishes to have a chat with you about it,' I said, to which Parker was very pleased, as was Miss Bellingford.

'It's all so exciting,' she said more than once.

THERE WAS ONE other development from dinner that I should note down before I get off to bed. We had finished eating and were preparing to go when Miss Bellingford slipped off for a few minutes. Parker was naturally very happy at the prospect of becoming an author and we were chatting away and smoking. But then, when I had just finished saying something, he leaned right over towards me and said, very quietly, 'You … you do like her, don't you?'

What a silly question, I thought. Of course I like her. 'My dear boy, she must be one of the most charming young ladies I have ever met,' I said.

Parker smiled broadly. He actually seemed very relieved. 'Oh, that's good. I'm glad, very glad,' he said, sitting back again in his chair. 'I do like her very much, and it wouldn't have been the same if you, well, if you didn't … if you hadn't taken to her.'

It is somewhat odd that he should have said this, for it is the sort of question that a young man would perhaps put to a parent in such a situation. But then again, who else does Parker have to seek such reassurances from? No one. And anyway, I am glad that he feels he can be open about such things with me.

I bid goodnight to the two young lovers outside the restaurant. They seem to go so well together – I am reminded now of how proud she looked when I mentioned that Mr Larwood was interested in Parker's Crimean project. I am so happy for them both.

I am also glad to have committed myself to making another speech before the Commons. It seems to have perked me up a bit, although I have to admit that the prospect both worries and excites me. Ah, but with Parker's fine intellect to help me along I am sure to make a good showing!

But I shall be nervous. I must try not to stumble. But I am getting ahead of myself. I should try not to think about it too much until I see Parker again, which will be very soon anyway. I should try to sleep now, but I know it will be difficult. Already I am imagining making such a fine speech that it moves the members to cheer and wave like they have never done before. A speech so focused and poignant that it turns the tide of the whole debate on India.

CHAPTER 12

THE SUNRISE THAT still morning was particularly spectacular. I was at the back of the line of camels, and as we descended a small hill I found myself looking out over a blissfully exotic vista – a single line of Bedouin enveloped in perfect gold. They were so regal looking atop their camels, each one of them swaying gently with the movement of his beast, their *courbag* rhinoceros-hide whips sticking up at an angle, thin dark lines against the golden sky and moving backwards and forwards almost in rhythm. It was one of those sights that makes a man stop and take stock of his position in life, and I have to say that it made me feel that despite the heavy burden of responsibility that I carried at this time, I was truly a lucky man.

To travel in the desert in the traditional Arab way is indeed a great privilege, and something that I have enjoyed enormously on the rare occasions when I have been lucky enough to experience it. It is the simplicity that I am drawn to. The only ambition is to reach the next watering-hole, the only problem how to do so safely. And so it was that I found myself engaged in just such a journey with these people on the latest stage of my hunt for Dawson.

I had travelled by steamer from Dongola to Korti, where, after some searching around – at one stage I felt sure that I was going to be stuck there – for the price of a few gold coins, I joined a small group of Bedouin for the journey through the desert. The leader of the group was a gentleman by the name of Mahmud. 'You English, you like to fight as much as the Arabs,' he said to me when we were negotiating my passage, even though I had told him nothing of my plans. Mahmud would turn out to be an indispensable guide in the adventures that were to come over the next few days.

There were six of them in total, all male, Mahmud being the elder. I believe they were all related in one way or another. They were transporting ostrich feathers mainly. We set off at dawn the morning after I arrived at Korti. Each man was in charge of three camels, two of which were fully loaded with goods, while the third carried some materials but was also used for transporting its keeper – although a lot of the time the men walked next to their animals. I was given a single camel for the purposes of the journey, which turned out to be an ill-tempered old thing that did not take to me at all, for it made the most awful noise whenever I wanted it to move somewhere.

Still, I could not complain. At least I was firmly on the trail of Dawson again, and there remained hope that I could redeem myself in the eyes of Major-General Kitchener. So all in all I was in rather a good mood as I set off into the glowing desert with my small band of Bedouin.

We stopped for a few hours that afternoon, when the sun was blisteringly hot, at a watering-hole that lay between Korti and the village of Gakdul. It was nothing but a small pool, a tiny hole in the vast desert, with some thin grass around its edge. It was so insignificant that the place did not even appear on any of our maps.

My parched mouth had been crying out for water and I drank feverishly, gasping loudly at the blissfully fresh feeling as I then doused my head and face. Satisfied, I thought I would take the opportunity to try and get on friendly terms with Mahmud, for I wished to ask a favour of him later and needed to lay the groundwork in the way of getting him on my side. 'You know the desert well,' I said, sitting myself down on the scrub near him and putting my metal cup down in front of me. The others were on the other side of the watering-hole, away from Mahmud, and were talking and laughing together. I got the sense that Mahmud always sat alone when the group stopped, for there was a seriousness about him that suggested he enjoyed no one else's company but his own. Indeed, he seemed a very lonely figure, sat as he was drinking his water, seemingly thinking his own thoughts.

'I have been travelling here for more years than I can remember,' he said, his eyes slowly scanning the desert.

'Do you ever tire of it?'

'What is there to tire of? The desert is my life, and I shall never tire of that.'

The travelling Arabs speak in such poetic terms. It is wonderful to listen to. Mahmud told me of his childhood, of following his father, together with his many uncles and cousins, on great treks through the desert. He even claimed to have been through the Arab Peninsula's Empty Quarter once, a most dangerous area that as far as I was aware no man had been through. 'But now it is all changing,' he said. 'Now men like you come here to start wars.'

'We are not here to make war with you,' I said. 'We are here only to defeat the Khalifa.'

'And why do you fight him?'

I began to tell Mahmud the story of how General Sir Charles Gordon had been sent to Khartoum in 1884 to organize the relief of the Egyptian garrisons there following the rise of the Mahdi, but that on a fateful morning in the January of 1885 an army of Dervishes had stormed the city. 'Gordon was one of our greatest warriors,' I said. 'He was sent here by the leaders of my country to defend the people from enslavement and persecution.'

Mahmud knew about Mohammed Ahmed – 'The Mahdi' – as everyone who travelled in these lands did, even if they did not count themselves as one of his followers. He knew how the people of Nubia, who were living under Egyptian rule, had awaited the coming of a second great prophet who would lead them closer to God – it is said that people would often ask the question, 'Art thou he that should come, or do we look for another?' He knew that the Mahdi had brought together the various disparate tribes of the region to fight as one against the 'Turks' – who were mostly Egyptians commanded by Englishmen – and that this new high priest had ruled the land ever since. And he knew that shortly after declaring victory and establishing his new desert empire, the Mahdi lay dying of fever in the new capital that he had had built for himself across the river from Khartoum, at a place called Omdurman. He knew also that the man's last words were that his faithful follower Abdullah – the 'Khalifa' – was his chosen successor. All of this he knew. Being unaccustomed to European civilization, however, it was the part that the British played in failing to stop the Mahdi's rise to power that Mahmud was not aware of, and so I endeavoured to enlighten him.

'This great warrior of ours established himself at Khartoum,' I explained. 'He brought peace and civility to the city, but it was not to last, for he found himself surrounded by the Mahdi's army of Dervishes. After a while the people of Khartoum, and Gordon's men, were running out of food. Back in England our politicians argued and talked continuously about what to do, but they did nothing. But then, when it was starting to look as if Gordon could not hold out for much longer, they decided to send an army up the Nile to rescue him. But it was too late, for when our great metal sailing vessels reached the city, they could see that Khartoum had fallen and that General Gordon was probably dead. So they returned, as our whole army did, to Egypt.'

'And did your great warrior man die an honourable death?'

Mahmud was clearly taken with my story. 'Oh yes,' I said. 'I have never heard of a death that came with such honour. The Mahdi gave him a chance to surrender, but he refused, even though he knew that it was his only chance of life. And when he heard that the Dervishes had embarked on their final attack he was not disturbed but calmly dressed himself in his finest garments before taking up his sword to face his enemy. Then he walked out on to the balcony of his quarters as the Dervishes swarmed through the courtyard. All that lay between him and the end of a Dervish spear now was just a single flight of stairs. "Where is your master, the Mahdi?" he shouted. And for a few seconds, do you know what happened, Mahmud?'

'What?'

'There was complete silence. For just a few moments the bloodthirsty crowd became quiet, and in that brief time General Gordon had them under his spell. But then, from one of the Dervishes at the bottom of the staircase, came a cry: "Oh cursed one, your time is come", and a spear was thrown. It struck our great warrior's chest and he fell, to be hacked to pieces by the crowd.'

Mahmud seemed most impressed. 'He must have been a brave man,' he said, 'a martyr to your cause, whatever it may be.'

'Yes indeed. He was a true martyr.'

'And are you going now to kill the Khalifa?'

I almost laughed at the thought of it. 'No,' I said. 'He will be killed, or captured, but another of our great warriors, a man by the name of Kitchener, will do it. I have my own enemy to deal with.'

We trekked the rest of that day before making camp close to Gakdul. Two of Mahmud's men then prepared a meal of rice and vegetables, which we all heartily shared. Afterwards I went again to talk with my host, just as the sun had almost disappeared from the horizon.

'Mahmud, I wish to ask a service of you,' I said, after we had been chatting a few minutes.

Mahmud smiled. He was a clever man. 'I have been waiting for you to ask something of me. What is it?'

I took a deep breath before answering. 'I do not wish to go to Metemma,' I said. 'My army is now far beyond there, and is now closing in on Khartoum and Omdurman. But I need to be ahead even of my own army. And if I am to do that then I need to cut across the desert directly for Omdurman, rather than going to Metemma. And—'

'And you need a guide,' Mahmud finished my sentence.

I nodded. 'Yes, Mahmud. I do indeed need a guide. Someone who knows the desert as though it were all his own small piece of land.' I said this with something of a hopeful tone.

Mahmud sighed and rubbed his face. 'It could be very dangerous. Leaving the trade route will be dangerous. If our camels were to be injured then we would be left to die in the desert. And then there is the Khalifa's men. If they found me with you then it would be my head.'

Despite his reservations I knew that Mahmud was interested in my proposal. I thought him an adventurous man at heart, and I believed he welcomed this chance to break with the monotony of his travelling life. 'Five more gold sovereigns,' I said to him, in the hope of clinching the deal, which indeed it did.

We agreed that we would take a camel each and enough provisions for a few days of travel. We would split off from the rest of the group the next morning, and as they carried on to Metemma we would move south-west towards Omdurman.

That night I slept on the desert floor with only a mosquito net above me. I closed my eyes to an image of sandflies dancing across the netting, set against a backdrop of exquisitely bright stars.

IN THE CHILL of the next morning, and over a breakfast of flat bread and sweet tea, Mahmud and I discussed how we would undertake the journey. I explained that I intended to swing right around the side of both the Anglo-Egyptian and the Dervish armies, and to approach Omdurman from the west. I did not expect Mahmud to accompany me all the way into the heart of the Khalifa's empire, for it was far too dangerous an under-taking to expect of a man. 'You wish to die, yes?' Mahmud said to me when I was explaining my plan.

It did indeed seem like something of a suicidal undertaking, but what else could I do at this stage? Dawson was at Omdurman and was intent on destroying our gunboats. I had to get there to stop him. But although the odds were certainly stacked against me, I sensed that there was some chance of success, for I hoped that I would not have to enter the city itself. Rather, I intended to reach the Nile near to Omdurman and try to dismantle whatever arrangement Dawson had put in place to sabotage the gunboats. Dressed as an Arab I might just get away with it. I needed Mahmud to escort me far enough through the desert so that I could safely navigate myself the rest of the way to the city.

With my plan roughly worked out, the question now was how I should attire myself for the journey. Should I remain dressed as an Arab in case we run into some Dervishes, or would I be better placed wearing my military uniform for the first stage of the journey in anticipation of stumbling across some British or Egyptian soldiers? In the end I decided it would be best to dress in the traditional Arab fashion, for I reasoned that Anglo-Egyptian soldiers would probably not fire on what they perceived to be Bedouin unless provoked. The Dervishes, however, would fire on anything they did not recognize as their own. Mahmud was good enough to furnish me with the appropriate garments – they were spare items that were the property of one of his young relations, who was not at all pleased at having to part with them.

As the sun was just rising above a cluster of rocks in the distance, Mahmud went around and embraced each one of his relatives in turn before mounting his camel to begin our adventure. I checked that my revolver was fully loaded and placed it underneath my garments.

'Are you ready?' I asked my companion, turning my camel to face away from the rising sun and wrapping my Arab headscarf across the front of my face.

'I am ready,' he said dutifully.

'Then let us go!' and we kicked our camels off to the cheers of Mahmud's companions.

We started the camels at a gallop before slowing down to a steadier pace, and I remember then, as we left Mahmud's companions far behind and rode out into the silent wilderness, a feeling of great anticipation for the journey ahead, tempered somewhat by a sense of foreboding at the thought of the dangers that would no doubt present themselves. It is easy for a man unaccustomed to desert travel to be completely overwhelmed by it; by its size and its emptiness; by its solitude and sterility. And yet, despite my years of travelling in such places, I could not help but be seduced and to a degree overwhelmed by the prospect of the adventures that were to come.

'Tell me about your country,' said Mahmud, once we were well on our way and ascending a small rocky hill. We were riding side-by-side, the ground a mixture of fine sand and flint. My field rifle and other kit were stored in various sacks that hung from my camel, but I was careful that nothing should be left showing that would give me away as being European.

'Ah, England,' I replied. 'It is a beautiful, beautiful place. Very green.'

'Lots of water?'

I laughed. 'Yes. Lots of water. Sometimes too much, when it seems to be falling for ever and ever, and the thick grey sky seems to be permanently wrapped around the land. But there are also lush meadows and forests of trees, which when the sun *is* shining look so beautiful that one could almost cry for them. And there are sparkling lakes also, and great cities and towns, and in the country there are armies of people working the land to grow food.'

He looked into the distance, as if he could actually catch a glimpse of England's shores. 'I would like to see that,' he said.

'Perhaps one day you shall.'

Mahmud shook his head. 'This is my homeland,' and he waved his hand.

'I wonder how you can feel so at home in this … this nothingness.'

He looked at me directly. 'When I am in the desert I am the desert. I am its sand and its wind. I disappear.'

These profound words made us silent for a few seconds, and when I next spoke I found myself quite involuntarily changing the subject. 'I see you carry one of our old Martini-Henry rifles,' I said.

Mahmud looked at the old British rifle that lay on his lap, many of which could be found throughout the Sudan from previous campaigns.

'I bought it in Assuan,' he said. 'Yours is better, yes?'

He was correct. His rifle was not nearly as advanced as my modern Lee-

Metford, with its lack of recoil, smokeless powder and magazine action. But I did not wish to offend. 'Not better, just different,' I smiled.

He was an interesting fellow, Mahmud. He had led such a simple life and yet there seemed to be a depth to him that one would associate with the most educated and worldly of men. Watching him then in his shining white robes, it occurred to me how striking and splendid he looked. He was sitting tall and proud in his saddle, his pointed, sphinx-like features dark and handsome, his piercing eyes, like two little black stones, seeming at once lifeless and yet also full of experience, as if they had recorded many of the twists and turns of human nature over a great many years.

We were silent then for a time, and it was Mahmud who next instigated conversation, when we were trekking across a flat plain that looked endless. There was not a hint of wind, the heat was furnace-like and the light as intense as though one were staring directly into a white candle flame. It was difficult to imagine how any human could choose to exist in such an environment. 'Have you killed many men?' he asked bluntly.

I looked at Mahmud. 'I have not killed many men, but I have killed,' I said. 'In fact, I had to kill a man very recently.'

'Recently?' Instantly he was interested. The Arabs are always interested in killing. It is one of their more unseemly qualities. 'And how did you come to kill this man?'

'I thought he was the man whom I am pursuing now,' I said, wishing I had given some other answer. 'But it turned out he was not, although he was also my enemy and deserved to die.'

'And did you shoot him, or cut his throat?'

'I shot him.'

He looked perversely impressed. 'The people in your army must consider you a great warrior.'

I smiled a little. My natural instinct was to be modest, and anyway, boasting about killing a man was not the sort of thing that I went in for. In this situation, however, in dealing with a man of this culture – who, although he sounded crude, was obviously very intelligent – I put aside these pre-conditioned ideas as best I could. 'I am regarded as being a skilled warrior, yes,' I said.

'And the man that you are seeking now, why do you need to kill him?'

'Because he is a traitor.'

Mahmud, who had been facing me, turned to look into the far away distance. 'Then you must kill him. He does not deserve life.'

The morning's trekking passed uneventfully. I estimated we were taking a roughly parallel course with the Nile now, at a distance of perhaps fifty or so miles from it. The thought that the river was not a great distance away gave me some comfort, for it meant that there was a chance of survival should we run out of water – although our chances of reaching it by foot should something happen to our camels were not great.

We did not stop to rest once the afternoon came. There would have been little point, for no shade was to be found anywhere. Instead, with our faces almost completely covered to protect us from the strong sun, we marched our camels on at a steady pace, careful that we should not drive them too hard. A few hours later and the landscape began to change and become more undulating. The camels found themselves having to contend with many loose stones and sharp flints, and occasionally we would come across an area of rough grass mixed with thorny bushes.

It was the following day that the first troubles – although certainly not the last – of our journey began.

We were ascending a stony incline, a large piece of grey rock sitting to our right, when suddenly the sun disappeared for a few seconds and, squinting to look at the crest of the hill, I spotted four men on camels. Instantly I recognized them, with their rifles and coffee-coloured helmets, as being British or Egyptian soldiers.

The trekking must have made me slightly dazed, for I did not respond immediately, and indeed for a brief second it escaped me that I was disguised as an Arab. I turned to say something to Mahmud, but then the sound of gunfire made me jolt. One of the soldiers had fired a shot at us. The bullet whizzed past my right side – Mahmud was on my left – and struck the ground behind me. The camels did not like the firing one bit, and before I knew what was happening my beast was careering off back down the hill and throwing me from side-to-side on its back. It was a real struggle to stay atop it. Another shot came.

'Stop firing, you bloody idiots! I'm British!'

Clearly I had been quite wrong in my theory that our soldiers would not fire on Bedouin. Once I was safely out of range and had managed to halt my camel, I turned to find Mahmud, calmly and with expert handling, riding towards me. I looked up and saw the soldiers still at the top of the hill. One of them, whom I assumed must have been an officer, seemed to be observing us through his spyglass.

'Shall we fight them?' Mahmud said, as he approached.

'I am afraid we cannot, as much as I would like to.'

I took off my white headscarf and began to wave it in the air towards the men in the hope that they would realize we were not Dervishes. It seemed to have the desired effect, for a minute or so later they began to descend the hill towards us slowly. Their rifles were lowered but were clearly still at the ready to be used. 'Remain calm, Mahmud,' I said to my companion. 'I shall talk to them.'

When they were around fifty yards off, and purely to make it clear that I was an Englishman, I shouted, 'Good afternoon.' They seemed surprised, as one would expect, but they at least kept their weapons lowered. 'My name is Major Winters,' I said, as the lead man got near. 'I am with the Intelligence Branch, hence my rather eccentric mode of dress. And this gentleman is an Arab companion of mine.'

The four men looked to be British. 'Lieutenant Watson, 21st Lancers,' said the lead. 'Sorry about shooting at you, sir. Didn't for a second think you were British though. Why the Arab clothing?'

'It is of no concern to you why I am dressed like this,' I said, immediately changing my tone to something more brusque, for now that we were safe I had no trouble at all making it absolutely clear that I was livid at having been shot at. 'Tell me, Lieutenant, are you under orders to shoot at anyone who is not dressed in British or Egyptian uniform?'

The lieutenant looked a little disconcerted as if I – *I* – had dealt *him* some kind of an injustice. 'Well, no … er, no,' he stumbled. 'Not exactly, but we simply assumed—'

'Precisely, Lieutenant. You assumed. Here I am winning the trust of the travelling Arabs of the Sudan and you are shooting at them simply because they are not European. It is not really the way to conduct things, is it?'

'No,' he said a little ashamedly.

I sighed. 'But anyway, you will know better now. My companion and I are travelling south. Tell me what you know about this area. Have you spotted any Dervishes?'

The lieutenant gave me a look that told me he thought I was absolutely barmy, but I had no interest in explaining myself. 'We haven't seen any as yet,' he said, 'but I believe some of them have been spotted around the area of the Kerreri Hills.'

My plan was to avoid this set of strategically important hills, which lay about six miles to the north of Omdurman, as I knew there would be a high probability of finding enemy there. Mahmud and I would skirt around them to the west. But if our forces were already at the Kerreri Hills, then this meant it would not be long at all until the decisive battle. 'When do you estimate the final move on the Dervishes will begin?' I asked Watson.

'I would say within the next two days or so, sir.'

If this estimate were correct then there was no time to spare. I simply had to get to Omdurman as quickly as I possibly could, even if it meant forcing the camels beyond their limits. 'We should go,' I said to Mahmud, in Arabic. Then returning to English I wished the men a safe time over the next few days. 'And remember what I told you,' I said as we started off.

'Wait! Sir,' said the lieutenant.

We stopped. 'Sir, I don't know anything about what you're up to, but I do know that it's extremely dangerous for you in this area. If the Dervishes don't get you then … well, we mistook you for the enemy, and I think others may well do also. May I suggest that you accompany us on the next stage of your journey? I assume you are moving towards the front line?'

I considered his suggestion then explained it to Mahmud. My intelligence officer instincts were telling me to turn down the offer, to remain anonymous and small in the desert. But as I thought about the real possibility of running into other soldiers or Dervishes, I knew that the sensible option would be to travel with the men towards the Kerreri Hills before splitting off on my own. 'You are travelling directly towards Omdurman?'

'As quickly as our animals will carry us, sir.'

'And you know this country? You could get me close to the Kerreri Hills without getting lost?'

'Indeed.'

That settled it. 'Mahmud,' I said, 'I think it would be better for us both if I accompany these men towards the Kerreri Hills. I should be able to move out into the desert and towards Omdurman from there on my own. I know our time together has been short, but I am most grateful to you. You have been a good guide. You can rejoin your companions now. And if you would be so good as to sell me this camel I would be most grateful.'

I went to open a pouch on the side of my camel to retrieve some gold coins but found Mahmud placing his hand up to stop me. 'You would die in the desert alone.'

'No, no, I shall be quite all right. Here—'

'No,' he said rather forcefully, pushing away the gold. The soldiers looked on bewildered. 'Do you know where the wells are? And what if your camel breaks a leg on the rocky slopes? With two we can still travel. Alone you would die a slow death. I will come with you.'

I must have endeared myself sufficiently to the man that he had decided his destiny would be entwined with my own until he felt he had fulfilled his part of our bargain. So it seemed that I had no choice but to retain Mahmud as my companion.

'Very well,' I said, putting away the gold sovereigns. 'And thank you.'

Mahmud nodded slowly and I turned to address Watson. 'We would be happy to accompany you. Thank you.'

'HAVE YOU BEEN involved in any skirmishes yet?' I asked Watson, once we were on our way, the afternoon drawing in and with the sun just hinting that it was about to lose some of its ferocity. I did indeed feel far safer with this escort of four British soldiers as we progressed into the vast desert interior. As well as Lieutenant Watson there were two Lancers and a particularly stern-looking sergeant, who said nothing except when giving his men orders.

'I'm sorry to say that firing at you is the first action we've seen,' Watson replied wryly to my question, but I ignored his attempt at humour.

'Indeed. Have you heard how the build-up is progressing?'

His smile dropped instantly as he tried to be serious again. 'No real action yet, as far as I know, but I think the build-up of our forces is virtually complete.'

'And the gunboats, what about them?'

'You know we temporarily lost one downriver?'

'Yes.'

'Well the others are in place and are providing the army with round-the-clock protection. All seems to be going to plan so far.'

'Very good.'

'And what about you, Major? May I ask what you are doing travelling alone through the desert with an Arab?'

'You may ask, but I'm afraid I can't tell you. All I can say is that I am an intelligence officer on a mission that was instigated personally by the *Sirdar*.'

It was at this point that Mahmud called my attention. I turned to find him gazing intently into the mammoth horizon, which in the flat plains that prevailed here seemed to be all the way on the other side of the world.

'The sky, it will soon fill with dust,' he said. 'We should prepare.'

He meant that a sandstorm was approaching. I squinted my eyes and looked into the distance. Nothing. All I could see was the infinite blue-white of clear skies stretching out for what seemed like thousands of miles.

'What's he saying?' asked Watson.

'He says there is a sandstorm approaching.'

Watson joined me in looking into the distance. 'I can't see any sandstorm. What's he talking about? There's nothing out there. It's completely calm.'

'Lieutenant Watson, these travelling Arabs have the keenest eyes of any men I have ever seen. They can sense where to find water and can spot those areas fifty miles before we could even see the outline of a bush or a darkened area of grass. If Mahmud says that a sandstorm is coming then we would – and you must trust me – be wise to listen to him.'

Watson looked at me for a few seconds then nodded his agreement. He was young and impatient. He still had some growing up to do, but he was willing to learn and his heart was in the right place – he was, after all, good enough to suggest that we accompany him and his men for our safety.

'Mahmud, what shall we do?' I asked. I had been through sandstorms before and knew that they had to be waited out, but I was more than happy to call on Mahmud's wisdom on this occasion. I think he felt somewhat honoured, for he smiled then.

'We must lay our camels down. We must take off their garments [he meant saddles] to use for shelter, and we must then cover ourselves with our blankets.'

I explained to the men in English what had to be done. 'Well, come on, get to it!' ordered Watson without hesitation.

We had the camels down and unsaddled in some few minutes, and looking up then I could see that Mahmud had shown remarkable observation, for the horizon was indeed starting to darken and turn a thick colour of brown. And there was wind also now, making my Arab clothing flap and already throwing bits of grit into my eyes and ears.

The wind gradually increased and the flying sand became more prevalent as the sun slowly began to be obscured by the rising tide of the storm. The men and camels had been put down in a kind of semi-circle, with Mahmud on an outer point and with me next to him.

I translated Mahmud's advice. 'Cover yourselves completely with your blankets. As long as you can breathe you will be fine.'

'But what about the camels?' asked Watson, apprehension prevalent in his voice.

'The camels are perfectly adapted to survive these storms,' I said, without the need to consult my guide.

And so I huddled down next to my camel's saddle, the rancid smell of the beast's coat at such close quarters being almost overwhelming, and with a nod to Mahmud covered myself with my field blanket. How I wished at this point that I had replaced it with a new one at Abu Hamed or Wadi Halfa, for I knew that the many holes in it would start to fill with sand. But it would have to do now.

I lay there then as the wind whipped up harder and began to beat heavily against the side of my blanket, the screaming sound outside that of an animal being tortured. I had been through similar storms further north and knew that they could last anything from minutes to hours, or even longer, and I must say that my principal concern was not for our safety but for the delay to our journey. How long would it be before Dawson destroyed those gunboats?

I emerged from my makeshift shelter, which was covered in a thick layer of sand, dusty and weary. I calculated that the storm must have lasted little more than an hour. We had been lucky. Mahmud was already outside, observing the retreating storm and the brilliant blue that was moving in to replace it.

'You may come out now,' I called to the other men, brushing my garments down. Each man emerged unscathed and with a little more knowledge of the trials of desert travel.

We carried on that day until, just before sunset, we felt that the camels could take no more. When we eventually did stop my grumpy old beast of burden released the most awful sounding groan, and I felt sure he was going to throw me as I got off him.

We could not light a fire to cook on for fear that it would bring us to the attention of some Dervishes, so instead we ate biscuit and some sort of dried meat that Mahmud kindly provided, and we had to make do with water rather than tea.

That night spent in the desert was particularly memorable, for, as the sun fell, a perfect moon rose to replace it so that the entire desert was bathed in pale blue-white. Before bedding down to rest I thought I would make the most of the illumination by taking my spyglass up the nearest hill to search for any signs of the enemy. And what a magnificent sight it was that awaited me – like catching a glimpse of another world. The dark valleys of the desert appeared as lunar seas, while the rocky areas cast great and unnatural-looking shadows on to the pallid dust. The stillness of that night and its contrast with the storm of the day meant that it left an indelible memory. There are times when the beauty of the desert can take one completely by surprise, even when one regards oneself as being well acquainted with all of its moods and secrets, and that night was one of those times.

Thankfully I spotted no Dervish – although there were one or two startling moments when I thought I had seen something move, but upon closer inspection it turned out merely to be the moonlight playing tricks with my eyes.

As I lay down to sleep, content that Mahmud and our little band were safe in our camp, I thought of our troops bivouacked this very night in or around the Kerreri Hills. Would they have time to contemplate how beautiful the desert looked under a full moon? I would have thought most probably not, for there would be far more pressing matters for these men's minds to be focused on. Those on stag duty would be avidly watching the plains for a night attack by the Khalifa's forces, while those lucky enough to have avoided this obligation would be lying as I was, trying to sleep but no doubt unable to, the excitement of what was to come making slumber impossible. And these men would also be listening for noises from the desert outside their position, fearing they might be called into action at any moment. Perhaps the men were even engaged as I lay comfortably on my field blanket. Perhaps they were in the thick of it and were slaughtering or being slaughtered. I hoped not, for if this were the case then Dawson would already have won our battle.

WE CAUGHT UP with the rest of the 21st Lancers early the following day.

'Just ahead, sir. Over the next hill they are,' shouted one of Watson's men as he trotted back from a short scouting trip.

It was still early morning, the sun low and friendly, the country peaceful, the cold of the night before yet to shake itself from our bones.

'Let's go!' shouted Watson, clearly exuberant at the thought of meeting his comrades once more. 'I wonder what news they shall bring,' he said, as we kicked the camels into action and began to ascend the slope ahead.

And then they were before us. In a crater on the other side of the hill, the entire regiment of horsemen, perhaps four hundred of them, all desert uniforms, riding boots and rifles, and of course their magnificent-looking twelve-foot lances, their sharp tips in the air glinting menacingly. The horses brilliant white, pitch black, every shade of brown.

I knew as soon as I saw the men that something was afoot, for there seemed a lot of commotion taking place. Rifles were being checked and loaded, water drunk, bully-beef hastily shoved down throats, orders given, saddles checked, the whole block of men alive and exuding energy. They were preparing for a fight.

The one leading these men, a Colonel Burton, looked most surprised at the sight of us, but Watson quickly filed a report. The colonel then galloped over. 'Going to Omdurman ... some sort of secret mission, eh?' He was tall and slim and had a solid bearing. He exuded confidence as he awaited my answer. Not a drop of sweat on the man.

'That's quite correct, sir, yes,' I said.

'Well, I wouldn't go getting ahead of us here. Bunch of Dervishes just over the next hill. Cut you to pieces. Best you chaps wait until we take care of them, all right?'

'Of course, Colonel. This is your territory, so whatever you think would be best.'

But he had no time to answer me and was off checking on his men again. I explained the situation to Mahmud. It looked as if we were about to bear witness to one of the first engagements of the battle to re-take Omdurman. There were lots of questions I wished to ask Burton, such as how far exactly we were from the Kerreri Hills, but now, just as the men were preparing for action, was not the time to do it.

No doubt the 21st Lancers would have taken more of an interest in us had their minds not been focused on the potential action ahead, but at this moment they paid Mahmud and I barely a second glance.

'We need not get involved in this, Mahmud,' I said. 'My mission is more important. It would be a disaster if I were to be killed or wounded now. We should stay close to these men, but not too close.'

'We will look after each other, yes?' he smiled.

'Indeed, my friend. Indeed.'

Watson returned. 'We are to follow on behind,' he said with a look of disappointment. 'It's the camels, you see. They could slow the others down. Damn it, I just knew I would miss it all.'

He was so young. 'So we should stay with you, Lieutenant?'

'Yes, if you wouldn't mind, Major, that's what the colonel wishes.'

In a short time Colonel Burton had his men ready to ride off to meet the enemy. He had them in a broad line of several horses deep, the animals quite still and well behaved. The colonel then rode along the line, utter silence but for his animal's hoofbeats, as we looked on, detached from the main body. 'You are a fine sight,' he then shouted to his men. 'We have come a long, long way for this moment. Some of you may not live to look back and enjoy its memory. But I cannot think of any better place to finish one's days than on the battlefield – than on *this* battlefield! This morning we may finally have a chance to show these savages what the 21st Lancers are made of. You will acquit yourselves well. I know you will. Sergeant-Major!'

From the end of the line: 'Sir!'

'When you are ready.'

'Sir!'

The sound of a British trumpeter at full blast rang in our ears and then they were off, these brave men with their brave leader, ascending the hill before us, all jolting and clanking together with their equipment, swords and rifles at the ready. Accordingly we six fell in behind.

I saw two patrols break off from the ungainly mass of Lancers and push on to the top of the hill. There they waited, closely observing whatever it was that lay ahead. And then they were over the lip of the crater with the rest of the regiment closely behind, and we also made our way up the slope.

The enclosed landscape of the crater opened out to a broad plain flanked by rocky *jebels* – hills – and it was then that I saw the enemy, several hundred Dervishes standing on the hazy open ground. I would later learn that they were Hadendoa tribesmen under the flag of Osman Digna, and indeed at the back of this block of white-robed warriors a black *rayya* flew.

But still there was calm, peace everywhere – how these moments contrasted with what was to come. And yet with this there was also a palpable feeling of incredible anticipation, which one could almost taste.

A shot rang out from the Dervish lines to break the tranquillity, but the 21st were still out of range and so it was ignored.

I was transfixed by it all, so much so that I almost missed what Mahmud, who was riding on my left side, Watson on my right, then said. 'We should be very careful now. When the English are after blood they might see our robes and shoot without thinking.'

'Quite right, Mahmud. We mustn't stray too far, and we should keep our eyes open.'

'You must stay close to me, Winters.'

It was the first time Mahmud had addressed me by my name. I looked at him. Why are you being so loyal to me? Surely I am nothing to you. I had these thoughts then but kept them to myself. If we both made it safely out of this battle and on towards Omdurman then perhaps I would ask him later.

On down into the plains, a feeling of being dreadfully exposed. And then our soldiers veered off to the left. Burton must have been planning a flanking attack, or at least he was taking the precaution of inspecting the left side for ambush, near the largest of the two hills that served as walls to what was effectively a fighting arena. An eruption of Dervish shouts and high-pitched war cries. The Lancers were at a trot now and moving across the enemy's front, little more than three hundred yards between them.

And now there came the almighty noise of a volley from the Dervishes, who had dropped to their knees to fire. Three, perhaps four of the British horses down, riders sprawled helplessly on the cracked, hard earth.

'Right wheel into line!' came suddenly from Burton.

The following minutes went in a blur. Serenely, as if they were a part of some perverse ballet, the Lancers wheeled round. They could have been performing to the beats of a soft adagio. But the noises which came now were utterly that of war. 'And charge!' from Burton, his glinting sword pointing straight ahead at the Dervishes.

The thunder of horses' hoofs and the gap between the Lancers and the enemy quickly began to close, while the gap between we camel riders and the 21st widened. And now the fire of the Dervishes came with furious torment, the smoke from their guns rising above the desert, the ground seeming to shake as the 21st Lancers closed in with vile determination.

The Dervish bullets struck hard around the Lancers, bits of earth flying into the air around them and the troopers having to bow their heads to protect their eyes. The force of the Lancers' advance now seemed unstoppable, and I thought the Dervishes stood little chance.

But then came their trap. As if straight from the ground, as if they had been sleeping warriors from many millennia before who had suddenly and magically been roused once more to battle, there sprang hundreds, many hundreds, more Dervishes.

We would later discover that a deep khor ran directly behind where the Hadendoa had been placed, and that this had been used to conceal the enemy fighters. Up they sprang, lithe and athletic and determined that the dry desert floor should soon be awash with the warm blood of many Englishmen.

The Lancers could not pull back now the energy of their advance was so great. For better or worse they were committed.

'Oh God, it's a bloody trap!' cried Watson, terrified.

Mahmud was more calm. I had noticed him check that his rifle had a bullet ready in the chamber. And now he brought out a long, curved knife from somewhere and placed it in his left hand.

'They should stop and turn back!' continued Watson, becoming more hysterical.

Automatically I said, 'No, they must ride through. Their only chance is to reach the other side.'

And so it was. To try to bring the mass of Lancers to a halt now would be chaos followed by death as the Dervishes swarmed in to cut and puncture. Their only chance lay in punching through the enemy's lines, as I was sure Burton knew perfectly well.

And indeed like an immense fist the 21st Lancers slammed into the enemy. The Dervishes who had acted as bait were thrown out of the way and trampled underfoot like rag dolls. The Lancers' momentum naturally slowed as from the ditch stormed the mad screaming horde, lances and swords swinging wildly, patches of white and black everywhere. Shouts and screams, of fear, of exhilaration, the clash of metal against metal. In the mêlée I saw one of our horses collapse, and in an instant the poor trooper it had been carrying was set upon by untold numbers of Dervishes. The ferocity of the hacking that then took place was shockingly gruesome. The noise of the battle was so loud that the unfortunate man's screams were not even heard. The Dervishes were slashing passionately at rein, at boot, at horseflesh. More soldiers fell, to be speared and dismembered.

But so too were many Dervishes falling, shot at point-blank range by a pistol or a rifle, hacked through the neck or shoulder with a lance. And then it seemed that most of our men were through the deadly crowd and were free. A few who had been brought down were still fighting and desperately trying to reach safety. Amazingly, some of them managed to hack their way through the violence to get to the other side of the ditch. I could see them emerge from that far side as if sprouting from the ground, swords dripping with blood and pistols smoking. Others, however, breathed their last in that disgusting place. I even saw one brave man return to the fray to attempt a rescue of a fallen comrade, only to quickly join him in death.

'To the left, the left!'

It was Mahmud who noticed them first. Swarming in to our left side was a small group of Dervishes, probably no more than ten men. Immediately Mahmud and I were off our camels. But Watson was too slow. They must have somehow made their way down from the hillside without anyone noticing them.

It all happened so quickly. They may have closed in secretly, but once they knew we were on to them they charged without hesitation. So quickly they covered the ground, like lightning. A flash then and I saw a spear fly up to hit poor old Watson in the back. There had been no time for him to dismount, and instantly he slouched forward on his camel. A diversion then as I noted Mahmud bringing down a Dervish with a rifle shot.

But now they were on top of us. I dropped one with a pistol shot at fifteen yards, another one at ten. I crouched to one knee as a crazy-looking Dervish came closer. I shot once, still he came, again and again and he fell, no more than a foot from me. I fired one more shot ahead, hitting nothing.

Out of breath now and sweating. No time to reload. I panicked, grabbed the sword from the ground where the Dervish had just fallen before me and a second later automatically raised it to block the downward swing of an enemy. This it did, but the ferocity of the blow knocked me on to my back. Blinding sun and a mad, tall Dervish standing above me, blazing eyes full of hate. A flash as he raised his weapon to administer the killing swipe.

But at that moment he flew back as if a rope had been secured around him and suddenly wrenched.

It was Mahmud. He had closed in from behind, and then they were rolling and struggling on the ground, fists and feet flying everywhere, flashes from blades. And Mahmud was on top now. There was a short scream as he drove his knife into the man's chest, who then lay still.

It was over then. The other men had taken care of the rest of the Dervishes, apart from one who had managed to run off. I was shaking and breathless, but my first thought was for Watson. Hauling myself up, noting that I was not wounded, I looked towards where the young lieutenant and his camel had been positioned and saw his body on its side lying deathly still in the desert, a picture frozen in time. His camel had bolted, as all our animals had. I went towards Watson and was joined by his sergeant and men, who had been engaged in their own small battles. None of them appeared to be wounded.

The young lieutenant was dead, the spear still in his back, wedged deep, blood oozing from it, and he appeared to have another cut on his chest, as if the Dervish had had a chance to finish the job. Poor, naïve Watson. He never had the opportunity to do that growing up that I thought he so needed. Such a waste. He would have turned out to be a splendid young officer.

But the main battle was still taking place and, as Watson's men knelt to check on their fallen comrade, I returned my attention to the battlefield. Burton's men were regrouping, as were the Dervishes. But now there came a brilliant and deadly stroke by the colonel. Rather than charge the enemy again, he led his remaining soldiers around to their right flank, from which position the badly mauled and disjointed group could dismount their horses and send volley after volley of fire into the densely packed mass of Dervish soldiers in and around the pit. The result of the well-grouped and rapid shooting was a rout, and those who did not manage to escape to the hills were slaughtered.

'OMDURMAN,' SAID MAHMUD, pointing to the east. I could not see the city from where we were, but Mahmud said it would be no more than a few hours by camel.

We had remained with the 21st Lancers for several more hours after the battle, and once the wounded were taken care of and Watson and the other dead buried, and with our camels recovered, we progressed further into the desert with them before splitting off on our own so we could box around Omdurman. We then spent a quiet night alone in the desert, speaking little of the battle that day. Several more arduous hours of travel followed the next morning and afternoon before we reached the point to which my Arab guide had promised to escort me. I thanked Mahmud profusely for all he had done to help me. 'You are a brave and a good man,' I said. 'You saved my life yesterday, and I shall never forget it. I expect no more of you now. I am forever indebted to you. We have come far over these past few days, and not just in distance. I will always think of how you have helped me.'

Mahmud smiled a little and bowed his head. 'I feel very honoured to have your friendship. You are a great fighter. But, Winters, you must listen now. I shall continue on with you. I must see you safely on to the end. I cannot go back until then.'

I had not thought for a second that Mahmud would have come up with such a suggestion, not this far into our journey and this close to Omdurman. 'That is really not necessary,' I said. 'It is much too dangerous. You would be foolish to go with me now.'

But, as I uttered these words, I realized that I had just made a mistake, for it was obvious that it was the very fact that I was undertaking such a dangerous journey that made Mahmud feel that he too should be able to face such a perilous enterprise. For such an intelligent fellow he was easily moved to action by his stubborn pride. 'I must reach the Nile now for water anyway,' he said. 'I travel in the same direction as you.'

Perhaps he was telling the truth, or perhaps there were many watering-holes in the desert that he knew of that would have served his needs. I did not know. But for now I was actually glad to have him continue to travel with me, for his knowledge of the terrain could yet be invaluable. Part of me did fear that he could eventually prove a burden, but I resolved myself to the fact that I would perhaps have to insist we go our separate ways at some point. So, for now at least, I felt safer having Mahmud with me. I said, 'Very well. But if you are killed then I shall take back my gold sovereigns,' to which my guide gave out a loud laugh, which rang through the desert.

CHAPTER 13

Diary of the Rt. Hon. Colonel Evelyn Winters, MP

27 April, 1935

THE WAR IN the Sudan has inevitably been at the forefront of my mind –
along with India – over the past few months, but today I had cause to
contemplate the campaign in a somewhat deeper fashion, for I attended a
memorial service at Westminster Abbey for those who lost their lives fighting
the Dervishes. Normally I would go to these sorts of things by myself, but I
decided to ask Parker to accompany me to this particular service – I thought
he might appreciate being there, as his father was killed at Omdurman.

I met him outside the Abbey. It was a fine, bright morning, and I found
him standing patiently by the entrance. It is the first time that I have seen
Parker wearing a suit. It was just a plain, dark effort, but I thought he
looked very smart in it, and I complimented him accordingly.

'Oh, you think so?' he said, looking down at his attire. 'Margaret's still
to see it. Hope she likes it.'

'I'm sure she'll think you most dashing in it. Shall we go inside?'

We were among the last to take our seats, so we placed ourselves
towards the back, with me next to the aisle and Parker to my immediate
right. The scale of the Abbey, with its massive columns shooting up to a
roof that seems a mile off, never fails to impress me. But along with this
there is, I think, also a coldness to the place. Perhaps it is the prevalence of
stone and marble that does it. But I do find it a little disconcerting on an
occasion like today.

I am always reminded of how unconventional my military career was
when I go to these things. Working in intelligence, often operating alone,
I never really had the chance to build up proper friendships. By contrast,

the other old soldiers there seemed to have many friends. Three or four men came up to greet the flat-capped gentleman standing in front of me, for instance, while we were waiting for the ceremony to begin. Still, at least I had Parker to accompany me.

Indeed there was one point today when I really was glad to have Parker with me – I hate to imagine what would have happened had he not been there. The ceremony was progressing in the usual sombre way. It must have been about halfway through and I was looking forward to its finishing. We were asked to stand. But then, when I must have been on my feet for around five minutes, something very unusual happened. I was looking towards the front, not at the altar but at the stooped backs of all the old fighters, wondering what their stories are, when suddenly I felt my feet start to wobble below me.

No sooner, however, had I thought that I would have to sit down than I felt Parker's strong arm go under my elbow to steady me.

'All right ... all right?' he whispered.

I looked up at him and nodded, my blurred vision clearing. 'Yes, yes, I shall be fine, I think,' I said, clutching the top of his forearm with my left hand. I let Parker take my weight until we were able to sit down again.

'Thank you,' I said, as we were walking out at the end.

Parker, I could tell, did not know what to say about it, but he was very kind, being careful that I should not feel embarrassed. 'Oh, no, no,' he said. 'We were ... yes, it was a long time, a long time that we were standing.'

My plan for the day was for Parker and I to return to my flat to do some work on my memoirs and my speech. But as it was such a fine morning I suggested we first take a walk through St James's Park before getting a taxi.

Although it is one of the smaller parks, I regard St James's as being probably the prettiest. The flowerbeds, so recently come to life, were a blaze of colours, the air sweet, and the view along the side of the pond, with Buckingham Palace lying at the top of it in the fine spring sunshine, was one of those enduring images of this great city that is so pleasing to see. The distant burr of traffic could be heard, but mostly it was the sound of birds singing that fell upon our ears.

Parker was quiet at first as we walked, as indeed was I. Thinking about those old soldiers like me, I was reminded, as I had on that first night that I met Parker at the British Library, of the real cost of war, and I could not help but feel somewhat guilty about dramatizing and romanticizing it, as I am doing in my memoirs. Indeed, many of the more grotesque aspects of the conflict, which I had forgotten, came flooding back to me today. I was reminded of how Kitchener, following his victory, had been less than benevolent towards the Dervish wounded, of how our forces had had to fire on civilians fleeing the city to try and check the Khalifa's escape. And I was reminded also of how, once he had entered Omdurman, Kitchener had had the Mahdi's tomb razed to the ground, his decayed and only partially embalmed body unceremoniously thrown in the Nile. I remembered how the Mahdi's skull had been spared a watery grave because Kitchener actually considered mounting it on silver and using it as an inkwell, but how Queen Victoria herself – no doubt reflecting the views of her people – had insisted that it be buried rather than be treated in any kind of inhumane way. There is indeed no chivalry in war, and even our greatest and most professional generals can turn savage in its midst.

It occurred to me then, as we walked silently on the newly cut grass, that there seemed also to be something on Parker's mind. He is not usually so quiet these days, and turning to look at him I thought him to be deep in contemplation.

'Everything all right with Miss Bellingford?' I asked.

'Oh, yes, yes … fine. Yes, she's fine,' he said, snapping out of it. But his eyebrows were furrowed a little. Then he looked at me directly and I knew that he was keen to tell me something. 'There's something … oh, I don't know,' – he looked really quite uncomfortable as he started, the poor boy – 'something I've been wanting to talk over with you for a few weeks now. Don't know why I didn't just come out with it to begin with. It's just that … well, my research on Omdurman … and the ceremony there reminded me of it also. Everything, in these last few months, has been … has been a constant reminder of my father. And … oh, it was the Royal Anglian Regiment that he was with, by the way. But it's simply that …'

'Yes?'

'Well, how should I say it?'

But I knew exactly what he wanted to say, and I was not surprised that the poor boy was too embarrassed to admit it. I thought I should help him along. 'You're being reminded of your father's death every time you pick up a book, or read a letter sent by some soldier from the Sudan, and it's proving difficult for you, yes?'

'Indeed, but—'

'Would you like to have a break from doing your researches?'

'No, no it's not that. It's just that—'

'Ah, I see. Doing this research has made you feel that you need to find out more about your father's adventures in the campaign and, dare I say it, exactly how he died. Quite understandable, my boy, quite understandable. And, I should add, rather gallant of you, too. Laying those demons to rest and all that. Am I correct?'

Parker went quiet for a few seconds and looked away from me towards the pond. I heard him sigh to himself. It must have been difficult for him. But then he turned, and with half a smile, said, 'Yes, yes, that's exactly it. I should find out a bit more about him. Yes, that's it. That was all.'

I have suspected for some time that researching the campaign would perhaps make Parker want to learn more about his father's activities in the Sudan. And I thought then that perhaps I had made a mistake in asking him along to the ceremony – I really should try to be more sensitive. The poor boy is being reminded often enough of his father's death.

'I'm so sorry for having you here today. It was probably the last thing that you needed,' I said.

He was quiet again for a few seconds, but then he said he was actually glad that he had attended, adding awkwardly, 'It was an honour really. Yes … indeed, it was very good to see some more of the men who fought there.'

I think it took a lot for Parker to admit that he finds conducting his research emotionally difficult, and that he wishes to find out more about his father, but I am glad of it. I hope he can find out enough about the man to acquire some peace of mind. At the moment I believe he knows little more than that he was an officer with the Royal Anglian Regiment and that he was killed at close quarters by the Dervishes on the battlefield at Omdurman. I must check my own research notes, though I do not recall the Royal Anglian actually being involved in the final battle, although they would certainly have been in the Sudan somewhere. Perhaps I'll have Parker check, once he feels a bit easier about things. I have offered to assist him in any possible way that I can when he is investigating his father's background – my army connections could prove useful, for instance.

RATHER THAN COME straight home I decided to treat Parker to a bit of lunch at a restaurant on Piccadilly. This perked him up somewhat, and he seemed in a far better mood when we arrived at the flat, fresh and ready to start work. 'Speech or memoirs?' I asked when we got in, to which Parker suggested we do some work on my speech.

Given how gloomy our feelings were in the morning, this afternoon actually turned out to be rather fun. We would work on a few lines of my speech and then I would deliver them as if I were standing in the House. I even had Parker reading out parts so that I could see what they sounded like. There he was, standing in front of the window in my study, the sunshine showing up a mini blizzard of dust around him, for all the world as if he had been speaking to Parliament for years – he even managed to replace his usual plodding speech with something far more eloquent. 'It is all very well,' he was saying in a low and serious voice, 'to state that a system of partially elected federal government in India, even with its limited powers, could bring a sense of honour to the country's people while retaining the efficiencies of British administration, but what happens in five, ten or twenty years from now, when the people no longer believe this to be adequate? What happens when they call on there to be formed some sort of United States of India, completely free from Britain, when the country does not have the expert administrators to govern itself? What will happen? Anarchy will happen!'

I think the boy might even be a natural, for as he finished the phrase he raised his voice just enough to deliver 'Anarchy will happen!' with real conviction. He even shook his fist for a few seconds as if he were a seasoned politician at the Dispatch Box – although I believe that, despite today's dark suit, he will always look more of an academic than a politician.

Parker's intellectual guidance – and confidence – was also brought to the fore, for when he had finished his little performance, he said, 'Oh, wait a minute. There's er, something not right about this,' and he stood looking at the written speech for a minute or so. He seemed to be ruminating hard, in a way that my older mind could probably no longer muster. Eventually he said, 'This part here, where we ... where we talk about a United States of India and put, completely free from Britain. It's too weak. I think perhaps ... hmm ... perhaps something along the lines of severing the umbilical cord with its mother country, something like that. Maybe that would be better. Something more descriptive. Would probably be more powerful.'

Of course he was perfectly correct. And so we progressed, reworking some parts, debating certain points and coming up with new ones. I hope that by the time I come to make the speech – on which I have yet to make a decision – it will be so polished as to be flawless.

I invited Parker to have some dinner with me, but he said he already had plans with Miss Bellingford. 'Give my regards to her,' I said as he was leaving, and off he went.

I dined alone at a nearby restaurant before returning to do a bit of work. I think I shall ask Parker if he and Miss Bellingford wouldn't mind a bit of company over dinner again soon, for I did so enjoy their company when we were last out together.

I may read what we have done of my speech again before bed. I think it is coming along wonderfully, thanks mainly to Parker's guiding me – or perhaps even his simply giving me confidence in what I myself am producing.

CHAPTER 14

THE VAST CITY of mud houses appeared as little more than a fine shimmering line of brown through the spyglass. Omdurman. The heart of the Khalifa's empire and the resting place of the Mahdi. And directly behind it, across the other side of the Nile, would be Khartoum.

'Can you see your army?' said Mahmud, his keen eyes squinting into the distance.

'No,' I said, lowering the spyglass. 'But even if they were there I doubt we would see them. We're too far away.'

We were to the west of Omdurman, trekking through flat and what seemed like ever more infinite desert plains. Before us and to the south lay only vast areas of emptiness, but to the north were the Kerreri Hills, jutting out of the wilderness like a ragged tooth in the mouth of some massive monster. But where was Kitchener with his army? Try as I might I could not see anything in the hills or on the plains immediately to the north of the city. We were simply not close enough. There could have been thousands of men there, but all that I was able to see through the haze was a blur. For all I knew the battle could already have been fought. Perhaps Kitchener was already installed in the Khalifa's palace, or perhaps, even, he had been driven from the battlefield and the Dervishes were celebrating another victory over the infidels.

'It is dangerous here. We should travel on,' said my trusty companion, his hawk-like features hard and uncompromising – I was indeed glad to have him with me.

I looked at Mahmud. 'Are you sure? I expect nothing more of you from here, Mahmud.'

'Winters, we waste no more time arguing now. We should move on.'

And so we set off further south, two lonely desert wanderers, mere specks in this vast world.

I hoped to circle around Omdurman and approach the city from the south-west unchallenged, but this proved to be wishful thinking.

It was a few hours later when it happened. We were tired, our camels even more so. I was saddle sore, thirsty and hungry. Even my eyes felt worn out from the constant squinting. We had stopped by a small and rarely occurring culvert to rest the camels and replenish ourselves.

They completely surprised us.

'Are you on your way to fight for the Khalifa?' came a voice from behind me, from the top of the culvert. Even Mahmud's sharp ears had not picked up the approach of the Dervishes' horses.

I was facing away from the voice. At first I remained with my back to our new guests, but I sensed Mahmud turning to face them. And then he answered, 'God be with the Khalifa in his fight, but we are only passing through this land.'

I placed my headscarf over my face before turning. Only my eyes could be seen. I hoped dearly that the men would not realize that I was European.

They must have been no more than twenty yards from us. Looking up to observe them I felt confident I would not be recognized, at least not immediately, as not being an Arab. I looked now upon five men standing in a line at the top of the culvert. Tall, wiry-looking figures, in white robes and with Arab turbans – *immas* as they are called – on their heads. The very dark skin of their bare arms seemed to almost shimmer in the sun. It would have been a beautiful sight were it not for the glinting of the rifles and spears that the men carried.

I was clutching my pistol under my robe. I could feel my hand shake a little around its grip. Should I bring the weapon out and fire on the men, in the hope of then making an escape? I would probably have time to hit at most one of them before we would have to make a run for it. But I did not rate our chances. There were too many of them. Better to try and talk our way out of this particular situation.

The Dervishes were looking at us suspiciously. 'A great fight is about to take place near here,' continued the same voice that had begun the questioning and that I could now see belonged to the lead man. He held his rifle at his side, its barrel pointing to the sky. 'We are going to drive the

infidel Turks from our lands. You should want to fight for the Khalifa and
the Mahdi's sacred cause.'

I remained silent. Mahmud would prove far more convincing than I.
'We are Bedouin,' he said. 'We fight for no land because we have no land
to fight for. We are travellers.'

The response from the lead Dervish came sharp and quick. 'In the name
of Allah you should fight. What are you carrying on your camels there?'

'Ostrich feathers.'

The Dervish's face looked petulant. 'Are ostrich feathers more important than the destruction of the infidels?'

'God willing the Turks will be massacred for the Mahdi's sacred cause,'
I said, having suddenly decided to intervene. I tried my best to mimic
Mahmud's accent. 'We shall fight with you. We would be honoured to do
so. Take us to Omdurman and we will gladly become martyrs.'

It seemed to work, for the lead Dervish smiled broadly. 'Come,' he said,
signalling for us to mount our camels.

I looked at Mahmud. His eyes asked me what on earth I was doing.
Obviously I could not explain my reasoning. That would have to wait until
later, once we had – I hoped – escaped. But I had decided to speak up
because I feared that the Dervishes would have killed us if we had not
succumbed to their wishes – these people give hardly any consideration to
the taking of blood; they place very little value on their own lives never
mind that of others.

And so we led our weary camels out of the culvert and mounted them
once more. I have never been so nervous in my life, for I was not sure how
long I could maintain my cover as a Bedouin. It would require only that
one of the Dervishes take a close look at my eyes, or ask to see my face,
and all would be lost. But one thing was clear: any escape attempt would
have to be undertaken soon, for the longer I waited the higher the chance
of being discovered.

Three of the men rode out in front, but two of them, including the one
who had questioned us, fell in behind. Clearly, as one would expect, we
were not to be trusted. I contemplated trying to whisper a message to my
companion to the effect that we must escape and that he should be
prepared for some form of action instigated by me. But then I thought
better of it. It was too risky. At some point I would simply have to try and
break off at a gallop and hope that Mahmud would be quick-witted

enough to react accordingly – I had enough faith in him to be quite certain that he would be.

We were moving east, towards Omdurman. So here was my enemy; Kitchener's enemy; Britain's enemy, these men who rode around the desert with their prehistoric fighting implements supplemented with modern yet ageing rifles. It was difficult to believe that they had already thrust the armies of the world's most powerful nation out of the Sudan once. And here I was riding with them, supposedly to fight for their cause.

The lead Dervish began to ask more questions as we trekked. He wanted to know where we had come from, why there were only two of us, and so on. He even enquired about the current price of ostrich feathers. He was certainly suspicious. I again deferred to Mahmud to talk for us. The poor man had to tell many lies.

But then, and without warning, when we had been trekking for an hour or so and the sun was starting to sit low in the sky, the lead Dervish moved up to ride beside me. He eyed me intently. I tried to take little notice. I still had my scarf over the front of my face, and with my dark eyes I hoped not to raise his suspicions. 'You say very little,' said the Dervish, looking up at me, for being on horseback meant he was closer to the ground than we camel riders.

'We have been travelling for many days and I am very tired.'

'Your voice sounds very different from your companion's. You are not related, no?'

'No.'

I knew now that I could not fool him for much longer. He was staring directly at me, trying to make eye contact, but I was looking straight ahead. 'What area of—'

I was off. With a swift pull to the left my camel and I were careering through the desert. I had no idea if Mahmud was following, but at this point all I cared about was putting distance between the Dervishes and myself. And for a brief second, as I bobbed up and down in the saddle, with my headscarf fallen away from my face to flutter behind me in the wind and with dust particles flying into my eyes, I thought I had actually pulled it off.

But then the shot came. My temporary sense of freedom fell as hard as my poor camel, which had been hit in the side. I would realize later that one of the Dervishes who had been ahead of me had instantly raised his rifle and fired – he was probably under instructions to react should either of us try to escape.

Thud; my camel made contact with the hard desert floor, and then I went forward, headfirst towards the ground. All was hazy for what must have been a few seconds before the senses began to feel, smell, see and hear again. The fall had flipped me completely over. I opened my eyes. Sky. Mostly blue but there was a bit of pink in there as the sun was beginning to set. Then I twisted my body around. I could hear the thumping of horses' hoofs. I thought that this was it. My time had come. I would not even have time to reach for my revolver to try and take one or two of them with me. It was not the first time that I had faced the possibility of death, but it is not a thing that becomes easier with practice.

And then came the shouts: 'He must be a Turk!', 'Kill him now!', and 'Infidel!'

I looked at my poor camel. The beast's head was no more than two feet from me. I could not see its wound but I knew that the animal did not have long to live. It snorted once or twice, slowly closed its tired eyes and died. I had not been at all good for the old thing. But, I thought, never mind, old chap, for I will no doubt be following you soon enough. I turned again to have one last look at the heavens and resigned myself to my fate.

They surrounded me, their grotesque faces blocking out my last perfect sky. But where was Mahmud? Had they already killed him? I dearly hoped not.

The Dervishes staring down at me looked astounded. For a brief second I was confused, but then I remembered that they were looking at what must have been a most unexpected sight – a white man dressed as an Arab close to Omdurman and, moreover, one who could speak their language fluently. I awaited a final thrusting of a spear. Any second now I would feel the sharp point touch and then penetrate my skin. I hoped for a quick death. I did not want the vultures to be pecking at me as I slowly bled my life away. Perhaps the Dervishes would cut me up into many pieces as they had done with General Gordon. Perhaps they would cut my head off and take it back to show the Khalifa. I expected no less than this level of savagery.

'English,' one of them said, the group's excitement now dissipated. They seemed not to know what to do. One of them brought his spear forward as if in preparation to administer the *coup de grace*. But then the leader put out his hand to stop him.

'We must take him to the Khalifa. He will tell us of the enemy's plans.'

Expecting to be run through with a spear, I was rather shocked instead to be hauled to my feet by the group's commander. 'Bind his hands,' he instructed one of his men, pushing me towards the man. I looked around for Mahmud. My eyes quickly found him in the same place he had been when I had attempted my escape. One of the Dervishes had remained with him, a rifle pointed at his head, while the other four had come to deal with me. My good companion looked perfectly composed.

I was stripped of my revolver, marched to one of the horses and unceremoniously placed atop it, as a child receiving riding lessons would be. One of the Dervish soldiers then sat behind me.

As we rode off in the sunset towards Omdurman, I glanced around at my dead camel. The solitary carcass looked as if it had been served up especially for the desert scavengers. Soon the vultures would be circling.

THE CITY OF Omdurman stood bleak and unpromising. I had expected to be overawed by the glimmer of beautiful and exotic palaces and temples, but, instead, my first impression of the fabled city, as we rode across moonlit plains towards it, was of nothing more than the smell of decay; a musty whiff that suggested putrefied flesh and human waste: the scent of squalor.

The single impressive aspect was the city's size. End-to-end it must have stretched to around four miles, the dark outline of buildings ceasing abruptly where the desert began. In the gloom there looked to be only one building that broke ranks in a city of single-storey mud huts, a large square block rising from the centre of Omdurman, with a single dome protruding from its top. I took this to be the citadel, which I knew housed the Mahdi's tomb.

And running past Omdurman, ahead and to my right, was the Nile, sparkling quietly in the blue-velvet night. Its position suggested we had approached Omdurman from the south-west. I followed the line of the river north of the city towards where I expected Kitchener's army would be placed, and I was startled then to see several beams of white light swinging back and forth on the Nile, seeming to emanate from nowhere. It took me a few seconds to work out that they were actually the powerful searchlights of our gunboats as they swept the banks of the river for the enemy. My eye was then drawn to the left by some other strange dots of luminance, which when I focused on them deduced that they must be the camp-fires of the Anglo-Egyptian forces. The Khalifa's armies would also be somewhere to the north of the city, possibly further to the west. And indeed, as I scanned the dense horizon I saw more little dots of camp-fire lights some distance away, signalling the presence of the Dervish masses – two great armies preparing to clash.

Our enemy was silent as we rode that final stretch, the only noise the rhythmic trot of their horses' hoofs. But as we approached Omdurman the sounds of a desert city at night gradually began to supersede. I heard the bark of a dog and then the answer of one of its fellow creatures.

A city wall presented itself as we moved in on Omdurman, running along its south-western fringe and, as we passed through an opening in it, I thought through my predicament. Here I was, a British major, bound and with little chance of escape, being taken to the Khalifa in the middle of his labyrinthine city. My mission to stop Dawson now seemed almost irrelevant. Simply staying alive would have to be my goal, and I was not at all confident that I would carry it off.

I was ahead of Mahmud as we entered Omdurman's dark and narrow streets. I had not even managed to exchange a glance with him on our journey to the city for fear of retribution from the Dervishes. And yet I wished dearly to have some encouragement from him. I wanted his stoicism to reassure me of our situation, and I also wanted to know that he did not blame me for this sudden bleak outlook to his fate – although I felt sure that his strong character would prevent this from being the case.

Inside the city the streets were much like those of Wadi Halfa – restrictive and gloomy. But there was a different feel to Omdurman. In the Anglo-Egyptian-controlled city I felt unsafe, as if at any moment some assassin would emerge from the darkness and bring about my end. But here, amidst the sense of squalor, there was also order. The irony of a despotic government is that extreme control can also bring safety for the population, at least for those who remain free of leadership torment. And so it seemed to be in Omdurman, a slum city of the oppressed.

We rode for a few hundred yards into the place, passing as we did so the occasional lonely soul patrolling the streets, head lowered and walking silently, keeping himself to himself, taking little notice of us. And after a few minutes of passing through Omdurman's slender alleyways, turning left here and right there, I was surprised to emerge on to a wide moonlit boulevard.

I looked to my left as we came on to the street to find rows of pale-white mud houses running down each of its sides. The place was empty of citizens. Turning my head slightly to the right, and trying not to alarm the Dervish soldier sitting behind me with a spear, my eyes fell upon the citadel that I had already glimpsed from afar. Sitting a few hundred yards to our front it seemed indomitable compared with the architecture that surrounded it.

The citadel's high walls cast great shadows along the avenue. It loomed massively as we approached, and the feeling of intimidation was compounded by the deep, rhythmic pulse of an *ombeya*, the African horn made from elephant ivory, emanating from deep within. I assumed we must be being taken straight to the Khalifa, for it was my guess that the citadel, as well as holding the Mahdi's tomb, would also serve as his successor's palace.

We marched right up to its walls. For a brief moment I could not see how we would possibly enter, for in the darkness it looked to be one solid mass. When we were close enough, however, the outline of what turned out to be a substantial wooden door emerged. The Dervish commander went forward, banged on it a few times and waited. A small flap in the door was flicked open. I assumed there were some eyes there but I could not see them. Next came the sound of bolts being drawn then a loud creaking noise as the door began to open.

Darkness. We could have been entering a cave in the middle of a forest there was so little light inside. 'Take them to the prison', I heard the Dervish commander say to one of his men as the blackness enveloped me. For a brief second I thought that this would be a perfect moment to attempt an escape. But then, just as I was coming up with reasons to discount the idea – my bound hands and the soldier virtually holding me in the saddle – I suddenly heard a commotion from behind, the loud neigh from a horse as if it were rising up on its hind legs. Then: 'Stop! Stop him!' from the leader.

I felt the soldier with me pull hard to the left to guide his horse around. It was now plain to see what all the fuss was about, for there was the flashing white of Mahmud's clothing as he sprinted gloriously through the bright moonlit avenue, his camel from which he must have just jumped standing placidly on its own outside the gate. As soon as I saw him I was certain that he would get away, for I knew that Mahmud would be an expert risk taker. I almost laughed I was so pleased. I wanted to shout encouragement to him as if he were an athlete competing at an event, but, I thought better of it.

One of the horsemen kicked off out the gate in pursuit – I imagined Mahmud must have been almost right beside him when he made his move – but no sooner had the hoofs started to lift up dust than my guide had disappeared down one of the many alleyways that led off of the avenue. They would never find him now. I felt very relieved, even though I would not have the support of my wonderful Arab companion anymore.

The Dervishes knew they had lost their prisoner for good, for the man who set off in pursuit did not even bother to enter the alleyway but stopped at its edge, looked in for a minute or so, then returned to the citadel – perhaps he even feared ambush from Mahmud.

'Idiots, idiots!' the commander shouted angrily. Then he began to berate his men, but he talked so quickly that I could not make out all of what he said. But he seemed to be blaming his men for what had happened. He rode out in front of the citadel's gate to meet his returning soldier. I thought he was going to hit out at him, but he did not, and instead seemed happy to wave his hands in the air and bluster vehemently. Then the two men came back in to the darkness to where I was still sitting looking out.

The commander was seething with rage, so much so that I feared he might even kill me on the spot in some sort of petty act of revenge. He came forward, disappeared from view in the dark. I sensed that something nasty was coming, but I knew not what.

The voice slowly began to penetrate the haze. 'Are you all right? Are you all right?'

'Where am I?' I stammered, coughing.

It took a few seconds to focus. 'You are in the Khalifa's prison,' came the voice again.

I seemed to have been left propped up against a wall. There was a distinct throbbing in the back of my head as I twisted to take in the person talking to me. There in the moonlight was the face of a wild-looking man, as if from another age. He looked, with his thick beard, long hair and sunken eyes, as if he had been deposited on some desert island and left to his own devices for a decade; a latter day Robinson Crusoe.

'How did you get here?' he said. I had not noticed the harsh accent at first, but now it became obvious that the man spoke English with a strong north European enunciation, probably German or Austrian.

'I was captured by them,' I said, not even sure if I was coherent and wincing at the pain in my head. I had obviously received a heavy blow, which had knocked me unconscious. 'I need some water.' The man understood, for he disappeared from my field of vision for a few seconds before returning with some sort of metal beaker. I winced a little as the water burned my parched throat. It tasted dirty, but I thought nothing of this and drank quickly, for I desperately needed the fluid.

The water did much to rejuvenate the senses. Now I could take in my latest predicament. The prison was not of the dungeon variety, which one would perhaps have expected, but rather seemed to be a mud-brick enclosure with no roof, winking stars being visible overhead. I saw no prisoners other than the strange man who had provided me with refreshment. 'Who are you?' I asked.

'My name is Karl Brenner.'

'What are you doing … why…?'

I coughed. I was still a little confused and could not quite formulate the words.

He tapped me on the shoulder a few times as if to say that he understood what I was getting at and that there was no need for me to talk. But I sensed that there was something strangely swift and shifting about his movements.

'I am a great explorer,' he said quickly. 'I am one of the best explorers. They brought you in a little while ago. But now I serve the Khalifa. They tied you here. This has been my home for many years.'

I tried to move but felt my hands grating off a wooden post behind me. I seemed to have been secured tightly to it. I would have felt sorry for myself were it not for the state of the poor chap in front of me now. 'How long have you been here?'

He sat back on the dirt and I noticed that he was wearing heavy iron shackles around his ankles. His skin was black with dirt. Then, very strangely, he laughed, a short snap of a giggle. Was he mad? 'My good Englishman I can't remember how long I have been here.' Then came the same jerky laugh once more. He must have been in the prison for years, and I could only conclude that it had driven him quite insane.

The last thing I needed at this stage was to have to deal with a madman.

He continued, 'Are you an explorer also? You can't be with the British Army or you wouldn't be dressed as an Arab.'

'I am a major in the British Army,' I said.

Suddenly his face lit up. One would have thought that it was the most exciting news that he had had in years – which indeed it may well have been. 'Then you must be a spy, yes?'

'Perhaps,' I said vaguely. 'Why haven't they killed you? Why do they keep you chained up here?' I hoped that by asking such questions I could gain some insight into what the Dervishes would do with me.

Brenner leaned forward quickly, which made me flinch and made him give out another nervous laugh. 'I told you, Englishman. I serve the Khalifa now. He relies greatly on me. He asks about European armies and how they fight and I tell him. I am very important here. Very, very important.'

To me it looked as if the Khalifa treated his camels and horses better than he did this poor, delusional wretch of a man. I asked him again if he knew roughly how long he had been a prisoner.

He looked about him before answering as if to check that no one was listening, even though we were plainly alone. 'Years. Seven years, perhaps eight. I wanted to reach Khartoum after the death of Gordon. I wanted to see for myself the Mahdi's new empire.'

'And he did not take well to you?'

A loud laugh. 'Did not take well! Ha, ha! No, Englishman, he did not take well to me. He imprisoned me, but then I became counsel to the Khalifa when he was chosen to succeed.'

I believe that then, in all my time in the Sudan, I was at my lowest. It seemed that I was destined to live out the rest of the war wasting away in the Khalifa's prison, open to the elements and with nothing but a mad German explorer for company. The thought of stopping Dawson blowing up our much-needed gunboats now seemed impossible.

'Do you have any food?' the German now asked.

'I am afraid not. Do the Dervishes not feed you? They must give you something to keep you alive.'

'Sometimes the Khalifa is kind and he sends food. But not always …' He trailed off. 'Where did they catch you?'

'Not far from here. About an hour to the south-west by horse.'

He looked surprised. 'The British, are they close? Are you here to destroy the Khalifa?'

I did not know how best to answer this question, for the man had displayed a strange allegiance to the Khalifa, and I was in no position to defend myself should he suddenly decide to pay some sort of honour to his master by killing me.

'I am not here to kill the Khalifa,' I told him. 'I am searching for another Englishman who has come here. But the British and Egyptian armies are marching towards Omdurman as we speak. The Khalifa knows this, and he must also know that very soon he will no longer rule Khartoum or Omdurman.'

At this point Brenner seemed to lose interest or concentration, for he suddenly looked up towards the starry sky and sat staring. 'Is there any possibility of escaping from here?' I asked, trying to gain his attention once more. He was not a reliable source of such information, but he was all that I had.

The shaggy chin fell and the little twinkling eyes that seemed so distant looked upon me again. 'There is no escape, never.'

No escape. The words rang in my ears like a death knell. 'Do you know what will happen to me?'

He laughed his erratic laugh once more and pointed a rancid, bony finger. 'Ha, ha. You will die, Englishman. You will die.'

PART III

Then roll on, boys, roll on to Khartoum,
March ye and fight ye by night or by day,
Hasten the hour of the Dervishes' doom,
Gordon avenge in old England's way!

Roll on to Khartoum – ballad sung by
British troops, 1898

CHAPTER 15

'ENGLISHMAN! ENGLISHMAN!'
The words pounded my head. I opened my eyes and immediately closed them again. Blinding sun. In those few moments before regaining consciousness I had dreamed that I was with Mahmud in the desert, free and still with hope of stopping the saboteur Dawson. But then the dreadful realization came that I remained a prisoner of the Khalifa.

'They are coming for you! They are coming for you!'

What was the mad German explorer getting excited about? With great effort I forced my eyelids apart. They felt as if entire sand dunes were weighing them down.

I tried to talk, but when I opened my mouth no sound emerged. I wanted to ask Brenner, whom I could now see was moving around excitedly in front of me, his bare and blackened feet twisting in the fine white dust, what was happening, but the inside of my throat felt as if it had been taken out and laid in the desert to dry for weeks before being put back in again. There was so little moisture in my mouth that I could barely swallow. 'Who is coming?' I eventually managed, although it was nothing more than a whisper.

'The Khalifa's men. They are coming for you, Englishman.'

'What men? Where are they?'

'There!'

He pointed to a wooden gate in one wall of our prison. It was the only entrance. In the daylight I could now see that the mud walls were at least twenty feet high. They enclosed an area not much larger than a dwelling house. Dotted here and there were wooden posts for shackling prisoners – Brenner, with his heavy leg irons which gave him a limited amount of freedom of movement, must have been getting special treatment. A most awful sight also presented itself to me in the form of the gallows. At the opposite end from the gate two tree trunks had been driven into the ground and another piece of wood strapped clumsily between them. And there, hanging down like sickening ornaments were the bodies of two Arabs. The sight of their limp corpses seemed to act as an automatic switch to my other senses, for no sooner had my eyes taken them in than the strong smell of death became all too apparent. It was almost overpowering. It was disgusting.

I did not contemplate the gruesomeness for long, for I had to see what Brenner was pointing out, and in the small gap between the ground and the bottom of the gate I noticed three pairs of feet shuffling around. They were wearing the distinctive Dervish *sayidan* – sandals. Then, just as I was registering the sound of street noises outside, came the sharp clink of metal against metal as a bolt was drawn.

Three Dervishes had come, looking not much different from the men who had captured me the previous day.

'Pick him up,' said one of them as they closed in.

My hands were unbound from the wooden post and I was hauled to my feet, my headscarf knocked off my head. At least they had not marched up and killed me outright, I thought. I had half expected to see one of them come through the gate holding a sword that would be used to cut off my head for presentation to the Khalifa. Then I thought that perhaps this *was* their intention. Perhaps they were simply taking me somewhere else to do it.

It was difficult to stand at first I felt so weak, mainly as a result of dehydration. And also my body was as stiff as wood, having not been able to move much the night before when I was dozing in and out of sleep. I believe I must have grimaced as those rough Dervish hands pulled at my arms, the sudden stretching of the muscles in my back producing a quick jolt of pain.

The German I noticed was now very quiet. He was sitting staring around himself as the guards prepared to take me away. One would have thought I had never been in the prison.

'Where are we going?' I ventured to ask the Dervishes in husky Arabic.

'No words,' ordered the man directing the proceedings. He was standing rather aloofly in front of us holding a short spear. As I was led across the tiny prison courtyard I glanced at the mad German, but now he was scratching his beard and looking at the ground. What a strange fellow he was.

I shall never forget the terror I felt as I was led out on to those streets, the mass of high-pitched voices and rancid smells hitting me like a heat-wave. Suddenly I seemed to be thronged by ghostly figures, the wretches of Omdurman, and I felt a thousand pairs of eyes upon me. In the past I had witnessed excited Arab crowds in North Africa cruelly beat criminals to death. In such situations the enthusiasm of one man would feed another until the passions of the whole mass of people would eventually explode with terrible violence. And no longer with my headscarf to disguise my European features I felt very vulnerable, as if this terrible fate would now befall me. In the oven-like heat I was cold with fear.

My instinct was to kick out or to run. But this would have been silly, and I knew I had to control my trepidation in those packed, bulging streets. The thin shoulders of my Dervish escorts crushed against me as they forced their way through the tightly knit crowd. I felt small and insignificant, like a child in a large group of adults.

But I was also confused now. I had imagined the gaol to be situated somewhere within the citadel, for my last memory was of being inside its walls. I had not expected to come out of the gate directly on to one of Omdurman's busy streets. Then I understood, for as I looked along the avenue I saw the towering walls of the citadel stretch to my right. The prison was indeed part of the structure, but it was accessed from the street, rather than from somewhere within. I must have been carried back outside of the citadel and around its outer perimeter to the prison once I had been knocked unconscious.

I was not sure if I was on my way to meet the Khalifa, to be executed, or perhaps to be tortured. But wherever the men were taking me I knew that my fate now looked bleaker than ever. I was sorely tempted to resign myself to whatever lay in store for me, be it instant death or pain then death. But I did not. Although I had given up on trying to stop Dawson, I was not yet ready to give up on life. And so as I was being marched through Omdurman's hectic streets I took in what I could of my surroundings with a view to possible escape.

My hands were still bound behind my back. My feet were free. But running in the streets with these crowds would be impossible. No, I would have to bide my time until an opportunity presented itself, and hope that I could stay alive in the meantime.

WHERE WAS THE opening into the citadel that would lead to wherever these men had been ordered to take me, either before the Khalifa or to some nightmarish torture chamber? We were approaching the end of the citadel's wall on the street where the prison was situated, the numbers of people thankfully beginning to thin, the avenue opening out wider to let the bright midday sun penetrate so that all was not in shadow, and yet I could see no other gate or opening. And then we were past the citadel and all that I could think was that I was being taken to be executed – perhaps to the Nile where my body could easily be dumped in the water to be washed downstream.

I recognized the wide boulevard that I was now being marched down, seemingly out of the city. There was no mistaking that it was the same one that had brought me to the citadel the previous night. The day brought it to life with the citizens of Omdurman, and I could see the desert stretch out beyond the suburbs of the town.

'If you are going to kill me, might I have some water first?'

I thought it worth a try. If these men planned to execute me then I would certainly attempt an escape, even if the odds were stacked so much against me that it would mean instant death. And if I were to exert myself in an escape attempt then I would fare much better if I could first quench my agonizing thirst.

'We are not taking you to your death, infidel,' said the leader, who was striding in front to ensure we had a clear path. The other two remained at my side and had an arm each. 'You are being taken to the Khalifa.'

Suddenly everything became clear. The Khalifa was no longer in his citadel because he was out in front of Omdurman with his army, waiting to take on Kitchener. My next thought was of the gunboats. Where were they now? Had Dawson already blown them up?

'Where is the Khalifa?'

'No more words.'

I thought it best to keep quiet as the streets fell away and the plains beyond Omdurman opened out to us. And it was then that I saw one of the most magnificent sights that I have ever witnessed. At first it looked as if the miles of plains ahead and stretching out to the Kerreri Hills were covered in a dense layer of thorn-bushes. But, as I blinked and squinted in the blinding sun, I realized that the big half-moon-shaped curve of darkness was not vegetation at all but was in fact the massed squadrons of the Khalifa awaiting their fight. Here, with Biblical magnificence, were all the armies of the Mahdi's successor, literally tens of thousands of men. Here were the Hadendoa tribes, the famous 'Fuzzy-Wuzzies' as the common British soldiers named them. Here were the Dangala tribesmen. Here were the Taaishi, the Jiadia and many thousands of others.

Despite the seriousness of my situation I could not help but be enthralled by the sight of this ancient-looking army, the many little specks combining to form a colossal dark carpet over the shimmering desert plains. It started about a mile from the city and seemed to stretch out almost all the way to the Kerreri Hills, a few more miles further north. I could see now that among the hordes of men many flags were flying. Later I would come to know which flag represented which *emir*. The bright green in the far distance was the sign of Ali-Wad-Helu with his several thousand warriors, who had mostly been drawn from the Degheim and Kenana tribes. In the centre there were formed large squares of black and Arab riflemen and spearmen under Osman Sheikh-ed-Din and Osman Azrak – easily more than twenty thousand men, I surmised – while in the rear flew the black flag of Yakub with his many thousands of swordsmen and spearmen.

My eyes watered as I scanned the horizon. The sandy desert plain, then a small hill – the *jebel Surgham* – until finally on the far right, camped by the shining line of silk that was the Nile and with the steeply rising Kerreri Hills behind it, was the Anglo-Egyptian army. Only a few miles separated the two forces, one the most modern and sophisticated the world had ever seen, the other like something from the Crusades. I could see the thin line of thorn bushes that made up the defensive *zariba* around the camp, and the many steamers and what appeared to be – for although I could not see them in any detail they looked to be relatively large – gunboats on the river behind. I could also make out the distinctive white of the hospital tents. And in front of this area there were groups of men scurrying around on horses – scouting parties of officers observing the enemy.

Away from the noise of the city now I could hear the slow beating of war drums from the Dervishes. The final battle could not be far off. It would be this very day, there was no doubt of it.

The men directing me wheeled around to the right as if to head towards the river. It was then that I spotted a small hill with a group of men standing atop it, about half a mile out from the outskirts of Omdurman and perhaps a mile from the Nile. It had to be the Khalifa and his men. It was a small group, perhaps ten individuals at the most, all of them on horseback.

The first sign that we were in the presence of the Mahdi's successor was when my two escorts lowered their heads in deference. The leader of the three then came and stood beside me, placing his spear at my throat, as if I posed some sort of danger to his leader when my hands were tightly bound behind my back. Some of the *mulazemin* then moved their horses to the side, and there, sitting defiantly on an almost completely black horse, was the Khalifa.

'We have brought the infidel,' announced the lead guard.

The Khalifa looked to have been discussing tactics with some of his men, whom I surmised to be his most trusted *emirs*. He turned his horse so that he was facing me. Some days before I had stood in the tent of the *Sirdar* as he sent me on this dangerous mission. And now here I was confronting his enemy counterpart. How different they were; one driven by religious fervour, the other by military glory; one believing that his God would win him a great victory, the other believing that his own tactical and administrative genius would crush his foe.

'Infidel, why have you disguised yourself as an Arab?' he asked first.

With his gleaming white robes he was illuminated like a beacon, the small skullcap placed neatly on his head blocking out the sun so that it shone around him almost as if he *were* blessed. His voice was softer than I had imagined it would be, seeming to float on the breeze that prevailed here in the open. The leader of the men who had found us in the desert must have told him that I could speak Arabic, for no one attempted to translate his words.

I required an immediate lie, and being an intelligence man this came naturally to me. 'I am travelling through here to report the news of the war to the people of England.' I was trying to speak up, but my voice was still low from lack of fluid, and I struggled. 'I am not a soldier. I am not here to fight, and I am not here to take sides. I am simply here to inform the outside world of what is happening.'

Here the Khalifa laughed. The spiritual leader of the Dervishes was actually mocking me.

'You say you are not an English soldier and yet you speak our language and you carry a rifle.' He stopped for a few seconds and turned to one of his cohorts to say something. I remained silent. Then he turned to face me once more. 'Bring the infidel closer and let us see him.'

I was led forward and it was then, as we moved a little to the side to ascend the small knoll, that I saw Dawson. There he was, sitting on top of a horse as if he were one of the Khalifa's most trusted confidants. With his white face it could only be him. Under an Arab turban was the same strong chin that I had noted by the light of a flickering candle back in Wadi Halfa. And even though he now wore Dervish dress, it was apparent that he was the same shape and size as the shadowy man whom I had confronted in the doorway of that hut.

Dawson observed me keenly as I was marched up the hill. His eyes looked cold and unearthly. Did he know it was I who had shot at him as he leapt on to that train in Wadi Halfa?

'Do you recognize this man?' the Khalifa asked the traitor.

Dawson looked me up and down for a few seconds. 'It might have been him. I cannot be sure.' Then he addressed me. 'What is your name?'

'Winters. Evelyn Winters.'

'Where did you learn to speak Arabic?'

'Cambridge.'

'College?'

'Trinity.'

'Ah, then you must have studied under Professor Henderson, as I did.'

I had put my foot in it. I had learned my Arabic in the Palestine and had never even been close to a Cambridge college. I had no idea if a Professor Henderson was teaching, or had ever taught Arabic there. For all I knew, perhaps even Dawson had not been to Trinity and was calling my bluff. One way or the other I had to gamble.

'Indeed,' I said with the utmost confidence. 'A fine fellow, a fine fellow.'

Dawson laughed. My gamble had not paid off. 'He is lying,' he told his master. Then he raised his voice so that I would hear clearly what he said next. 'There is no – and as far as I am aware there has never been – a Professor Henderson at Trinity. You must be a British soldier. Are you an intelligence officer? Did Kitchener send you to track me down?'

'I have no idea what you are talking about.'

Addressing the Khalifa he said, 'I would suggest we waste little time with him if he continues to lie. You should have him killed. There are more important issues at hand.'

The decision on whether I should live or die lay with the Khalifa for little more than a second. 'Kill him,' he instructed one of his bodyguards casually before turning to face the Omdurman plains once more.

A tall and rather mean-looking fellow immediately dismounted his horse and drew a long, curved sword. The next few seconds went in a blur as my mind raced to come up with some sort of plan – anything! I glanced at the man's dark eyes as he strode towards me. He looked calm, but there was fire in there also. He had executed before. I believe my first thought was of running, but I would certainly have been shot or cut down after only a few paces.

The men flanking me forced me to my knees, and I faced death for the second time in little more than a day. I felt utterly vulnerable. I looked blandly at the dry desert dust. Soon my blood would be seeping through its fine particles. I had not expected my life to end this way – the first casualty of the Battle of Omdurman.

I was about to hang my head and await my fate when a vague idea came to me. I shouted, 'If you kill me now then your plan to destroy the gunboats will never succeed!' It was a last-ditch attempt to regain the attention of Dawson and the Khalifa.

But it worked.

'Wait!' came from the Khalifa. Then he spoke to Dawson, but I could not hear what was said.

I raised my head and looked at my executioner. He was dressed all in black and was holding the hilt of his sword with both hands, legs apart, slight movements from side-to-side, looking at his master as he awaited the final command to strike the blade through my neck. I could smell the animal ruthlessness in him.

I put my head back down and gasped. My heart was racing. A bead of sweat sped down my forehead then dripped off the end of my nose to splash into the dust. I looked up at Dawson and the Khalifa again. Was there hope?

'What do you know about the gunboats?' asked Dawson, dismounting his horse and walking towards me.

'I—'

But before I had had a chance to say anything he had me by the neck.

Then came a blunt feeling of pain as the man's fist connected with my exposed chin. I would have expected him to be more calculating, more subtle. 'Tell me what you know!'

Suddenly he seemed like a madman. 'I know that you have set charges on the Nile to blow up the gunboats. Yes, yes, I am an intelligence officer! Yes, yes, I was sent to stop you! And yes, yes, I have sabotaged your explosives!' I was passionate as I said this, but I calmed to finish, and I quietly said, 'Rather ironic, isn't it?'

A statement like this could have got me killed, but I could not help but indulge, my hatred for the traitor coming to the fore. 'How do you know about the gunboats?' he asked angrily.

'The French have told us everything. You didn't really expect to get away with it, did you, Dawson?'

He looked surprised that I knew his name. Suddenly a nervousness seemed to overcome him. He took a step back and looked to his master. All of our exchange had been in Arabic, so the Khalifa knew as much as Dawson. 'Take him to the river,' he ordered. 'See if he is telling the truth. Make him show you what he has done to the charges. The ships *will* be destroyed.' And with that the Khalifa returned to observing what would soon be the battlefield.

SO HERE WAS the man who had brought so much trouble to Kitchener in his efforts to retake the Sudan. Dawson. Finally I had a chance to try and question him. Even if death was now my not-too-distant fate, I still wanted to understand how an Englishman could turn traitor and support the Mahdi's cause. But as we walked upon the open plains towards the Nile with an escort of two Dervishes, Omdurman to our right seeming strangely peaceful, it was Dawson who spoke first.

'How did you discover the French were involved?' he asked. He was perfectly calm now.

Dawson was ahead of me and to my right. It was still morning, and with the sun not sitting too high in the sky, his tall, slim and wiry body, which was much like the Dervishes he had fallen in with, cast a long shadow in the sand.

I explained how I came to meet Portart – I had no reason to lie now, other than to maintain the pretence that I knew the details of the explosives on the Nile and that I had sabotaged them. Then I asked for some water. 'I fear I may not even make it as far as the river if I do not drink soon,' I said.

Thankfully, and to my surprise, he relented. We stopped, perhaps a half-mile from the river, which at this time looked to be free of much commercial activity, the upcoming war having no doubt driven many of the usual traders away. One of the Dervishes produced a water-skin and then, holding it above my head, he poured liberally. Ungainly and rather seal-like I had to push my chin in the air and move it around to catch the falling liquid. I regretted every drop that missed my mouth to bounce off my chest to eventually water the desert. I felt I could have drunk for days, but all too soon the Dervish had taken the supply away again.

'What turned you?' I asked Dawson in English, lowering my chin breathlessly and looking into the distance too see what was happening with the armies. Here the sun reflected off the tips of the many thousand Dervish spears to create a strange glimmer, a white haze above them. But the haze seemed to be moving – moving to attack or merely regrouping?

Dawson began walking again, one of the Dervishes prodding me in the back to get me going also. He did not answer my question at first, and seemed to be considering whether I was worthy of a response.

'You could never understand. You are blind,' he said eventually, looking ahead, across the water and into the distance. He seemed peculiarly calm, given the events that were starting to unfold on the plains to our left.

'Please explain. I really would like – in fact I need – to understand.'

He stopped for a second and turned his head to look at me before continuing on. 'You and your armies … Kitchener … you march into these peoples' lands, utterly convinced of your superiority, as if God Himself has decreed that you should be here. You have no appreciation whatsoever of the beauty of this culture.'

'A culture which is barbaric?' I interrupted. 'This morning I saw two Arabs hanging dead in the prison. Were they perhaps political opponents of the Khalifa, or had they merely committed some petty crime? Such things are wrong, and I cannot see how one could argue otherwise.'

'That is not the point. The point is that it is not for us, who are equally if not more flawed … it is not for us to judge this land, this culture, this civilization. The peoples of these lands have evolved in a certain way, which happens to be very different from our own, but who is to say that our way is any better?'

'Fine. You do not agree with the Anglo-Egyptian position, but why directly fight against us? Why did you choose to remain here to take British lives? Why did you not return to England to make your views public there?'

The glittering water was getting closer. Soon my chance to get information out of Dawson would be gone and I would have to again concentrate on my own survival.

Dawson gave out a sarcastic laugh. 'Ha, England! I will never return there. This is my home now. And as to why I took British lives, this is war, and I have chosen the side for which I want to fight.'

'Indeed you have.' I wished my hands were free and that I had my revolver, for I would have liked nothing more than to have shot him on the spot. But all that I could do at the moment was try to learn more about the man's motives, so I asked him at which point he decided to bring together the band of Arab fighters.

To my surprise, Dawson actually seemed keen to detail his traitorous activities – perhaps this was because he felt sure that I would soon be dead. 'You are an intelligence officer, did you know that I, too, served with the Intelligence Branch in North Africa?'

'I was aware that you had some sort of intelligence background, yes, but in what capacity I had no idea.'

'I was something of an Arabic scholar at one point you know. I did study at Trinity, and so, the Intelligence Branch were keen to exploit me. It was then that I first began to feel that what we are doing in Africa – our entire attitude to the peoples of the countries that we administer – is quite wrong. I did not suddenly wake up one morning and decide to switch to Mahdism, you know!'

'No, no, I'm sure you didn't.'

I could now see the calm expanse of the Nile just ahead of us. I had to plan what my next move would be, but Dawson was still talking. 'This is something that has taken many years for me to come to terms with, and I have now reconciled myself to being what you would describe as a traitor, but what these people regard as a holy warrior. It has not been easy, turning one's back on one's family.'

'You have family back in England?'

'Yes, but …' He looked away to the distance. 'It is of no consequence. When the railway was being built I was placed in charge of a number of men engaged in its construction. We were based to the south of Wadi Halfa. But by this time my hatred of what we are doing in Africa was complete, and with each new sleeper that we laid and each additional foot that we pushed further into the Nubian Desert my feelings of guilt and foreboding increased, until eventually I formed my little resistance movement and managed to contact the Khalifa and persuade him that I was intent on helping his cause. It has been most effective, don't you think?'

'You have certainly been effective murderers, yes. But how did you contact the Khalifa?'

'I sent one of my Arab men to Omdurman as a messenger. After that it was all very simple.'

'And the other men you recruited, are they here in Omdurman?'

He smiled. 'Why do you ask such questions? You cannot escape.'

'I am an intelligence officer: I am naturally curious.'

'They are there,' and he pointed towards the plains in front of Omdurman. 'They are ready to give their lives for the Mahdi's cause, as I am. But now it is time for you to answer my questions.' The hand that was pointing north fell to grip the hilt of a dagger that stuck out from Dawson's belt. I was under no illusion what would happen if I did not co-operate.

There were three of them. Three almost completely submerged boats in a line across the Nile; three metal turrets, the waters of the river lapping gently just a few feet below them, the light reflecting strongly off their sides. They must have been the only metal ships that the Khalifa had.

I understood immediately what Dawson had arranged. The boats were about 100 yards downstream from us. They were situated at a small bend in the Nile, where the river jutted to the west before extending north again, to disguise them from boats coming upstream. I could just make out two planks of wood extending out from each side of the river, perhaps ten feet or so, towards the boats. Although I was not close enough to see them, I presumed that electric fuse wires ran along the top of the wood and out across the water to the turrets of the boats. Each boat would probably have a few barrels of dynamite in their hulls, for that's what it would take to destroy the gunboats. If ever they went off the explosions would be enormous.

'What have you done to my fine arrangement?' asked Dawson. 'Have you severed the fuse wires? Tell me, or I swear you will be killed right now.'

I sighed as if I were reluctant to divulge my secret. 'I have not cut any wires. I have been far more subtle than that. If we go closer then I can show you.'

'Very well. Move.'

Now there was no more time for questions or contemplations. I had to make some sort of escape attempt. But what could I do? I was tempted to simply jump into the Nile in the hope that I could stop myself from drowning long enough for the waters to carry me downstream towards the British positions. The water was a mere three feet away. But it was not flowing nearly fast enough, and anyway I would have been shot before I got fifty yards.

The banks of the Nile were empty of people. As we walked north across the dry bank, occasionally crossing little clumps of grass, I looked longingly towards the Anglo-Egyptian Army. It was then that for the first time in any detail I saw Kitchener's gunboats, floating on the metallic flatness downstream. They must have been the largest vessels ever to glide along this part of the river, although from this distance it was still somewhat difficult to appreciate their size. There were at least three of them, distinguished by their guns and by being much bigger than the other craft around them. Their metal hulls shimmered, while great plumes of black-grey smoke rose from their funnels. Soon they would be steaming south to bombard Omdurman, steaming towards their destruction by Dawson!

'They are coming,' said Dawson, who had also noticed the ships. He said this in a satisfied way. 'Hurry!' he commanded me.

We seemed to close in on the area where the charges had been laid quicker than I had expected. I had no plan prepared. But I did know that I needed my hands to be free. At the bank where the fuses started there was situated a clump of grass, quite significant by the standards of the area. It ran for perhaps twenty yards along the bank and was several yards in width. As we got to within a few yards I suddenly had a vague idea of what my next move would be. 'Stop!' I said loudly.

Dawson and the Dervishes duly halted. 'I have set a device in this area so that whenever someone goes forward to ignite the dynamite they will be blown apart before they have a chance to. Do not move into that area of grass or we will all be blown to smithereens.'

Dawson looked a little sceptical, but I was confident that he would not risk doubting me. 'Cut me free for a few minutes and I will disarm the device,' I said calmly.

He hesitated. 'Where can I go?' I added. 'I have no weapons and your men have rifles. And I will only be a few feet from you. But if you don't believe me then send one of your Dervishes in there. Then we shall see how much you care for these people. But I warn you that we should all stand well back first.'

'I see no explosives in there.'

'What kind of a saboteur would I be if they were noticeable to anyone who happened to pass?'

He still wasn't sure. 'What sort of device is it? How can it be made to go off just by someone walking in there?'

'It is quite simple really. It consists of a small dynamo attached to a very short fuse wire. The movement of the wire causes a few sparks and that is all that is needed to set off the dynamite.' This was all completely made up, but it had a certain logic to it.

'Very well,' said Dawson. 'But be warned—'

'Yes, yes, I know. I will be killed outright. Rest assured I do not wish to die here.'

He took his knife out of his belt. It was a traditional Arab curved variety with a fine gold hilt – a present from the Khalifa?

My hands were cut free and I tentatively stepped forward into the grass, which came up to my knees. I walked out into the middle of the area and saw where the fuses began, at a square detonator box. All it would take to blow the dynamite would be one push on its handle once the fuses had been connected.

I had to act now. The Dervishes began raising their rifles to cover me. In a tenth of a second the idea for a possible escape came to me, and in even less time I had decided what I had to do.

CHAPTER 16

Diary of the Rt. Hon. Colonel Evelyn Winters, MP
15 May, 1935

I AM SO happy tonight that I can barely write in my diary. Parker delivered some news this morning. I knew as soon as I saw him that he couldn't wait to tell me something, for he literally burst out of the train carriage and on to the platform. I was afraid for a moment that in his excitement he would slip, as the constant drizzle today made the platform look most treacherous – not at all the sort of weather we should be having in May. But thankfully he did not fall, and instead came bounding towards me with his little suitcase that I am now so accustomed to seeing down here in Wiltshire swinging by his side. 'Hello, hello ... nice to see you, nice to see you!'

'And you, my boy, and you. Pleasant journey?'

'Oh yes ... yes indeed. Wonderful journey.'

I knew that whatever it was that Parker was so pleased about would come out soon enough, so I did not press him on it as we motored back to the house. Once inside, however, and over some tea that Mrs Jenkins had waiting for us, he finally came out with it. 'Getting married ... I'm getting married!' he said.

Well, I almost dropped my steaming cup. I thought that perhaps his investigations into his father's background had produced something positive, and that this was what had led to the gleam in his eye, but I did not expect this. But as shocked as I was I was also overwhelmingly pleased. Miss Bellingford is delightful, and I think she will make Parker very happy.

They plan to get married in June, up in London. 'And I hope ... that is to say, you must come along,' Parker said to me. Indeed, it was more like a command, and his eyes shone with happiness.

I said that I would be delighted. And I have to say I feel very honoured, for very few people will be there. I think that other than myself and a few young friends of his, there will be no one else there to support Parker as he enters this period of his life, which I am sure will be his most content.

There was little possibility of us getting any work done for a while following the great news. We took our tea to the study as we always do, Parker taking his usual seat at the other side of the desk and I sitting myself down in my old study chair. But we didn't so much as glance at our notes, and instead talked and talked about the forthcoming event and Parker's plans for the future; where they will live – Parker wishes to move out of London to the suburbs; when they will have children – he is keen to start a family as soon as possible.

'I hope ... and not long from now, you *will* see children running up and down the lawns here,' he said, which pleased me immensely.

'Well, I should certainly hope you will bring them to visit,' I added. 'After all, who else will they have to teach them what grumpy old soldiers are like?' at which he laughed vigorously.

AS I HAVE noted, one of my first thoughts when I saw Parker this morning was that he had discovered something new about his father. It reminded me that I have been meaning to ask him how his investigations have been proceeding, but my memory is terrible these days and I keep forgetting. But it did remain in my mind over the next few hours until I took the opportunity to ask him about it after lunch.

I think he sounded a little disappointed when he said, 'Oh, well, no ... no. Haven't really managed to come up with anything yet.' Then he came out with something quite interesting. He was standing looking out of the bay window at the grey and the drizzle that is currently plaguing the countryside, and without turning to me, mumbled, 'I, er, I did speak to someone from the Royal Anglian, but ... well, he said there is a record of a Captain Parker having served with the regiment in the Sudan but that was all he could tell me really.'

I thought this seemed highly unusual, as I should have thought that all the regiments that took part in the Battle of Omdurman would have detailed records of the action from the perspective of each of their officers.

All that I can think is that whoever it was who checked these details for him did not do it properly.

'Probably an administrative error,' I said. 'I suggest you try to visit the regimental headquarters yourself – see if you can't personally check its history.'

'I don't think there's much more I could find out about him. I should probably just leave it … now, I think. Not much point trying to get anything else really. I never even knew him, after all.'

'But I think you should, my boy. If your father's glories have not been properly covered in the other history books, then I think it is our duty to make sure he gets appropriate mention in my memoirs.' I knew this would please him, and he smiled a little when I said it. But I was looking forward to seeing how he would react to what I said next. 'And I was thinking, perhaps we could even dedicate the book to your father. You know, dedicated to the memory of Captain Parker of the Royal Anglian, whose son contributed so much in researching the military history that has gone into these memoirs. That sort of thing. What do you think?'

He was rather shy about the idea, but I think quietly pleased. 'Yes, very kind,' he said.

'Oh, but that reminds me. Would you mind checking on exactly where the Royal Anglian Regiment were placed at the start and then during the Battle of Omdurman? I don't recall reading about them in any of the official histories. Must have been overshadowed by the 21st Lancers and the like, the poor chaps. Still, we'll make sure they get their appropriate mention in my memoirs.'

THERE WAS ONE other development today. It seems like an awful long time since I have seen the Reverend Richards, but purely by co-incidence he dropped by for a visit – it is uncanny that he should stop round on the very day that Parker informs me he is about to be married before God.

'Not a particularly nice day to be doing the rounds, Reverend,' I said when Mrs Jenkins announced that he had called and I went to meet him in the hallway. His dark raincoat and hat were absolutely dripping with water.

But he was his usual cheery self. 'Makes me feel more pious, Colonel,' he said, with that foggy voice of his. 'Suffering for my work and all that. But how are you? Seems an awful long time.'

'As a matter of fact,' I said, 'things could not be better. Will you stay for a cup of tea? Good. Let's go into the study. There's someone I would like you to meet.'

Parker was sitting at the desk reading a part of my memoirs. He got up to shake hands with the reverend. 'He's just arrived this morning from London with the news that he is to be married,' I said.

Naturally the reverend was most pleased, and Parker was again subjected to explaining all about his plans for the future. Thinking about it now I hardly gave the lad the chance to explain things himself as I kept stepping in. 'He's keen to have children, aren't you, Parker? This place will be simply buzzing with life, Reverend,' and much more talk like this.

Eventually I stopped long enough for the Reverend Richards to explain why he had come by. He wanted to discuss a town fête that he wishes me to speak at next month. Of course I readily agreed – one must always jump at these opportunities, for they will undoubtedly secure a few votes at the next election.

I think I let the news of Parker's marriage go to my head a little, for when I was walking the reverend to the door I was amused to find him asking me if Parker and I are related. 'A nephew of yours, is he?' he said, placing his sodden trilby back on his head.

'Oh no,' I laughed. 'He's just my research assistant and no relation. No, I don't think his kind of brains run in my family line.'

'You just seem so very proud of him getting married that I assumed you must be related somehow.'

'Well, he's ever such a good chap and we have become firm friends since we started on this writing project of mine. And yes, I am very proud of him.'

This last statement from the Reverend Richards has really got me thinking. It has been on my mind for some time now that Parker and I have become quite close, but I never thought of it in terms of us getting on so well that I would be as proud of him as if he were family. I am not sure I would go so far as this, but if I am being honest with myself – and I would never admit this to anyone – I think a relationship of this nature has gradually developed. Call it a coming together of personalities or even mere circumstances, but I do care for the boy. And I think he respects and appreciates me in some way, which I find comforting in my old age.

Diary of the Rt. Hon. Colonel Evelyn Winters, MP

22 May, 1935

Today should have been a wonderful day, but it has been tinged with a bit of worry also. I shall note down the positive first.

I think we've actually done it. Finally, after weeks of polishing and of adding new parts and taking other parts out, I think we've finally got my speech just how I want it. I am really rather pleased with it, and I feel sure it will make a difference to the India debates. My only regret is that Parker will not gain any official credit when I finally deliver it to the Commons a couple of weeks from now.

Ah, but Parker. I am somewhat worried about him. We both knew we would complete the speech this morning, and I expected him to turn up and be virtually bursting with enthusiasm. He seemed happy enough when he first came in, but now that I have had a chance to think about it, it occurs to me that he may well have been putting on a brave face.

Once we were inside and working on the final polishes to the speech, it was plain to see that he was not himself and that something was weighing heavily on him. He seemed distant. He was sitting by the window with some papers on his lap. I was standing at the desk, and whenever I asked his opinion on something he would mutter, 'Hmm,' while continuing to stare blankly at my speech. Then eventually he would catch on and say, 'Oh ... erm, sorry, sorry ... what was that?'

I wondered if perhaps the thought of his impending marriage is beginning to trouble him. But then I thought it more likely that it has something to do with the research that he has been doing on his father. Perhaps he has discovered something that has upset him. I always expected that the reality of his father would prove to be less pleasing than the immaculate image that Parker must have built up in his mind over the years.

Eventually I decided that I had to ask him directly what was troubling him. 'You're not your usual self. I know you're not,' I said.

He said everything was absolutely fine, but I pressed him. 'What about the research that you've been doing on your father? Have you come up with anything new?'

'Oh, well ... nothing significant, exactly.'

I was determined to break his reticence. 'But what about that relative of yours down in Kent? Have you talked to her yet? Did she come up with anything new?'

He remained silent for a second or two before answering, 'Oh, no, I haven't talked to her. Oh, sorry … erm, yes. Sorry, forgot to tell you. Yes … talked to her briefly on the telephone. Bit of a waste of time really. Hadn't seen much of my father at all. No, she hadn't.'

'Tell me what she said.'

Finally he actually looked up and gave me his attention. 'Well … just … she just had some vague memories of seeing him when she was very young. She was taken to see him when he went off – off to the Sudan.' But then he looked a little awkward for a second, and putting his eyes back down towards the speech, said, 'She … she said she remembers he looked very handsome in his uniform. That was all, really.'

So this was why he was not his usual self. I think this image that he was presented with by his relative, of a gallant man going off to a far away land to fight for his country, leaving his loved ones, has particularly upset him. It is quite understandable really. I hope he will get over it soon enough.

We continued working on the speech for an hour or so, until we were completely satisfied with it. Then Parker announced that he had to be going.

I must say he is doing a splendid job editing this first part of my memoirs. Even today, when all that I could think about was my speech, Parker still remembered to check on a particular detail with me. It was as he was putting his jacket on to leave. He stopped for a second and said, 'Just reading over some of it again last night. Yes, the part where you met Dawson and the Khalifa, just outside the walls of Omdurman.'

'Oh yes.'

'Yes, just wondering … I was just wondering if it was definitely Trinity College. Where Dawson studied Arabic, I mean?'

I was rather surprised that he bothered to ask about such a trivial detail. What will it matter to the readers whether he went to Trinity or Clare or Emmanuel? I am glad, however, that he is making such a detailed examination of the text.

'Yes, I'm sure of it,' I said. 'It's one of those things that has stuck in my head all these years.'

When he left I returned to the study to read through my speech once again in its entirety. I think that by the time I come to speak I shall know every single word off-by-heart.

CHAPTER 17

ITS BOW APPEARED as a vague flicker in the side of my eye, a dark patch in the sheet of light reflecting off the waters. I turned my head slightly just as the Dervishes started to raise their rifles – a boat, gliding around the corner of the Nile as if God himself had suddenly placed it there as my own personal saving grace.

Why had I not spotted it before? Mine was not to reason why. Here was my chance of escape, and I literally leapt at it. As soon as I hit the water I got my arms and legs moving as fast as I could.

The Dervishes did not fire at first. They must have been waiting for the order from Dawson. But then came that awful crack that signalled the onslaught of hot metal projectiles. The water splashed on each side of me. Miraculously both bullets missed – but they had come so close! If the Dervishes had time to reload and fire again I felt sure I would be hit.

The breeze was stiff enough to make the white triangular sails of the little boat puff out in the direction in which it was travelling, which was south towards Omdurman and Khartoum. Not that I had time look up and observe it properly. I had my head down in the brown water, swimming as fast as I could, occasionally glancing up to check that I was propelling myself in the right direction. The water was relatively calm but I managed to create turmoil in the area where I was swimming. I was taking water in through my nose and my mouth, sputtering and gulping to get air.

And then a surging pain came as I heard the duller, water-muffled noise of rifle fire once more. The bullet tore through my clothes, ripping a small chunk of flesh from the outside of my right arm. It felt as if I had been punched. I was lucky it had not hit the arm directly – I was lucky it had not been a few inches higher or it would have been my head!

174

I believe the Dervishes may have fired one more time before I reached the boat. I had perhaps only swum thirty or forty feet, but the speed of the exertion combined with my fear of the Dervishes' bullets meant that by the time I reached the side of the vessel I felt as if I were about to faint.

I did not look up to observe what was happening inside the craft, and instead dived down underwater, underneath the boat and back up at the far side. At least now I was shielded from the bullets. I came out of the water gasping, for my heart was beating so fast that after just a few seconds of holding my breath I needed more air.

The boat was only travelling at a few knots, but it would be enough to speed me away from my enemy. My problem now was how to safely get aboard. And then came my second piece of good luck that day. Hanging from the side of the craft was a rope, trailing tantalizingly in the water. I reached for it, grabbed it and clutched it to my chest. Now for just a blessed few seconds I could rest my wrecked body as the boat carried me south.

I was lying on my back in the water, the smooth wood of the boat rubbing off my left shoulder, the cooling water flowing along my body, as we glided along the river, looking up towards the immaculate sky. I closed my eyes for a second, took a deep breath and opened them again. Suddenly a face had clouded my picture. It was the face of an Arab youth, his keen little eyes staring at me in wonder. Then came the shouts: 'Here, here! Down here!'

I reached with my left hand, grabbed the side of the boat and began to haul myself up. I had to use my right arm also, despite the searing pain from my wound, for I did not have the strength to manage the task without it. Then, just as I had popped my head up over the side to catch my first glimpse of whoever and whatever else was in the boat other than the boy, I was shocked to see a man rushing towards me wielding a sword.

It must have been the boy's father. The figure closed in quickly. The sword was above his head. I glimpsed his face – a calm determination. I saw the blade flash as it came down towards me. I felt like a piece of meat awaiting the butcher's chop. My instinct was to let go of the boat, but this would have left me dreadfully exposed to Dervish fire from the bank. I threw my weight to the left side, my injured arm flailing out to balance me. My timing must have been perfect, for not a moment later the sword struck wood.

I gave no thought at all to my next action. I reached across with my injured arm, the pain incredible and, grabbing the Arab sailor by the wrist, hoisted him out of the boat. He keeled over and plopped into the water as elegantly as a diving water bird.

I watched as he disappeared below the murky water only for his head to re-emerge a second or two later. As he began to swim after his boat I threw my legs up over the side and rolled into the craft. Next came a thudding pain in the back of my head. I had knocked it on the side of a wooden crate.

I raised my head. The boy was cowering at the back of the boat. 'Out!' I shouted in Arabic.

It was cruel to force the boy into the river, but I felt I had no choice. I knew that the father would most probably stop swimming after the vessel with his son in the water. The boy immediately obeyed and leapt over the side. I sat up and saw the father swimming towards his son, who was floating in the wake of the boat.

And now there were more shots – the Dervishes had begun firing on me once more. A piece of wood splintered just a foot from me. Bullets whined through the air and into the water. Head down again. The boat was on a steady course, and this part of the river being straight, I hoped to eventually outrun Dawson and his men.

'You won't get far, Winters!' It was Dawson, shouting across to me. 'I hope you are ready to die for your queen!'

And still the bullets came whizzing past, some of them drilling neat little holes in the vessel. While remaining low I piled some crates up on the side of the boat that was open to Dervish fire. They were packed full of dates. In the next few minutes I was to discover that they offered surprisingly good protection from the flying metal, for every few seconds I would hear a dull thud as a bullet cut through the wood of first the boat then the side of a crate, finally to come to rest in the fleshy fruit.

I spent the next several minutes lying low, until the sound of gunfire had abated and I felt confident that I could safely take a peek over the side of the boat. My enemy was a good few hundred yards along the bank. I was not as yet out of range of their fire, but I doubted if they would waste any more ammunition now, for the chances of hitting me were very slim. Dawson was shading his eyes with his hand and looking upriver towards me. The Dervishes were standing with their rifles by their sides.

Now I turned to see what my boat was sailing towards. Ahead and to the right was the brown mud city of Omdurman. But a bit further south again the waters seemed to spread out wide as if flowing into a sea. Here was the mighty confluence point of the Blue and White Niles. And sitting at the tip of that point, like a mythical island, was Khartoum.

It was the first time I had glimpsed the city. Khartoum looked very different from Omdurman. It stood grey-white rather than brown, its decaying whitewashed buildings, many of which I knew would have lain empty since the fall of General Gordon, seeming to have an air of forgotten greatness.

This was where I would land my boat. I knew from intelligence that we had gathered in the years before the war that the city had all but been abandoned by the Dervishes in favour of Omdurman. But more importantly, this was my best chance to get away from Dawson and his men. To get to Khartoum they would first have to find a boat to get across the Nile, and by that time I would have melted into the streets.

THERE WAS NO jetty or obvious other landing place that I could use, and so instead I had to crash the boat into the sands that emerged gradually from the water, as a fisherman would on a beach. It was as I was doing this that I heard an almighty roar from behind me. I would find out later that it was the Dervish armies, firing a triumphant volley of shots into the air before marching forward to confront the 'enemies of God'. There was no time to spare, and I wasted none in getting ashore, stopping only to lift a piece of material lying in the boat to use as a headscarf and a water-skin that I was lucky to find at the bow.

The bank of the Nile rose steeply, then there was an area of dry scrub, which led to a crumbling wall of mud bricks painted white. I set off at a run for the wall, for I felt dreadfully exposed in the open by the bank. There were a number of large windows that seemed to have been partially bricked up set at intervals along the wall. I scrambled through the one closest to me. It was an empty building that had no roof and looked to be slowly disintegrating. The last men to have set foot inside it may well have been the Dervish soldiers who overran the place on that ominous morning when Gordon was murdered.

I seated myself on a pile of rocks by the window. At last I had time to stop and take stock. Impatiently I opened the water-skin and drank and drank until it was almost empty. It was the first proper fluid that I had consumed in more than a day, a long time in the relentless heat of the Sudan. It felt wonderfully restorative. But now for the wound to my arm.

A large patch of blood stained my Arab robe around the shoulder. I shook with nausea as I took it off to find that the blood had started to congeal around the wound, which looked as if some animal had taken a bite out of it. It was still oozing liquid. I tore a strip of material off my headscarf and used it as a bandage, wincing as I tightened it around the damaged area. The dirty white material quickly turned crimson. It would have to do for now. My guess was that the battle for Omdurman would take place within the next few hours. Perhaps then, if Dawson or the Dervishes had not managed to kill me, I could secure some proper medical treatment.

But before I could even fully contemplate the outcome of the battle there remained the problem of Dawson and his system of river sabotage to deal with. I would have to make my way back down the Nile and either disarm his explosives or, if that were not possible, at least make my way further north to warn our forces of the danger upstream. If Dawson's timing was right, I knew that there would be enough explosives in the Nile to completely destroy our gunboats, and it would be these vessels that would make or break our advance.

Looking at the bandaged hole in my arm, I realized that I was in no state to be setting off on such a dangerous mission. Although I had managed to acquire some water, the effects of heat and dehydration were slowing me down. Combine this with the loss of blood that I now had to deal with, and I could not help but question my fitness for the task. And I was not armed: I did not even have a knife, much less a firearm.

But I was not about to sit out the rest of the war in a crumbling old colonial building in Khartoum. I was not about to wash my hands of the situation and let Dawson's explosives tear apart Kitchener's gunboats. I decided then how I must act. I would go into the heart of Khartoum. Surely there would be some people around. There I would have to, by any means possible – even if it meant by murder – acquire a rifle. I would then use my boat – if it was still there – to sail north to the sabotage area. As to what I would do then, as yet I had no idea.

I took a few minutes longer to rest and drink before setting off into Khartoum. I wrapped the material I had taken from the boat around my head as if it were an *imma*, draping part of it over my face so that only my eyes could be seen. I must have looked like little more than a wretched beggar.

I stuck my head out of a doorway and observed a vacant street, strewn with rubble, empty windows and crumbling walls. It seemed that I had the entire city to myself, with nothing for company but the wind, which was whipping up little columns of dust to transport them along the avenue. But I could hear now the distant sound of artillery being discharged – the battle must have started.

I sauntered along the street, in a direction leading me away from the Nile. By all accounts my situation now was still extremely dangerous. After all, I was a wounded man in enemy territory, quite possibly still with Dawson and his men in pursuit. But at this point I felt lucky just to have freedom of movement, and to have escaped being shot by the Dervishes.

I followed the empty street until it opened out to a dusty and dismal-looking square. Immediately I recognized that this must have been the area in which General Gordon had been killed, for there, at the other end of it, was the cracked and worn balustrade that fronted the balcony on which he would have faced the Dervishes. But also, and significantly, here there were also people; groups of between three to five scattered here and there of what I took to be refugees, finding shade where they could, awaiting the outcome of the war. All wars come with their refugees, and I am not afraid to admit that by this stage I had now seen so much of Arabia and North Africa under conflict that the sight of these wretches with their drawn faces, their ragged clothing covered in desert dust, did not shock me. I spotted no Dervish soldiers among them.

There were two ways in which I could attempt to acquire a rifle. One was to somehow steal one, which would be risky. The other was to use some gold coins that I had strapped to my inside leg, and which the Dervishes had failed to find, with which to buy one. This, too, would have its dangers, not least my being discovered.

Tentatively I entered the sun-bleached square, slowing my walk and bending my frame to give the impression of a decrepit who posed no danger to anyone. Some heads turned, but no one seemed to take more than a passing interest in me. I moved my eyes from side to side, observing everything. Which group should I approach?

They were mostly women and children, and the few men whom I did see looked to be very old. I walked further, in the direction of Gordon's balcony, my eyes constantly scanning. And then I focused on him.

He was standing alone, leaning against one of the pillars that propped up the balcony. He had a stick in his other hand, and my immediate assumption was that he had a problem with his leg that was keeping him out of the war.

He did not notice my approach. 'This war will be the death of all of us,' I said with a deliberately weak voice, by way of an introduction. I had my head lowered and was only half-facing the gentleman.

'I am not sure which will kill us first, the Turks or our own empty bellies,' he said in reply, emitting an almighty cough.

I looked at him. His sunken eyes, set in a face that was so thin as to be almost skeletal, stared towards the barren ground. 'I might be able to help you,' I ventured.

He continued to stare for a second, but then he seemed to switch on and moved his head to look at me. 'I need a rifle. I have some gold that I will trade you for it. You will be able to exchange them for food. You want to eat, don't you?'

'Do you have food?'

'No. But you can easily trade the gold with the soldiers.'

I left him to decide whether I meant the Dervishes or Kitchener's troops.

His weary eyes observed me suspiciously for a few seconds, and I hoped dearly that he would not discover that I was an outsider and announce it to the rest of the inhabitants of Khartoum.

'Show me,' he said.

I glanced around. 'In here,' and I motioned for him to follow me behind one of the columns. 'Three for a rifle and some ammunition,' I said, showing him one of the shiny gold pieces that I had retrieved from underneath my clothing.

The dazzling metal seemed to have an almost hypnotic effect on the man. Suddenly his half-dead eyes opened wide, and he actually licked his lips as he stared at it. 'Yes,' he said, with what seemed like a small amount of wonderment in his voice. 'Yes, I think I may be able to help you. How many of these will you give me if I can find you a rifle?'

'Three.'

'Six.'

I made a look as if I was not sure what to do. The truth is I would have happily paid all the gold sovereigns that I had left, which I hoped was at least ten, for a rifle, but the Arabs feel a need to bargain over trade before a settlement is reached. I had to play the game.

'It will take four for me to buy it,' continued the man. 'Then I keep just two for myself. It is not easy getting a rifle here ... Englishman.'

So he had seen through me. Of course he had. It seemed I had little choice, for my fate was now in the man's hands. It was probably my Arabic accent that had given me away. 'Very well, six,' I said. 'But I will need ammunition too. At least forty rounds.'

He nodded. 'Wait here. I shall return shortly.'

And so I waited, knowing that I was only a few feet from where General Gordon had been hacked to pieces by the Dervishes. For an awful moment I imagined that the same fate could now befall me, if it turned out that the man I was attempting to trade with was more interested in upholding the Khalifa than in making money.

But he was not, and after only a few minutes he returned and produced a rifle from underneath his robes. 'You are lucky that I have a family to feed,' he said as he handed it to me, 'otherwise you would have been killed.'

'And the ammunition?'

'You will only have twenty rounds this day.'

I could not argue. At least the rifle was modern. It was some sort of European make that I was not familiar with, but it had a magazine action. It seemed to be in fine working order.

I handed the man the gold sovereigns. Then I held up another two. 'You see the avenue at the other end of the square there?' He nodded. I was pointing to the street that I had come down earlier. 'I will leave these two gold coins at the end of it by one of the doorways. Keep quiet about what you have seen, then go there half an hour from now and you can collect them. The street is deserted. No one else will find them in the meantime. But if I leave this square and am followed by anyone then you will get no more. Understand?' And he nodded once more.

I loaded the gun and let it hang by my side, then calmly walked out of the square the way that I had come in. With a rifle in my hands I now felt far more confident about the task that lay ahead. A plan began to formulate. I would take the boat that I had stolen and sail back down the Nile, but only far enough that I could dock again on the other side of

Omdurman and to the north of the confluence point of the two rivers. I would then walk towards the area where the explosives had been planted in the knowledge that Dawson and his men were most probably on the opposite bank. Perhaps, I thought and hoped, they had even returned to the plains in front of Omdurman to lay down their lives for the Khalifa in the final battle.

THANKFULLY THE BOAT was where I had left it. I estimated it was now mid-morning. I could not see the battle from where I was but I could certainly hear it: explosions, firing and shouting.

I stood on the bank and observed my little boat, its triangular sail waving to me in the breeze. I looked at my shoulder and saw that blood was once again beginning to come through my clothing. And then I looked up towards the sky, squinting so much that my eyes were almost completely closed, and saw three vultures circling ominously. Perhaps they had already smelled my blood. Perhaps they had already sensed a soon to be dead animal below. I looked again at my boat and the gently flowing Nile. Must I go back out there? Clearly I had to. What choice did I have?

My wounded shoulder throbbed as I pushed the boat back out on to the water, and my feet felt particularly heavy as I jumped into my vessel. I was tiring.

But then I was sailing once more, only this time going north, my good arm controlling a small rudder at the back of the boat, my rifle leaning against the other, weaker arm. Even here on the water the wind was so hot and dry that it felt as if a raging fire was close by. I spotted no activity by the sides of the Nile, where the bank would rise to a few feet here, creating a drop to the water, or where the tiny waves would lap the gradually sloping land.

Naturally the boat travelled faster downstream than it had up, and it was not long before I had passed the confluence point of the two rivers and I began to see the first signs of the battle that was now most definitely in full swing, for all over the horizon there were dotted clouds of smoke and dust from artillery explosions. A continuous roar emanated from the area, and the anthracitic smell of modern warfare hung heavy in the air. But I did not have time to look for long as I had to find a place to land the boat.

And it was just as I thought I had spotted an appropriate position when my next set of troubles arose. I looked towards the right bank and saw an area where it fell away to a rocky beach and began to steer towards it. And then I glanced over towards the left bank for no particular reason. Something caught my eye so that when I looked away I instinctively turned my head back again. It was a Dervish, standing on the opposite bank, a foot or so above the waterline, his arms raised and aiming a rifle.

I ducked just in time. The bullet came so close that I am sure I felt a wisp of wind at my ear as it passed. It struck wood on the opposite side of the boat and then splashed into the water. I let go of the rudder, the pain from my shoulder now a distant memory. I lifted my own rifle and aimed. The Dervish was reloading. I fired. For a split second a puff of smoke appeared in my line of sight, at the end of my weapon, and when it drifted off the man was leaning forward. He fell into the river, his rifle falling with him. And then there was another Dervish soldier, appearing as if from nowhere, then another and another, until a small group stood in a line like a firing squad, which indeed it was.

The good news was that I was speeding towards the empty right bank. My head moved left to right left to right, my mind instantly working out distances and times. The bank seemed to be only a few seconds away. But now the Dervishes were raising their weapons. None of them, apart from that first man whom I had felled, fired at will. Clearly they were intent on firing one single and deadly volley. The hail of bullets would surely be my end.

I looked again at my enemy. Now they all had their rifles raised. Surely just a few seconds more to get to the bank! I jumped up and rushed towards the front of the boat. I was still perhaps ten feet from the bank. I did not look back now. I leapt across the boat, along the line of the sail and across boxes of dates. There was one box just behind the bow. I put my right foot on it, at the last second expecting it to go through. But it held. And then I was flying through the air as I dived for the bank, my arms out in front of me, my rifle still in my hand.

As I hit the dirt of the bank I heard an almighty snapping sound as the riflemen fired simultaneously. I kept my head down, expecting to be hit but only acknowledging the whine of the bullets as they skimmed near me.

And then all was relatively quiet again, but for the dense roar of a distant battle. I turned. The boat was sitting at an angle to the bank, the sail preventing me from seeing the Dervishes – and crucially preventing them from seeing a target. The holes where the bullets had ripped through the material gave out sad sunlit winks.

In a second I was on my feet. The ground rose gradually for a bit, then there was a small hill, behind which I thought I could find some cover. I zigzagged towards it, expecting another volley. But nothing came. And, as I leapt up its side again, all that my ears were tuned to was the soft tones of the flowing river.

I reached the other side of the hill, sweating profusely, out of breath. Here I could see nothing ahead of me but slightly undulating desert. It came as a welcome view and told me that for the moment at least I was out of danger. But I had to find out what the Dervishes who had fired on me were up to, and so I made my way north for perhaps fifty yards before risking a glance over the hill to observe them.

Tentatively I lifted my head above the crest of the hill, half expecting it to be shot off. There they were, the white-robed fighters, standing at the same spot on the opposite bank from which they had fired. Meanwhile I could sense a great battle taking place just a few miles to my right, shouts and wild screams, bursts of fire and explosions, but I could not take my attention away from my immediate threat. I counted nine Dervishes in total. Some of them were pointing to the boat that I had just abandoned, while others looked to simply be milling around.

And then I spotted Dawson, standing away from the others, intermittently kicking the scrub and looking across to the other bank, his white face so out of place among the dark soldiers he was leading.

But here I had an opportunity. I looked at my rifle and back at Dawson. He was within range. It would be a difficult shot, but it was certainly possible. My mission had always been to stop Dawson, and although my main priority now was disarming the explosives he had left in the Nile, there was no question that I would not take this chance.

I sat up a bit further and brought my rifle to the fore. It was time for the traitor to pay for his crime. I raised the rifle to take aim; firm against the shoulder; eye by the sight. But I was shaking. I doubted it was nerves – more likely dehydration and exhaustion. I lifted my head from its firing position for a second, swallowed and took a deep breath. Back again and I was steady.

I put the sight as close to Dawson's heart as I could manage with him standing almost side on to me. He was staring out across the water as if deep in thought. Perhaps he was thinking about the mess that his bombs would make of the men in the gunboats. I was.

I rested my finger on the trigger. One last breath and that would end it.

CHAPTER 18

Diary of Mr Wilfred Parker

18 May, 1935

I'M NOT NORMALLY very good at keeping my diary up-to-date, but I feel I have to note down my troubles somewhere. What a silly muddle I have ended up getting myself into. Why wasn't I simply honest with the colonel from the start? He is an understanding man. But now, however this turns out, whether he finds out the full truth or not, I have proved myself to be deceitful and to be a liar. And all this when the only thing that I should be thinking about is my wedding next month. I wish I could just block it all out, even if only for a few seconds.

I took the train down to Kent today, and I must say I was full of anticipation. As soon as I had taken my seat at Waterloo I was fidgeting and drumming my fingers on the train's wood panelling. But then I did manage to relax a bit. I think this was down to the carriage not being too busy and those first stirrings of summer sunshine that were streaming in through the window. In fact, I would go so far as to say that I began to look on the bright side of my situation. In a few years from now, myself, Margaret and the Colonel will all be looking back on this silly situation and be laughing at it, I thought, as the train left South London's neat suburbs and steamed into Kent's rolling hills and farmland. But these feelings were only temporary, and after a little while I returned to worrying again. Not even the normally pleasing sights of the country, of the farm labourers out tending the fields, of the quaint little thatched cottages and old churches, could take my mind off the pathetic matter.

The one-and-a-half-hour journey seemed to take forever. But then I was opening the gate to Cousin Janet's house and walking up that well-tended garden path, the sight of which had not blessed my eyes in so many years. With its little porch and ivy growing up its side, it's the sort of place that I could see Margaret and I living in very happily.

I knew it was going to be awkward meeting Janet again. I wish my extended family had been closer when I was growing up. But things were never quite the same after Father went to the Sudan. Mother shut herself away in a box, and now that I am older I can see that it would have been near impossible for her to continue with family relationships as they had been before.

I have to say that Janet has been wonderfully supportive since I telephoned her. She could easily have turned her back on me and once again forgotten about the whole thing, as everyone else in the family had. But she has been so understanding of my situation. It heartens me. And having only been a child when my father left for the Sudan, she is also learning a lot about our dark family secret.

My first impression when she opened the door was that she looked a little sad somehow. Perhaps she felt sorry for me, and didn't think it would be appropriate to show any signs of being happy.

'Hello, Wilfred. My, you are looking well. How wonderful it is to see you again. Please, do come in,' she said a little sombrely, but she was smiling also.

I remember it was exactly midday because an old grandfather clock standing in her hallway gave off a few deep chimes, breaking the silence, as I walked past it to the living-room. As I expected her home was spotless. Like Cousin Janet herself, there was not a thing out of place, not a speck of dust on the mahogany furniture or the little ornaments of birds on the mantelpiece. It's the sort of tidiness that I think comes from living alone.

I wonder if living by oneself is perhaps a family trait with us lot. I'm sure Janet will never marry now, not at her age. It seems a pity, because even today I thought she seemed quite pretty in her petite little flowery dress with her dark hair – and not a trace of grey in it – neatly worn up. But perhaps members of our family are just meant to be lonely ... ah, but I should stop thinking these sorts of worrying thoughts, especially when I'm just about to commit myself to marriage.

Two china cups were sitting side-by-side atop of saucers on a little tray on the coffee table when I entered. Cousin Janet was so organized that a pot of tea was brewed and sitting under a tea cosy waiting to be poured.

'Now, how are the marriage plans coming along?' she asked, lifting her cup and sitting on the sofa opposite me.

I told her that everything was going really quite well on that front.

'And what about your research?'

'Well, it's definitely him,' I told her. 'There's no doubt about it.'

'Definitely?'

'Definitely. Where should I start? I'll tell you about my trip to Cambridge first.' Janet sat back on the sofa to listen. 'I met a professor who's been at Trinity for over fifty years. He actually remembered teaching my father, if you can believe it.'

'Amazing.'

'Indeed. Anyway, it seems Father was one of his best students. Said he was very committed to his work, one of the few to really become fluent in Arabic. I was pretty sure it was Father at this point, especially when he told me – and I thought this was most interesting – that Father took his studies to the utmost extreme. In his words, he said Father would study "for days without taking a break, and heaven help anyone who disturbed him when his mind was engaged in his work". But it wasn't until I visited an old soldier from Father's regiment, that I knew for certain that it was him. I showed him that old photograph I've got of Father, from years ago, and he said he knew him. But *he* knew him as a Captain Dawson. He said there was no mistaking it. He said Father was attached to the regiment, but that he hardly ever saw him. Until they had to start building the desert railway in the Sudan, that is, when he was put in charge of some workers. Then he said he just disappeared one day. So you see, there's no mistaking it, Captain Parker and Captain Dawson were one and the same.'

'But why the two names, Wilfred?'

'I can only think it was something to do with his intelligence work. I think, from what the colonel's told me, that a lot of the intelligence officers would adopt different names, especially if they had families, when they were recruited to that part of the army.'

'It's all so incredible.'

'But the thing is, all this running around that I've been doing to confirm things, I needn't have, you know. What I mean is, I knew from the start. As soon as the colonel told me, that night when we first met in the library, that the focus of his memoirs was on how he tracked down a traitor in the Sudan, I knew then that he was writing about Father. I mean, how many traitors could there have been there? Mahdism was such an extreme cause that I would not have imagined there were any others. But I think I've been using this whole need to confirm thing as an excuse to delay telling the colonel what I already knew was most probably a certainty.'

'And you still haven't said anything to the colonel?'

'Oh, no, no. No, I couldn't. Not yet. I did try to actually, but couldn't in the end. And as I say, I was using my need to confirm that it was my father as an excuse I think. No, I haven't even mentioned it to Margaret yet. She doesn't need to be bothered with all this when she's looking forward to our wedding day. And as for the colonel, he's due to give a big speech in Parliament soon. I should tell him after that. I just hope he understands why I've found it so difficult to be truthful. Poor Colonel Winters, he wants to dedicate his memoirs to my father too.'

'No!'

'Indeed. What an irony that would be. But it won't happen of course. I'll have to be honest with him before then.'

'Oh, that reminds me. Your mentioning that old photograph reminds me. I found this yesterday, up in the loft.' And she got up and went to one of the cabinets.

She opened a little wooden door and brought out what looked like a photograph, which indeed it turned out to be. It was of my father. It was obviously from his student days at Trinity. There must have been twenty of them in it, in three lines, all dressed in jumpers and scarves, the leaded windows set amongst the fine stone of the college their backdrop. I spotted my father straight away. He had my strong chin, and I thought he looked to have a similar build to me.

'Ah, yes, yes … this must be him here, isn't it?' I said, pointing.

Janet was standing next to me and I was seated. 'That's right,' she said. 'It says it on the back.'

I flipped the picture over. It was marked 1891 and all the names were there in order, the name Parker corresponding to the man I had pointed to. I flipped it back again to look properly at my father. Such innocent-looking eyes he had. And he looked to be so full of life and joy.

How could it all have gone so wrong? How could he have turned his back on his family and on England to support Mahdism? How I wish Mother and I had talked about it more before she died – although I knew she felt too hurt by it all to press for further details from the army. Anyway, they would probably never have told us any more than that Father was killed disgracefully, and that he had turned traitor. If I had known the whole story before, it would have saved me a lot of searching around now to confirm what I already essentially knew. At least the colonel's memoirs are giving me some kind of insight into what made him do it. I actually wish Mother had been alive to read them. Perhaps they would even have given her some peace of mind, although Mother obviously just wanted to get on with her life afterwards, even though she was heartbroken.

And now his treachery has come back to haunt me also all these years after Omdurman. I only hope the colonel will not be too disappointed in me.

CHAPTER 19

Diary of the Rt. Hon. Colonel Evelyn Winters MP
20 May, 1935

I WENT AND sat in the House today and tried to imagine how tomorrow will play out. I hardly even listened to the debate that was taking place – something about housing for the working classes. Thankfully the House was very quiet, and I was able to find myself a seat at the back, near the entrance, so that no other MPs were around me.

I sat in that corner looking out over the entire Chamber and tried to picture what tomorrow will be like. Today there must have been at most forty MPs in the House, but tomorrow I expect it to be packed. The Government is intent on getting the India Bill through within the next few weeks, which has resulted in the recent heated debates, especially when Mr Churchill has been involved.

I believe I must have looked a rather queer sight on that bench. I had my speech in my hands and was intermittently looking across the floor then putting my head down to close my eyes and test myself on some part or other. The other MPs, most of whom were of my generation, were spread out sparingly throughout the Chamber. And I have to say that the Speaker looked really quite bored by it all.

But it suited my needs perfectly, as it gave me a chance for quiet reflection and final preparation.

After a while I folded my speech up and put it in my inside pocket – I think I've known it off by heart for the past four weeks or so anyway – and decided to just sit back and imagine my giving a stunning performance. I believe it was a member for one of the northern constituencies who was speaking, from the opposite side, on the need for proper sanitary conditions in working homes, that sort of thing. He was standing about four rows from the front, austere in his black suit – which clashed wonderfully with his brilliant silver moustache and hair – his hands up by his chest, elegantly making his points in a well-ordered sequence. There were a handful of other members sitting around or near him. One or two of them had fallen asleep, their heads hanging as if an undertaker had just stopped by to drop them off. Others were clearly listening as they nodded in agreement every time the member speaking made a point that they particularly liked.

'And I must say,' he croaked, 'that this is not simply a question of money or of resources. It is also a question of progress.'

But I hope that my performance tomorrow, despite my own advanced years, will be more spirited. I pictured it as I sat there. I shall be standing directly behind the Dispatch Box, just a few rows from the front. Baldwin will be there, as will Sam Hoare and Stafford Cripps and, of course, Mr Churchill and the rest of us rebels. I shall rise up slowly when called to speak and glance casually around the House, for it is always good to start a dramatic speech with a bit of silence to build up the tension. I shall look at the Speaker, then take my eyes across the packed benches opposite. I might have a little smile on my face.

'The Montagu-Chelmsford reforms,' I shall begin, 'set forth a process of the partial Indianization of provincial governments in British India … and now this government wishes to force yet more of our Western doctrines of democracy upon this nation. But I say what right do we have to do this?' And so I will go on.

I hope it will be well received.

I EXPECTED PARKER to be in touch today, but I have heard nothing from him – not even a telephone call. It seems a little odd. I thought he would want to check that I was ready for tomorrow. Perhaps he had plans with Miss Bellingford – although if he had I would have hoped he would have let me know that I would not be seeing him today.

Still, he will be around tomorrow. We will be leaving together from here, and I shall make sure he gets a good seat in the public gallery.

CHAPTER 20

I COVERED MY head and put it to the ground, my nose touching the dirt. I breathed in a second too soon before raising my head again and found myself choking on the dust.

There had been two bangs, one from my right side, downriver, the other to my front, which had a deeper, thudding sound. I turned my head and saw the mass of a British gunboat steaming up the Nile, three plumes of white smoke hanging above it testimony to the shells it had just fired towards Omdurman. The missiles had landed across the river from me, short of the city. I looked across and saw three mushrooms of dust rising in the air on a plain that rose gradually towards Omdurman's brown mud walls.

And then I turned to face Dawson and his men once more. They were looking north towards the gunboat. I had missed my chance to shoot the fiend, and by now a Dervish soldier had moved to stand between my target and me. Damn it, I thought. He should have been mine.

'Over there! Over there!'

One of the Dervishes had spotted me. I was about to crawl back down the slope but anger made me fire a shot before taking cover. I sat up quickly, aimed and hit nothing. And then some of the Dervishes were raising their rifles, while others had started to run along the bank in my direction.

I crawled backwards down the hill and out of harm's way as a couple of shots rang out and flew over my head. I was angry that I had not shot Dawson. This only lasted for a second, however, for taking stock of the situation I realized there was no time to lose. The gunboats were steaming towards Omdurman to shell it, and soon they would fall into Dawson's trap. I had to get there first.

I got up into a crouch position and made my way further down the incline until I felt sure the Dervish bullets would not get me. Then, still crouching to ensure I did not present a target, I started running north in parallel with the bank. Looking up I could see the smoke from the steamer and estimated it to be about a mile away, which meant it was perhaps half a mile from the danger area.

I picked up the pace, wondering how far behind – or to my front – Dawson and his men were. I found out soon enough, however, as the small hill that had acted to shield me from the Dervishes dropped away suddenly, the land bordering the river becoming as flat as a table. I slowed for a second as I came upon this more exposed area. Looking to my left there was no immediate sign of the enemy. But to my front I saw the gunboat. The way that the river meandered here meant that the vessel was actually facing me directly, so that it looked as if it was sitting still in the water even though it was actually driving upstream at full speed. I have to admit that despite the precariousness of the situation, the sight of that great armoured boat, following my internment by the Khalifa and my narrow escape, warmed my heart. It looked impenetrable with its shiny steel hull and bellowing funnel. But I knew that Dawson's explosives would rip it apart as easily as if it were made of paper.

But there was something else also. In the haze that floated off the Nile it looked almost like a shadow behind the vessel. But then I noted a second great column of smoke immediately behind the first gunboat and realized that another vessel was also steaming towards us. The prospect of not one but two gunboats being blown to smithereens filled me with dread.

At this point I lost any notion of thinking about my own safety, and instead of plodding along in a crouch, straightened myself up and started to sprint as fast as I could towards the gunboats.

After just a few seconds I was panting terribly, but I pressed on regardless, my shoulder gnawing like a toothache once more from the natural arm movement that comes with this sort of exertion. As I closed in on the area where the charges had been planted I glanced over my left shoulder. Dawson and his small band of Dervishes were a good few hundred yards upstream from me. But they had clearly seen me and were in pursuit. I would not have much time. I would have to get out into the river and cut the wires that connected the charges.

Thankfully I was out of range of the Dervish rifles and so had no flying bullets to contend with, just my own wrecked and exhausted body. I was taking long and quick strides across the desert, jumping left and right here and there to avoid tripping on rocks. I was panting so hard that my entire upper body was moving forwards and backwards with my breathing. But it was not far now, just another two hundred yards or so. I could see the tops of the three funnels sticking out of the water, and the little clump of grass on the other side of the bank that I had escaped from earlier.

I glanced over my shoulder again. The Dervishes did not appear to be gaining on me. The land rose a bit before dropping down again towards the point at where the explosives had been planted. I scrambled up the incline, pushing with my left hand against the sometimes sharp, grey rock. And then I was running down the other side and through a patch of grass before the bank.

I threw down my rifle and dived into the water. As soon as I surfaced I began to swim towards the funnels of the deadly little sunken boats. A rush of pain shot from my arm and up my neck. I could have screamed. But despite the agony it took me a mere seconds to reach the first funnel. It was the one furthest from me that I needed, however, for if I could cut the wiring at that point, at the first stepping stone out from the bank where the detonator box was located, then all three devices would be disarmed. But it seemed so far away, and it was so close to the other, more dangerous bank.

I stopped and reached up to grab the top of the first funnel. Glancing up for a second in my exhaustion, the top was almost completely lost in the bright yellow of the sun, which was directly overhead. Then I looked upriver and saw the group of white figures hurrying along the bank towards me. I had little time. I took a deep breath and continued on.

My damaged arm was now becoming so weak that I could hardly keep my head above the river's small waves as I swam. If Dawson and his Dervishes didn't get me then some water-borne disease probably will, I thought, trying not to gulp in water as I went. I was swimming directly below the fuse wire, which hung around a foot above the water.

But then I was quickly at the next funnel, right in the middle of the Nile. I grabbed the top of it with my good arm. The metal of the funnel pressing against my body was cool from its contact with the water. I gasped as I clung there, and felt as if I were using the last of my energies. For a brief second I wished only to lie back and let the waters consume me. But I snapped myself out of it and got on with the task at hand.

I was now faced with deciding whether to go on to the last funnel. I looked again towards the approaching enemy. I estimated I had about a minute before they would be on the bank opposite me. Clearly there was no time to reach the furthest funnel. It was all that I could do to cut the wires on this middle charge, thereby at least disarming two of the three bombs. But then I suddenly remembered that I had no knife or other cutting implement.

I was almost overcome with panic. The metal fuse wires would be too strong to be ripped apart by hand. I would have to think of something else. I hauled my body up the side of the funnel while keeping check on the progress of my pursuers and, momentarily forgetting about the pain in my shoulder, swung my legs over to balance precariously on the side of the shaft. Two thin black fuse wires ran out to the funnel. One of them disappeared into its innards while the other continued on to the third set of explosives. I looked into the funnel. At first I saw only blackness, but after a second the corner of a box of explosives appeared in the gloom. Dawson had somehow managed to sink the vessels while keeping the area where the explosives were housed dry.

But now for the wires. I glanced around me. How on earth would I cut them? My eye focused on a seam in the metal funnel of the boat. It was my only chance. I would have to rub the wires off the edge of the seam, where two pieces of metal had been riveted together, and hope that they would break.

I grabbed the first wire and frantically got to work, moving it back and forward against the metal. The black waterproofed cotton that coated the metal quickly came away to reveal the copper wire underneath. I looked to the Dervishes. They were fast moving north. Soon I would be in range of their rifle fire.

The first thread of the wire snapped. What I would have given to have had a knife at this point! I moved the wire even faster and more threads began to break in two. And then the whole wire was in two pieces. That took care of the set of charges immediately below me. I let them go, one end falling into the blackness, the other into the Nile, grabbed the second wire and began to repeat the tedious cutting process.

The now familiar sound of a Dervish rifle being fired rang out. I ignored it, for I knew they would still be out of range. Again the cotton wrapping came away quickly and it took more work to get the wires to start to sever.

I glanced at the Dervishes. They were certainly within range. I had only a few more seconds of safety left with which to work. The muscles in my arms ached. Then suddenly I heard a twanging sound as a bullet struck the metal of the boat's turret just in front of where I was sitting. I did not look up but kept working. A few more strands broke away, and then my hands flew apart as the wire split into two parts.

No time to think about what to do next. I fell backwards into the water, the brown murk enveloping me and instantly making me feel safer. Below the water I felt with my feet the flat metal of the turret and used it as a platform to fire me away from the boat. I surfaced face first and instantly rolled over and began to swim back towards the turret on the far side. And now I could hear a voice shouting. 'He's out there somewhere. Can anyone spot him?' It was Dawson.

For a few seconds the turret that I had swum from must have given me cover, and I heard no firing. But then sure enough there eventually came the sound of what seemed like a small barrage. How none of those bullets pierced my body I cannot say, but by some miracle I managed to reach the next turret unscathed.

I swam around the turret's side and got behind it so that I was gloriously shielded from the Dervish bullets. Here I trod water for a few seconds before swimming on to the bank, taking the opportunity to check on the progress of the gunboats. They were steaming forward, almost side by side now. At their current speed I estimated they were no more than a few minutes away. And there remained one set of explosive charges on the Nile!

I did not look back at my enemy, and ignoring their bullets swam to the bank, got out, picked up my rifle and began to run as quickly as my tired legs would take me. Bullets were striking the earth left and right, and yet still I was somehow managing to avoid them. As I ran north I also veered off to the right, away from the Dervish fire, until I was pretty much out of range.

The desert here was very flat and I made good speedy progress across it. And then, as I got closer to the gunboats, I looked over my left shoulder and saw that Dawson and his men had halted the pursuit. Clearly they did not wish to get too close to the immense firepower of our mighty river vessels.

When I was sure that I was safe I could not help but slow down to almost a walk, for I was so exhausted that I felt ready for collapse. I trundled along those last few hundred yards like a man who had just crossed all of the Sahara. And then I was alongside the gunboats. I turned directly to my left and faced them. They were powering along, and as I started to make my way to the bank to try and signal to them, their guns with an almighty boom once again opened up on Omdurman. But this time they were close enough for their shells to reach the city. Several clouds of dust appeared in an area perhaps a few hundred yards in front of the Mahdi's tomb. Kitchener must have given orders that it should be destroyed to try and break the morale of the Dervishes, I thought. But the boats were not yet within range. I pitied the poor civilians, the women and the children, whose mangled bodies I knew would already be littering the streets, cut to pieces by our shrapnel shells. Such is war.

I reached the edge of the river and began to shout to the boat, but my voice was hoarse. I forced a few coughs and tried again. 'Hello!' I cried. 'Over here! I'm a British officer!' I saw a few men at the front of the bow of the boat closest to me. Most of them, however, would be on the other side and manning the guns that were firing on Omdurman.

Nothing came of my shouts. 'I'm a British officer, of the Intelligence Branch! Stop the boat or you'll be blown sky high!'

The guns were firing continuously now, and their pounding noise was drowning out my cries. I was about to give up and jump in the water to try and swim to the first boat when I noticed a sailor at the bow turn and stare.

My frantic waving had caught his eye. He approached the port side and put his hands above his forehead to observe me. He looked to be a young sailor. Still I waved and shouted, not knowing if I was being heard or not. 'The boat is in great danger!'

I watched as the sailor put his hands down and walked to the stern of the craft. I thought he was going to summon one of his superiors, but was surprised when he returned alone. Next thing I knew he was holding a rifle before him and was about to take aim. 'No, you silly bugger! I'm British!'

But it was no use. He obviously could not hear me. I turned and zigzagged away from the bank. The man must have fired, but my ears picked up no sound of gunshot above the noise of the boat's artillery and the battlefield beyond.

Out of range of the bullets, I sat myself down on a rock facing our gunboats and seethed with rage. It was all I needed; having escaped Dawson and his Dervishes, to now be running from my own side's bullets – although in hindsight I could not blame the young sailor, for all he would have seen was a man dressed in dirty and torn Arab dress and with a face so filthy and sunburned that he probably looked just like a Dervish.

To the side of the gunboats I could see some part of the battle that was now taking place on the other side of the river. A strong whiff of cordite drifted across the water to pierce my nostrils and the noise from the other bank was hellish, the deep roar and boom of full-scale war. On the far right, thick clouds of smoke hung above the Anglo-Egyptian *zariba*, out of which volleys of artillery were being continuously launched towards the enemy. But it was out in front of this area, and to its left by the Nile, that the real action was taking place. For here, on the mostly flat and lightly grassed ground the Dervishes appeared to be falling in their thousands. Forward they streamed, these brave warriors, in a hopeless attempt to break through into the *zariba*. But out in front there were lines and lines of our Sudanese riflemen and a number of Maxim guns, driving thunderous barrages into the savage hordes. I would see a mass of black and white patches charge forward to then suddenly and all at once drop, only to find others immediately jumping over them to continue the charge, spears and swords raised in the vague hope that they might get close enough to kill one of our troops.

I had no idea how the battle was going overall, but from what little I could see it seemed that at this stage we certainly had the upper hand. But what could I do now? An idea suddenly struck me. The men on the gunboats were sailors and would know Morse code, as I did. If I could communicate with the ship using this method then the men would surely realize that I was British, or at least not a Dervish, for the chances of one of the natives knowing Morse code were practically zero. But what could I signal with? I had no looking glass or any other obvious reflective implement.

I looked around me at the grey rocks and the dry, cracked earth. Nothing sprang to mind. But then I looked down at my rifle straddled across my lap. In the game of cat and mouse that I had played out with Dawson and his men it had become covered in a layer of fine desert dust. I rubbed the stuff off from around the firing mechanism to reveal the metal part of the gun. It was a dark iron colour. I knew, however, that if I stripped the rifle down, then beneath its wooden casing I would be likely to find a shiny metal plate extending out from the mechanism along the underside of the barrel.

I quickly got to work, trying to block out the awful noises emanating from the other side of the river, and quietly rather pleased at my inspired thinking. First I stripped out the firing parts. I could then slide off the wooden casing. It did indeed come off to reveal a flat piece of shiny metal that twinkled in the sunshine. It might just work. I looked up and found the ships were a further hundred yards or so upriver from where I sat, so I jumped up and ran off in pursuit. Reaching the bank, I held the piece of metal up and angled it so that I was sure the sun was reflecting perpendicularly off it towards the Nile. I began to signal ... BRITISH OFFICER ... BRITISH OFFICER ... DANGER ... DANGER.

I saw one or two men walking up and down the port side of the vessel closest to me. At first there was no response, but then one chap seemed to take notice and came and stood looking across the water to me. Then I saw him wave to a colleague, who came and joined him.

DANGER ... DANGER. TRAP ... TRAP.

Next came flashes from the boat – one of the men was using something to send signals back to me. It told me to identify myself. Walking along the bank to keep up with the vessel, I signalled: MAJOR WINTERS ... INTELLIGENCE.

At this point I looked to my left to check on the distance to Dawson's charges. It wasn't far – perhaps a quarter of a mile. There was little time left. I signalled: DO NOT FIRE ... DO NOT FIRE ... COMING TO YOU. Then I ran along the bank so that I was ahead of the gunboats, threw my signalling metal to the ground and dived into the water. Again I would have to fight the pain of my wounded shoulder.

But I was happier now. I felt that at least now there was a chance of stopping the gunboats being blown up.

The metallic sides of the vessel reared up as I closed in. I looked up and saw some heads leaning out over the bulwarks to observe me – I was grateful that none of them was firing on me. I tried waving when I was about twenty yards off, and shouted, 'Lower a rope! Lower a rope!'

The boat had ceased firing its missiles on Omdurman, although I could still hear the continuous pounding noise of guns from its sister vessel. I did not know if the men would trust me and lower a rope, or simply steam past, but I swam on anyway.

And then I saw the end piece of a rope falling in front of my eyes to almost touch the water. What relief I felt.

But now I was not even sure if I would reach it. The boat was moving steadily, and its great size meant that it was casting off waves of perhaps a foot in height to its side, which greatly slowed my progress. I gritted my teeth and with complete disregard for my shoulder fought on. I would see a little wall of brown liquid rise up in front of me to break over my face, lifting me as it went. It felt like incredibly hard work. And then when I was alongside the rope and thought I had it, I found the vessel moving forward so that I lost it again. With what little strength I had left I kicked with my feet and moved my arms frantically.

And then the rope was in my hands. It was like a repeat of my experience earlier that day with the small wooden trading boat, only on a much grander scale. But I had made it, and after a few seconds of hanging there in the water I felt a jerk as the rope went taught and I was hauled out of the Nile and up the side of the vessel.

I did not even have the energy to add my right hand to the rope, and instead hung there helpless, letting the sailors do all the work. I had my back to the metal hull so that I was looking out over the flat haze of the desert. And then I felt the strong grip of several sets of hands around my shoulders, and the next thing I knew was standing on a flat wooden deck, feeling dazed.

'Winters, is it? You look like you've been to hell and back. What on earth is this all about?'

The blood was rushing to my head from my exertions, and for a second I thought I was about to faint. My eyes clouded over and I did not respond to the questioning. But then I felt the smoothness of a metal cup at my lips. Someone was feeding me water. I took a sip then put my head back to gulp down the rest. It was magnificently restorative and immediately brought back my wits.

Now I could make sense of the situation. Four men surrounded me. Three of them were sailors and one was an officer, who was immediately to my left and stood taller and broader than the others. I presumed it was this man who had questioned me. I turned to face him. He was indeed a very tall fellow and stood a good four inches above me, a lick of greasy-looking black hair hanging across his forehead.

'You have to stop the boat,' I gasped. 'And you must instruct the other gunboat to stop too.' I pointed to the sister vessel, forcing my hand out between the shoulders of two of the sailors. It was sailing about twenty feet off the starboard side.

'What do you mean, stop? Why should we?'

I did not answer, for before I had a chance to I noticed, over the officer's shoulder, that we were fast approaching Dawson's trap. 'That's why!' I said, pointing again, only this time out over the bow of the boat where, as we rounded a bend in the river, the three turrets which had been filled with explosives were coming into view.

Quickly I tried to explain the situation. 'I have uncovered a plot by a traitorous British officer to blow up the gunboats. There is enough dyna- mite in those half-sunken ships there to blow us all out of the water. I've disarmed two of them, but one of them is still live.'

I looked at the officer, the backdrop of the blue sky and the smoking city of Omdurman behind him moving steadily to the left as the vessels turned in the river so that we were now directly facing the charges. There was a few seconds of silence as he contemplated my story. I would not have blamed him in the least if he discounted it on the basis of my being a madman and instructed his men to throw me off the side.

'Shut off the engines,' he commanded.

Then from one of his subordinates, 'But, sir—'

'Shut them off, now! That is my order!'

I was impressed by his quick decision-making. Only later would he realize the significance of what he had just done.

The order was passed to the bridge, and there was a flurry of activity as the officer – whom I had now surmised was the commanding officer – went about communicating with the other gunboat to have it too come to a halt. The guns of the sister vessel fell silent, and this was followed by the groaning sound of our ship's massive engines coming to a halt.

And then I heard one of the cruellest callings of my life. From the bridge, which rose up in levels to my right, came a shout. 'It's no use, sir. We won't stop in time.'

The large vessels were so heavy that coming to a stop from going at full steam was no easy task.

As all this was going on I hobbled to the front of the gunboat. We were closing in on the danger area fast. I commanded a view now of the three half- submerged boats straddling the Nile, sitting like pieces on a chessboard, and the clumps of grass at each side. And then, as I was looking at the area of grass to the right, to see if I could see the detonator box, I noticed that some sand bags had now been placed there. They had obviously been built up around the detonator box, and I had no doubt that Dawson would have placed one of his Dervishes behind the sandbags, ready to set off the charges once we were up next to them. I could see no more of the enemy.

I now scanned my eyes left across Dawson's deadly construction, following the thin fuse wires, which I could just make out, along to the next and middle set of charges. I almost took my eyes right past it. But then I stopped.

For there was Dawson, sitting atop the middle funnel, side on, as I had been no more than ten minutes before. I blinked, staring in disbelief at the man. He was fiddling with something, working quickly, occasionally glancing over to observe our progress.

He was splicing the fuse wires together again! And after I had just risked my life to cut them.

'Can you turn your guns on that set of sandbags there, by the bank?' I asked loudly, not addressing anyone in particular.

I turned. Several Royal Navy staff were scurrying around the deck. A young officer approached to look out over the Nile. 'There,' I said, pointing to where the detonator box was located.

The officer, a short and portly little fellow, was silent as he contemplated the target. 'Well?' I said, a little agitated that he seemed not to fully appreciate the seriousness of the situation.

'We're too close,' he eventually responded. 'Yes, far too close. We won't get the trajectory.'

'But don't you realize that we're going to be completely bloody blown apart?'

Nothing from the man but a blank stare. I could have pulled my hair out. I tutted and turned to look out at Dawson once again. 'Get me a rifle,' I ordered. 'I need a rifle. Bring one to me right now!'

The officer went to totter off, but then I heard another voice from behind me. 'We have one here.'

It was the commanding officer again. Thankfully, he seemed to have a better idea of the urgency of the situation. A second later a sailor ran forward from the stern carrying a rifle.

I snatched it from him and made the weapon ready to fire. This time I would not let Dawson escape, definitely not.

I raised the rifle over the front of the boat and rested my elbow on the very tip of the vessel, pleased at least – despite the persistent danger of our situation – that Dawson and I had now reversed our roles and that he was the one being fired upon out there in the Nile.

But the movement of the boat meant that the end of the rifle was moving from side to side and up and down. I stood up straight to see if I could steady the weapon. It was better, although still not ideal, and I had to try and let my body move in rhythm with the boat.

I brought the rifle's sight down on Dawson. We must have been no more than a hundred yards off now at the most. He had his head down, his headscarf and *jibba* wet and dirty looking from the murky waters of the river. His hands were together as if he were praying, but I knew that he was actually splicing together fuse wires.

It was a difficult shot. His body kept moving in and out of my circular sights with the motion of the boat. There! Fire now! No, gone again. This time! No, again too late. I took a deep breath, and at the first hint of his dirty-white *jibba* in the left side of my sight squeezed the trigger.

The bullet went wide, hitting the water at Dawson's side. He looked up, but only for a second, his head dropping again to continue with his work. I could only commend his courage, despite my hatred for the man. The sight of our gunboats bearing down directly on him must have been awesome and terrifying.

I reloaded and took aim again, and again missed my target.

'Let me try,' said the commanding officer.

'No!' I said, reloading again. 'I'll have him.'

'Get more rifles up here!' shouted the commander to his men.

I took aim again – but now he was gone. I lowered the rifle.

I saw the white of the turban in the water a few feet away from the turret. He was swimming towards the right bank. My heart jumped. It meant that he had successfully repaired the fuse wires. In just a few seconds we would all be blown out of the water.

But I had not come this far to let my enemy beat me now.

Forgetting about Dawson I took aim at the set of charges closest to the right bank. Our last hope of survival lay in setting off the dynamite before we reached the danger area.

I fired and hit the turret. No explosion. The bullet must have been too high to connect with the dynamite. I would have to aim lower. I reloaded and aimed once more, noting in my peripheral vision our sister gunboat, which seemed little more than fifty yards away from Dawson.

We were now so close that I was leaning right out over the bow. I placed the vertical metal that was in the centre of the circle of the sight back on the turret and just above the water-line. I could sense Dawson swimming to my right, but could not see him. I rested my finger on the trigger, blinked once then fired.

A wave of energy enveloped me. I fell back on to the deck and, opening my eyes, saw a mountain of brown water rising vertically before us. The boat was still moving forward at quite a speed, and the next thing I knew a shower of river water was falling gloriously upon us.

I lay still for a second. We had made it – made it by the skin of our teeth! Getting to my feet, almost slipping on the drenched deck, I felt myself starting to grin broadly. And then I was laughing out loud like a madman, amazed at our good fortune. I hobbled over to the side of the ship to look over just as we were passing by the middle turret. The explosion had bent and twisted its metal.

The water below was moving in waves to hit off the side of our vessel, while our sister ship was now gliding directly over the area of the explosion. It did not seem to be damaged.

But what of Dawson? The size of the explosion would surely have torn him to pieces. And it was then that it suddenly dawned on me. I had fulfilled my mission. Dawson was no more, killed by his own deadly explosives while the rest of his saboteurs were out on the plains seeking their martyrdom. There would be no more acts of sabotage.

I leaned forward and put my hands on my knees, the laughter gone, emotion starting to overcome me. I felt like weeping.

A voice came from behind me. 'I believe we owe you a great debt.'

It was the commanding officer. I turned to find the tall gentleman grinning broadly, his black hair and naval uniform absolutely dripping. The deck all around him was awash, the other sailors pale with shock.

I said nothing in reply. I had no words.

'WHAT HAPPENED TO your shoulder? Have you been shot?'

It was the commanding officer, a Captain Daniell, as I would later discover.

My body, which seemed to have gone on working throughout my

adventures seemingly with some kind of superhuman strength, now took this moment to give in, and I fainted.

I was brought round some short time later by the stinging whiff of smelling salts and found myself in a small room within the gunship, a tall, grey-bearded medical man leaning over me, a small pair of round silver spectacles sitting neatly on the end of his nose.

'Cleaned and patched you up as best as I can, young man. You should be all right, but try not to use this arm too much.'

I realized as I heard these words that the doctor was actually shouting, for the background to his words was the relentless roar of the ship's guns as it fired shell after shell. 'Try and sit up for me, young man. There we go.'

His voice, despite it being raised, was wholesomely soft and calming, and wonderful to listen to after my tribulations. 'What's happening?' I asked, sitting up and signalling with a move of the head that I was interested in the battle outside.

'Oh, we're right up by Omdurman now. I think they're shelling the Mahdi's tomb.'

'I must go and see what's happening,' I said, going to get up.

'Just a minute there, lad. Let me tie that arm up for you.' He made a sling from a bandage and hung my arm in it. 'There you are. Now try not to move it too much. Don't forget now.'

I realized when I got back on deck why the doctor had been so calm and had taken so much time over my care, for there was no other work to do. The firepower of the gunboats was so superior to anything that the Dervishes could muster that the men were quite safe on the deck, free to load and fire the howitzers and to spray the banks of the Nile with their Maxim guns as if they were on exercise.

I emerged from a side door of the vessel to look across the water and up the rocky slopes towards the walls of Omdurman and found them pockmarked with shell holes, a large plume of red dust floating away down the plains. And I had time now also to observe the tremendous battle that was taking place over to our right.

The front I judged to be four to five miles long. The Khalifa's armies, at the rear, looked to be composed of large masses of men joined together by smaller lines, and by the flanks there appeared to be large numbers of standing reserves. The British and Egyptian forces were by comparison a far smaller affair, facing away from the river and also arranged in line.

From the left there was, I would later learn, the Rifle Brigade and the Lancashire Fusiliers, then came the Northumberland Fusiliers, the Grenadier Guards and the Maxims of the Royal Irish Fusiliers, the Royal Warwickshire Regiment, the Cameron Highlanders and the Seaforth Highlanders, and also the Sudanese fighting line. To the right I could see the Camel Corps and out towards the front I would later discover was stationed the 21st Lancers, as always in the thick of it. But it was at this point that I fully realized, as I took in the great scenes that confronted me, the utter folly of the Khalifa's battle plans for, as his brave warriors were streaming forward in their thousands at a time and in seemingly well-ordered battle array, they were being slaughtered to the man. What is more they were being cut down in their droves long before they had even had a chance to thrust a spear or lay down fire anywhere near our troops. As a gap in the smoke and dust would appear I would see a line of wild Dervishes, all waving spears and leaping like leopards, and perhaps with a flag bearer at their front, rush forward to then, just a few seconds later, fall *en-masse*. And no sooner would these fearless ones have succumbed to our overwhelming firepower than a fresh line of brazen fighters would follow on behind and bound forward at an equally suicidal rate. The reserves must have known that they were waiting to be funnelled into certain death.

Why hadn't the Khalifa kept his army within the walls of Omdurman and forced Kitchener to take the city house by house? Or why hadn't he, even, taken the initiative and attacked the Anglo-Egyptians at night? His only chance lay in drawing us into close-quarter fighting, for that was where the wily Dervish, with spear and sword, was at his best. When it came to the hand-to-hand stuff there was probably no more terrifying and effective foe than the valiant fanatic, fighting not for a queen nor for country, nor even for a way of life, but for God and a religion that was put above everything and anything to an extent that we simply cannot conceive. But the Khalifa, rather than playing to his own strengths, had naïvely played perfectly to the strengths of his enemy and, as a result, had served his men up for the slaughter on that great plain between Omdurman and Kerreri.

I watched, mesmerized, as the shells and bullets whizzed and pounded, and as the Dervish left began to stretch out towards the Kerreri Hills. Perhaps the Khalifa had a plan after all. Perhaps he hoped to draw out his enemy into the desert to then send a force round to outflank it. But I knew, as I watched those maniacs push forward and fall in wave after wave, the smoke from the Anglo-Egyptian guns rising up in industrial quantities, the deep rumbles echoing around the hillsides, that the outcome of the battle was already decided, and that before the day was out the *Sirdar* would be riding triumphantly through the streets of Omdurman.

I turned away from the fighting, unsure whether to be proud of our efficient performance or to be sick to the pit of my stomach at the butchering of so many undoubtedly brave, if misguided, poor Dervishes.

The gunboats, once in range, rained down destruction upon the Mahdi's tomb. The banks of the Nile were continuously swept with the deadly wind from our Maxim guns to clear them of any enemy, and then the shells began to fly towards the resting place of the man who had raised a religious army to bring down Khartoum; the man who had killed Gordon and in the process aroused the world's mightiest empire to reek its cruel vengeance.

The first few missiles landed short of their target. The next volley, however, produced a large and impenetrable cloud of dust around the dome of the tomb and, when it cleared, the resting place of the Mahdi was flat topped rather than rounded. There followed several more direct hits that left gaping holes in other parts of the structure.

'This will take the fire out of the hearts of those damned Dervishes,' said Captain Daniell as our gunboat turned to steam back downstream.

The rest of the day turned out as I had foreseen, with the annihilation of the Khalifa's armies. The gunboats supported our forces on the field wherever they were called, and there was one particularly hair-raising moment when the Camel Corps looked as if it might be in trouble from a few thousand Dervishes who had somehow managed to appear at its flank, near the river. But the firepower of our gunboats once at the scene cut the enemy down in minutes, and in a short time that part of the field lay white with *jibbahed* corpses.

As the tumultuous day wore on the lines of Dervishes thinned out to a trickle until those who hadn't fled and were still determined to fight were being picked off one-by-one by our rifles.

But what of the Khalifa? Kitchener would soon discover that he had fled with a band of diehard followers, and it would be another few months before he would finally be tracked down and slain. He had failed to die with his brave warriors.

We were now moored by the *zariba* at this point in order to take on more ammunition. It seemed relatively peaceful now compared with the carnage of the previous hours. Already men were starting to engage in the usual post battle routines of eating, sleeping and gathering in groups to discuss their experiences of an historic day.

I looked then at the final result of the battle of Omdurman. Thousands of bodies lay like a meadow of snowdrift on the vast plain. Here and there a moving patch of white, a wounded man on all fours trying to edge his way towards the river to drink, to die.

I looked at the glorious abomination before me. 'Truly now he is avenged,' I said to the desert.

THE FOLLOWING DAY, with Omdurman now secure and all resistance vanquished, a memorial service was held for General Gordon in Khartoum. I had spent the night aboard the gunboat with Captain Daniell and his men. They were eager to know how on earth I had managed to get wind of the explosives that had been meant to blow them out of the water, but until I had reported to Major-General Kitchener I, as standard good practice, could still not talk about my mission. They understood, however, and after a hearty dinner I spent the night playing cards with Daniell. Some of the men went ashore to view the battlefield in detail and to hunt for souvenirs. They returned with stories of ruined dead Dervish heaped three or four deep around the standards of their *emirs*, of acres and acres of corpses, and with descriptions of the awful wounded whom no one could help. Early the following morning we then disembarked by the ruined city for the ceremonials.

'I know you can't tell me anything about your mission,' said Daniell, as we walked along streets which the previous day had been deserted but were now throbbing with battle-worn British troops, some carrying large Union Jacks or other regimental flags, 'but I've been around long enough to recognize when a man has been wearied through the bearing of great responsibility. And from what I saw of you yesterday, you've certainly been wearied a great deal. I don't know what you've come through, though I'm sure it will come out in time. But I do know one thing, the *Sirdar* will have your chest decorated with medals before we return home for what you did yesterday. You saved our necks, Winters, and I'll be certain to make sure old Kitchener knows how splendidly you performed on our decks. They'll write about you, Major. You will be read about in the history books.'

I laughed at the thought of it. 'Our work has a tendency to remain secret, no matter how dramatic it appears, so I think I'll have to leave the glory, quite rightly, for the 21st Lancers.'

It was marvellous to see the sun shining off our finally restful gunboats, now moored alongside a crumbling stone quay, and the happy faces of the soldiers who knew they would soon be heading home, having come safely through perhaps the most trying days of their lives. The atmosphere was joyous, despite many of the men having lost friends, although there was also a hint of the solemn – it was after all a memorial service.

'I heard the Sudanese troops had a bit of a party in Omdurman last night,' continued Daniell.

'A party?'

'Yes, went on the rampage, the bloody savages. Probably killed hundreds. Seems a lot of them had old scores to settle. Don't think the officers did much to try and stop them either.'

I sighed. 'Not how one would have wished the day to end.'

'Not at all how one would have wished for the day to end. But today is another day, and it is, Major, a glorious one. Look at the flags flying there.'

We had entered the area in front of General Gordon's old palace, where the day before I had acquired a rifle, and on top of the main building the Union Jack and Egyptian flags flew. At this moment the Guards' band launched into the poignant sounds of the Dead March in Saul. I had time now to properly observe the place, and my first thought was that there was a genteel loveliness to Khartoum compared with the mud hovels of Omdurman. Lush undergrowth had sprouted up to completely cover the stables and the outhouses of the palace so that only the front façade remained exposed, while a luxuriant, healthy smell wafted from a large acacia tree that was growing next to the Nile. The refugees were gone now to God knows where and had been replaced by shabby-looking British and Egyptian troops formed up as three sides of a rectangle. A gentle breeze fanned us. The scene and atmosphere I could only describe as being haunt-ingly romantic.

It was then that I saw the *Sirdar* for the first time since he had sent me forth on my mission at Wad Hamed. He was standing proudly in front of his troops, in splendid shining uniform, directing the proceedings, forever in command. Daniell and I stood atop a small mound of rubble and watched the service, the sad music wiping out the smiles and the laughter so that the men's faces now wore sombre and serious expressions. The padre then read out a passage from the Bible, and we all joined in saying the Lord's Prayer.

Next it was the turn of the pipers, who, to the steady beats of a drum, played the *Coronach* as a lament. We then sang Gordon's favourite hymn, Abide With Me. The following minutes were surreally emotional. There was not a man among us that did not feel the weighty sentiment of all those years of Mahdism finally being crushed, of comrades fallen and of Gordon avenged.

Heaven's morning breaks, and earth's vain shadows flee;
In life, in death, O Lord, abide with me.

I remember then casting a glance towards the *Sirdar*. Amazingly, this indomitable soldier, a machine of warfare, was standing there with tears streaming down his face. It was a sight that I would never in a million life-times have expected to see. And I wondered then, as I stared at Kitchener, what his tears were for. Were they for Gordon? For his men? For Britain? For his own glory? I could not hazard a guess. But really, it would have been silly to do so, for whatever reason that great man stood there with eyes watering in the blazing sun, to his men the sight was undoubtedly moving. Indeed it was all that I could do to stop myself from letting my emotions overtake me, and I must say I had never felt so proud to be an Englishman.

Kitchener, unable to do so himself, turned to one of his deputies and asked him to dismiss the parade. And it was at this moment that I went forward, leaving Captain Daniell.

'Major-General,' I said, as he was walking through an overgrown area that used to be Gordon's garden. He was accompanied by a few colonels, and the group stopped accordingly.

'Ah, Winters, Winters.' His voice had softened since the last time we had spoke, and indeed it seemed to be a different man who stood before me now. He seemed happy and unafraid of sincerity. There was not a hint of the old harshness, and his face looked piously gentle. 'What a good job you have done.'

He was shaking my hand vigorously now, having actually stepped forward to do so. I was dumbfounded. 'You saved the gunboats. We might never have been here if it weren't for you. I always knew an intelligence man would be up to the job. Well done, Major. Well done indeed. You must provide me with a full report later, but tell me, who was responsible for the sabotage?'

'You were perfectly correct, sir. It was one of our own. An Englishman. A Captain Dawson.'

He nodded a little, and it was at this moment that I sensed a presence approaching and, turning to the side, found a tiny old black African man clutching the arm of a British soldier being led towards the *Sirdar*. He was horribly thin, so much so that his cheekbones bulged out and his eyes looked unnaturally big and round. His scrawny body was covered in tattered rags. Instantly all attention went from me to this pitiful-looking person.

'He was General Gordon's head gardener,' said the soldier. 'He's remained here all these years, since Gordon's death, trying to tend the gardens as best he can, living off nothing.'

I glanced around at the area that the old man treasured so much. The place was terribly dilapidated and tumbledown – but it was also beautiful. The deluge of greenery, which for some reason I had not picked up on until now, flooded the senses, a complete contrast to the constant glare of the desert. Thick grass interspersed with pink and yellow flowers covered the ground, and some sort of creeper had grown to almost completely cover the white palace wall at the far end. It seemed cool and refreshing here, and there was the sweet smell of oranges and pomegranate blossoms. There was a small, and in comparison to what was around it, rather tidy vegetable garden stuck in a corner, little rows of leaves sticking out from its yellow dirt. And there were fig trees and bananas and tamarinds spread here and there.

The old man began to speak in Arabic, and Kitchener understood his words perfectly having, as I had, learned the language in the Palestine. 'So many days he stood up there,' and he pointed weakly to the roof of Gordon's crumbling palace, his voice very low indeed. 'So many days he watched the river, waiting for your boats to appear and save us. But they never came, until it was too late. Then came the darkness. I try to keep the gardens but I am so old now. I do it for him. I can still feel his spirit here.'

As he finished a single tear appeared in the corner of his left eye, spilling out to roll down his cheek. How he must have loved Gordon. Kitchener, again out of character, was very kind. He took the old man's arm from the soldier and said soothingly, 'I am sorry we didn't come before, but we are here now.'

I had been so controlled throughout the ceremony, but the sight of that proud old man brought a great lump to my throat and then, I must admit, a tear to my own eye.

But it was a happy tear, for Gordon had finally, and at long last, been avenged.

CHAPTER 21

Diary of the Rt. Hon. Colonel Evelyn Winters, MP

21 May, 1935

A MISTY RAIN HAS descended upon Wiltshire, its fine particles falling in continuous sheets against the windows of my study. We have consumed a thoroughly good dinner, Parker and Mrs Jenkins have retired to bed and, as I sit here writing my diary, all seems to be thoroughly well with the world.

I feel lighter tonight, lighter than I have felt in many months, the weight of expectation having been lifted. But what a most extraordinary and illuminating day it has been. Indeed, it has been a truly unbelievable day. I should start at the beginning and try to note down in every detail the amazing events, lest they should become a dim memory in my aged mind.

I awoke in the flat to sunshine shooting in between the bedroom curtains and instantly felt ready to take on the world and give my political opponents a good bashing. My spirits were really rather high, and, as I read over my speech at breakfast, I was pretty confident that things would run smoothly.

I took my time dressing, taking care to get the knot in my tie the right size and shape. Such little details, tedious as they were, helped build my confidence, so that by the time Parker came round I was most eager to get to the House.

'Good morning, Parker,' I bellowed, as I opened the door to his smiling face.

'Indeed, good morning, Colonel.'

I led Parker into the study, as I wished to go through my speech with him one last time before we left. 'I thought I would perhaps see you yesterday,' I said, as I fished around my desk for my notes.

'Oh,' he said, 'I ... er, thought you might want to have a bit of time to yourself before your big day. And also Margaret had some plans for us.' He was standing behind my green leather armchair.

'Oh well, not to worry. Do you think we might go through my speech one last time before we leave, just to make certain it's all ship-shape?'

'Certainly.'

I was about to start reading my speech aloud when I remembered that I wanted to ask him about the Royal Anglian Regiment. It could easily have waited until after I had made my speech, but I knew I would most probably end up forgetting to ask at all if I didn't do it while the thought was still there. 'While I remember, Parker my boy, I ran into an old officer the other day whom I served with in the Sudan. Yes, chap by the name of Lloyd. But anyway, this business about your father's regiment at Omdurman. It's been on my mind. And as' – I laughed as I said this – 'you seem determined not to find out what part exactly they played in the battle, I thought I should ask him. He wrote a book about the campaign a few years after we came back, so you see he does know an awful lot about it. Anyway, he says the Royal Anglian most certainly did not fight at the Battle of Omdurman, but that they were stationed further to the north, near Wadi Halfa, when the battle was actually taking place. So I'm wondering what your father was doing at the front at all. Did he perhaps specialize in something? Signals perhaps? Was he attached to another unit for some reason?'

At the time I presumed that Parker was perhaps beginning to get nervous at the thought of me making my speech, for he became noticeably flustered as I said this, but in retrospect it was quite obvious why this was so.

'No, no, he ... wasn't attached to any other regiments. Listen, Colonel, there's something that I've been meaning to go over with you for ... for some time now. It was my father, he—'

Suddenly a thought flashed through my mind, and in that awful way that I know I sometimes have I cut him off. 'Oh, was he an intelligence man?' I said excitedly.

Parker mumbled somewhat. 'Er, yes, yes indeed he was.'

'Well why didn't you tell me before? Or have you just come up with this from your research now? Oh, look, time is getting on, my boy. I'll tell you what, shall we talk about it later, after we've been to the Commons? You can tell me all about it then. I just wanted to mention the Royal Anglian thing while it was on my mind. But let's get through this blasted speech one more time, though, eh?'

He smiled, and now that I think about it I recall him also looking a little relieved. I have to say that, what with the huge anticipation that I felt for what was to come, I did not for a moment comprehend what should now have seemed a very reasonable probability. Instead I blindly picked up my speech and got stuck into reading it, with every word that came out making me feel more and more certain that I would put in a good performance.

'Wonderful,' said Parker, once I had finished. 'Love it ... they'll love it.'

'Well I do hope so, my boy. And it is in no small measure your doing. Don't think I don't know how difficult it must have been for you to help an old imperialist like me with something like this.'

'No, no, of course.'

'I don't know how to thank you. But, what's this? Is that the time? Let me get my coat. We should go. I can't be late for my own comeback speech.'

A curious thought came to me as we were leaving the flat. It was a fine sunny day, and as we were coming out of the main door I naturally glanced at the little garden out front. I have come out of that door so many times to observe the garden, and indeed there was no difference in its layout today. Because, however, I recall the story in my speech of that place in Khartoum where General Kitchener met Gordon's old head gardener all those years ago – and which I shall also write about in my memoirs – I was quite suddenly taken back to when I was standing in that place amongst the ruins of the imperial city. I suppose the size of the garden in London and the fact that it is getting a bit overgrown and needs some attention must have been what vividly brought back to me the image of that old gardener weeping for his long dead master. And in some ways I felt that here, even at my age, I am continuing with the struggle, continuing to fight for what that old gardener had so poignantly shed tears.

Parker had waved down a taxi for us and stood now with the door held ajar waiting for me. I took a deep breath and, thinking about that gardener's tears and about Gordon and his ideals, I went forth to fight what could well be my last battle.

We were soon at the House, and I got out of the taxi to take a long look at the Gothic façade of Westminster, set against a bright blue May sky.

'Best we get in,' said Parker, placing a hand on my shoulder.

'Indeed, my boy.'

It was as we were walking through the wood-panelled hallways towards the House that I had the first stirrings of nervous tension. My fellow rebels were patting me on the back and wishing me luck as we passed them, and this suddenly made me think about the weight of anticipation that now rested upon me.

'Here we are, well … well, best of luck,' said Parker, shaking my hand at the bottom of the stairs to the visitor's gallery.

'Yes, and thank you again, Parker. You've been ever so good to me.'

I must admit that, alone now, I did not feel nearly as sure of myself as I had back in the flat. But I had to focus, so I turned away from the stair and walked briskly into the House.

I took my seat as I had planned near the Dispatch Box and looked across at a wall of black suits, white collars and grey hair. I thought they all seemed to be looking at me as if I were some sort of exhibit in a zoo. Another member was speaking to my right, but I did not register anything that he was saying, my mind being focused only on the first words of my speech.

Quite a number of rebels had turned up to listen, and I had noted some of them smile encouragement as I was sitting down. Once settled I looked towards the front benches and saw Mr Churchill's distinctive glabrous head and large frame a few rows away. And there too was the more mouse-like Mr Baldwin, sitting nearby. I looked up to the gallery then and spotted Parker straight away, seated right at the front and leaning on the railing, the usual assortment of newspaper reporters with their notepads and pencils and members of the public seated around him.

I fished the notes that I had out of my pocket and, as I glanced over the sentences and words, most of my speech began to logically formulate itself in my head. I have practised it so many times over these last few weeks that I felt sure I would remember it word-for-word. This realization, that the speech was still in my mind and that nervousness had not caused me to draw a blank, boosted me somewhat, and I began to feel calmer. Indeed I was now once again looking forward to getting up to speak.

Then suddenly the House fell silent. I felt a nudge on my arm and discovered that I was being called on to get up. I looked around. All eyes were upon me. I saw those of some of the rebels twinkling at me, encouraging me to stand and face the enemy.

Slowly I got to my feet. I shuffled my papers around in my hands a little, looked around at the House, then up to the public gallery again to observe Parker smiling positively at me. I coughed twice, suddenly noticing that I had broken the silence, as the first words of my speech came into my head, the part about the Montagu-Chelmsford reforms.

I glanced at the Speaker, then at the back of Mr Churchill's quite still head. He could have been waiting for a train, and the silence at this point seemed eternal.

But I began as planned. 'Mr Speaker, Honourable Members, as we are all perfectly aware the Montagu-Chelmsford reforms set forth a process of the partial Indianization of provincial governments in British India. And now this government wishes to force yet more of our Western doctrines of democracy upon this nation. But I say what right do we have to do this?'

I began thus, and I think I successfully put across the point that the westernization of the countries that we administer may not be as morally enviable as many would make out, and that indeed it could do more harm than good, to both the administrators and the administered. I then went on to state that we British have reached the pinnacle of civilization, and that the native peoples of less-sophisticated lands on the whole feel very grateful for, and benefit greatly from, our civilized leadership.

I continued: 'If I may, Mr Speaker, illustrate my point. Now, some of the honourable members may know that for the last several months I have been busy writing my memoirs of the 1898 campaign in the Sudan, in which I was privileged enough to serve as a major in the Intelligence Branch.'

I had planned now to give a very brief history of my time there before recounting the story of the old gardener in Khartoum, shedding tears for his benevolent master, Gordon. But it was at precisely this point that the most amazing realization, which I should have caught on to this morning from what Parker said – and what in retrospect had been staring me clear in the face for some time – finally came to me.

'Many members of the House may not know the circumstances of my time in the Sudan. I faced a most dangerous foe – and I do not mean the Dervishes. No, this was an Englishman. A traitor. A former intelligence officer who ...' It was as I was uttering these words that quite suddenly everything began to fall into place. I believe I stopped talking at this point, mid sentence. Thoughts raced through my head. I was reminded of what Parker had said this morning, about his father having been an intelligence man. And then I recalled how unwilling Parker has been to tell me about his father's activities. I was reminded of our walk in St James's Park and realized what he had actually been trying to tell me that day, and of the times when I have questioned Parker about the Royal Anglian Regiment. How blind I had been. Suddenly it all began to make sense.

Every man in the House must have been wondering why I had stopped talking, and why I was now standing in silence with a very perplexed look upon my face, as I am sure I must have had.

Quite naturally I now began to raise my eyes to look at Parker. And it was as I was following the dark wood of the Chamber up towards the viewing gallery that the *full* implication of my discovery came to me. As my eyes fell upon Parker's face my first sense was of the rigidity of his mouth, the thin lips.

And it was then that our eyes connected.

The following few seconds must surely rank as being the strangest moments of my life. Immediately before I had looked at Parker, some part of my brain had started to doubt my thinking, and I thought I must simply have got horribly mixed up. But then, in that instant, as I stared into those severe eyes, more stern than I had ever seen in Parker, I knew definitely that it was his father who I had killed on the Nile all those years before. I cannot quite explain why I knew this with such certainty. All I can say is that the confirmation lay in Parker's eyes and, what is more, I sensed that just then both of us knew exactly what the other was thinking. I knew that Dawson was Parker's father. Why hadn't I seen it until now? And Parker knew that this realization had just dawned on me. I could read it in his hollow eyes as plainly as if I were reading a newspaper.

I had killed poor Parker's father – Dawson and his father were one and the same. The fact that their surnames differed was practically irrelevant, for many intelligence officers changed their name as a matter of routine once they were employed by the service. As incredible as it all seemed it was also now plain to see. What a shock all of this came to me. Indeed, I am positively glad I did not faint as the image of that explosion on the Nile that killed the man flashed through my mind. It is all so confusing and there are many questions yet to be answered – but will they ever be answered? – that I can hardly absorb it, even now after a day of difficult contemplation. But now here I was, all these years after Omdurman, looking … Oh why shouldn't I simply admit it? Here I was looking into the eyes of a boy who in these last months I have become so very fond of, to the extent that my affection for him makes me feel as if he were in fact *my* son.

I think I almost gasped at the realization of the tangled web that we were now thoroughly caught in. But then I noticed Parker's expression change. His eyes widened slightly and I believe he moved forward in his seat a little. He was willing me on to finish my speech.

All of this happened in mere seconds, although it seemed like far longer. But thankfully the change in Parker's expression shook me out of my near stupor. I lowered my eyes away from him and scanned the stern faces of the House. I believe there may even have been a little emotion showing in my eyes. I heard a cough from behind me, and then my thought processes truly began to return so that before I knew what was happening I was back into my speech again.

I told the House that after a great struggle I finally defeated the traitor. 'And afterwards I encountered an old man who had tended General Gordon's garden, and indeed since Gordon's death had continued to do so for many years, as if to somehow honour his old master. It was the benevolence and inherent goodness of Gordon that had produced this incredible loyalty. And it is that spirit – the spirit of Gordon – that now blesses the many millions of peoples of India. That spirit cannot be allowed to die there. The Indian people deserve better than that. The Indian people deserve our benevolent leadership.'

I shall not cover here the rest of my speech, but overall I think it went really rather well. Certainly, once I had finished and had departed the Chamber I was given some very positive responses from my fellow rebels – although it shan't be until tomorrow, when I see what the papers have to say about it, that we will know how successful I have been.

But now that my speech was out of the way all that I could think about was Parker and the fact that I had actually killed his father. And now also I kept thinking about the fact that the poor boy has been helping *me*, his father's killer, to write a story that in some ways celebrates and glorifies that death. What an incredible and utterly strange situation to have found myself – ourselves – in.

But before I had time to dwell on it for too long there was Parker standing before me, a few feet away, having come down from the viewing gallery. It was noisy, as the outside of the Chamber always is after an important speech, and I was surrounded by many of my fellow rebels, all of whom where clamouring to congratulate me. But I must say I was taking little notice of them. Hands were clasping mine and patting me on the back with many shouts of, 'Well done, Winters! Splendid job! Summed our thoughts up beautifully!'

But I was barely registering it all, my attention instead being focused only on my dear boy Parker. An awkward few moments ensued, when neither Parker nor myself knew exactly how we should react to our meeting again.

In a short time, however, he was moving towards me, his tall frame squeezing past the other MPs. 'Well done,' he said calmly, putting out his hand to take mine. As I go over it now I don't recall even responding to this at first. Instead I believe I simply stood there motionless, so that Parker actually had to take my wrist with his left hand to direct me in a handshake.

'Oh, er, thank you, my boy,' I mumbled.

'Yes, very good, very good.'

'Thank you,' I said again. Would he acknowledge what we both now knew? Should I? I couldn't think properly there was so much going on.

There was some suggestion from the other rebels of my waiting around to meet Mr Churchill, but I had had enough for today, so I said it could wait until I returned to London. 'Do you still wish to come down to Wiltshire?' I then asked Parker tentatively, for I really had no idea how he would feel.

'Of course,' he said simply and quietly. And so we set off for Victoria Station, and after a quick taxi journey, during which none of us said anything, we found ourselves in a private train compartment.

I have never experienced such awkward moments in my life. I could barely look at Parker. Yes, his father was a traitor, and yes, Parker never knew him. But still, I would not have blamed him if he hated me for having killed the man, especially when Parker's own liberal instincts must make him feel that the Sudan campaign was morally questionable. And yet, despite all of this, he seemed not to hate me at all. It was all so strange.

Not long after we had sat down Parker got up to open the window as the sun had made the compartment uncomfortably warm. 'Terribly stuffy in here,' he said.

'Indeed.'

He sat down opposite me again and was illuminated by the glow of the afternoon light. I thought at this moment that the uneasy atmosphere was becoming really rather silly, and that I should pluck up some courage and just say something.

'Parker, I …' But I am afraid to admit that I could not bring myself to do it, eventually just saying, 'So you thought it went well then.'

'Indeed. Splendidly, splendidly.'

But then again silence prevailed. As the train started off I lit a cigarette, which at least gave me something to occupy myself with.

It was as the first green fields of Surrey were coming into view that we finally came to talk, in a way, about the situation, and it was Parker who started us off.

'Yes, I don't think it could have gone better, really.'

'Thank you.'

'Yes, and I thought that … well, that part towards the end, when you said that although you regard the actions of those MPs who are trying to have the India Bill passed into law as being misguided, that … that you still respect their point of view and accept that the world is changing, but that these changing attitudes should not be allowed to hurt the Indian people, and that we should stop and think before turning them into action. Made your position more credible. That bit, I mean. And I think your opposition saw it too … how tolerant you are of other people's opinions that is, and—'

'How tolerant I have *become* of other people's opinions,' I interrupted, for I had to acknowledge that this enlightened strength in my speech, and indeed perhaps in my thinking, came as a result of what I have learned from Parker.

He smiled a little and looked to the carriage floor. 'Yes … yes.' Then he looked directly at me. 'But that tolerance it … it must come from all sides. That is, I mean, from those against the India Bill and those who, well, I suppose like me, who would really like to see things change. And take the Sudan campaign. It was so long ago. Even back then people thought differently. Some people thought in extremes that … well, we wouldn't even see today. And, of course, people died as a result. Wives lost husbands and … and sons lost fathers. But, as I say, we should be tolerant, we should understand. Colonel, I understand how extreme the situation was in the Sudan and that enemies had to be faced and people killed. I understand … and, and I'm sure that in Parliament many people understand that nothing is as easy as simply right or wrong, which is why I think your speech was well received.'

I could have wept as I listened to him make this short and admirable statement, for it was plain that he was telling me that he did not feel any animosity towards me for killing his father. He understood and he accepted, and yet again dear Parker's strength of character impressed me enormously.

I think I simply nodded once he had said this and mumbled a thank you. I was very touched, and suddenly now everything seemed to be all right again. We both understood each other perfectly, and I believe our friendship remains as strong as ever. Perhaps it has even been strengthened.

I am reminded now of what Parker said a couple of months ago, when we were out in the garden here. If I recall correctly he said that I reminded him of his father and that he took some comfort in the thought. This seems incongruous when one recalls his father's ideology, which stood in complete contrast to my own thinking. But perhaps what he meant that day was that I remind him of how he would have liked his father to have turned out. I have no doubt he must wish that his father had not become such a fanatic. And perhaps there is a feeling also that he would have liked to have had a father who, in the best traditions of the generational gap, he could clash with intellectually, a father he could argue and debate with while remaining on good terms.

It has been a turbulent day, and even though I know that the India Bill will eventually be passed into law, I am content that I have done my bit to act against it. Perhaps some day Parker and I shall have an open and frank discussion about his father. Or perhaps we shall simply put it behind us and move on. It is too early to know. But more importantly I retain Parker's friendship, and I can still look forward to seeing his grandchildren running up and down the lawns of the house here. I should go to bed now as it is getting late. Despite all that has happened this day, I feel I shall have a restful night.

Author's Note

Readers familiar with military history will note that the significant engagement by the 21st Lancers took place on the day of the Battle of Omdurman itself rather than as in *After Omdurman* before the Battle of Omdurman.